The Circadian Anomaly

Written by David Villegas

with contributions by Heidi Babin

Special thanks to Sergeant Mark Tapps of the Alpharetta Police Department for allowing me to name the K-9 hero of this novel after your incredible retired K-9 Officer, Mattis.

Thank you to Jay Little for permission to adapt the subject matter of your game, The Coriolis Defect.

ISBN: 979-8-218-41212-8 (paperback)
ISBN: 978-1-7338218-8-9 (ebook)
ISBN: 978-1-7338218-7-2 (audiobook)

The Circadian Anomaly

*For Cindy, the wind in my sails, and
Tay, my beautiful daughter.*

Chapter 1

The Chase (Day 0)

To everyone at the FBI K-9 skills competition in Grant Park, it is another normal, cool, windy day near the lake in Chicago. People mill about, unconcerned with the sight of a young woman having fun with her parents. The reality of the situation is quite different.

Dan tries desperately to keep up while running into people, but his daughter Jeanne's face is resolute and unrelenting. He has seen it before when she is trying to solve a problem that is stumping her. Sometimes she melts down, but occasionally the dogged mentality shows up and she won't ever give up. He sees her face stiffen as she bites her lower lip slightly, and he instinctively lets out a long sigh and a subtle shake of his head as he thinks, *the bulldog is about to show up*.

Jeanne moves purposefully across the food truck area. She makes her way through the vendor tents and away from the so-called event organizers. She motions in a not-so-flashy way for her dad to follow her as she searches for her pursuers, who must be hunting her. Her intuition tells her they are lurking around the corner or on the other side of the trucks. She has the advantage, but they are after her and her gift…again! She looks for her parents in the crowd and pauses just long enough to spot them, faces straining as they try to cut through the masses.

Dan and Lynn are vaguely aware of who their daughter is trying to flee from even though they can't understand how she came to the realization. Now they are caught in an impossible position as he reaches for her, fighting through the throngs of people. He turns back and sighs as his little girl is slipping further away from him. His mind races to weigh the possibilities and consequences of the next decision he has half a second to make.

The celebration continues all around him. The sights and sounds of glee and the smell of food mix with his adrenaline and indecision to almost overwhelm him. He finally lets out a visceral bellow, "Jeanne your mom and I can't keep up! Stop!"

Her eyes dart back and forth, scanning for threats that might emerge at any moment. She responds, "No Dad, they are not going to capture me again, I won't go to their lab, I know the way out this time, you'll have to find us on Roosevelt!"

She turns to resume moving as two men with radios appear on the other side of the pavilion and she pivots back towards Lake Shore Drive. *Found them. Now, where are they going?* The smell of popcorn and funnel cakes fills her nostrils as she makes a momentary note of where she is going to go next.

Usually, her mind runs away with her when her plans change, but somehow she is focused on her task this time. She peers one way and thinks *open field, that's going away from Roosevelt.* She looks back to the food trucks and tents and says to herself *here come all the people between events to eat, I can hide in the crowd.* She hunkers down and waits for Carlo to pull the car around.

While Jeanne is finding a way to elude her potential captors, Carlo has attracted some unwanted attention. He's picked up an agent from the VIP area following him towards the bushes where he stashed his rental. *Why did the girl talk to me?* He thinks to himself as he continues toward the well-hidden vehicle barely visible from the street.

He's been through this timeline before. This is supposed to be the getaway route, but things all of a sudden changed when she recognized him and told him to be ready with the car. That single event drives him to question his entire plan and his ability to anticipate the endgame. This is the first time he is trying to surprise a person who possesses the same gift of time travel he has, so his mind wanders for a moment.

He turns the corner and snaps back to his pursuit mentality because he is only about 100 yards away. As he approaches, he decides to turn into the foliage to try and lose his pursuer. His thoughts momentarily disengage again as he thinks to himself, *how am I in this position? I swore this could never happen again!* The agents at the tent are tracking her and now, because of one brief conversation he did not instigate, they are on to him as well.

He has one thing on his mind: shake this guy so he can make it to the car and make it to the north side of the fountain to

Lake Shore Drive where the dog and handler will be waiting for him. His thoughts wander again. *How could it have all gone south so fast? This is my third time through this, what changed and how did the girl come by this information?*

Tons of questions are running through his head, but he's getting close and is smacked back into reality as he runs face-first into a fairly thick clump of leaves concealing a branch that strikes him with some force in the face. As his cheek warms with the fresh blood extracted from under his right eye, he remembers to search for a fundamental item he needs.

He grabs for his jeans. *Where is my damn key?! Why did I put it in my back pocket?*

On the east side of the massive opening, Tony and Mattis are trying to walk along like they don't have a care in the world, just a cop taking his K-9 officer through the park looking for nefarious goings on but are dead set on their objective of getting to Lake Shore Drive.

Tony is perplexed as they move through the foliage, *How did that girl know what was about to happen? Do I believe her? Mattis took to her, maybe he's done this already? Why does the FBI want to kidnap my dog, why not grab us in the tent? This seems way too elaborate to capture an animal they could have had at any time.*

Right now, one non-negotiable thought keeps running through his head; he will die before he allows any government agency to use his doggo as a gross science experiment. Still, his questions are doing battle in his head but as he goes further, his brain arrives at the conclusion he believes her and everything else does not matter.

His only objective is to find the car the girl said would come, the blue sedan with Michigan plates and an old man at the wheel named Carlo. As he begins to gain some mental clarity and works through all the uncertainties still biting at his psyche, one thing remains clear: as it relates to Mattis, nothing is outside the realm of possibility.

He's seen way too many things that can't be explained. His dog has a gift no one understands and it's time to keep him safe. They continue their brisk walk, but his senses pique and the hair on the back of his neck starts to stand up, so he turns to see a man wearing a properly tucked-in polo shirt and blue jeans with a belt that looks entirely out of place following behind. He thinks to himself, *this is a man working way too hard to blend in at a yacht club that is nowhere to be found*. His cop instincts tell him this guy wears suits for a living and can't dress casually if his life depends on it, so he holds his stare on him and raises his hand to his mouth, simulating a communication device in his hand. The man who is walking with the same form and purpose suddenly looks down and engages a small transmitter on his shirt collar. Tony thinks to himself, *FBI. Great.*

He starts looking to the north where the car should be coming from since they are only about 200 yards from the sidewalk adjacent to the street. He's beginning to make a plan for an alternate escape route as a blue Ford fishtails around the corner a couple of blocks up the road, drawing his gaze.

"That has to be the guy buddy," he says as he looks down at Mattis, "let's go!" Tony breaks into a sprint to meet the man who is moving at high speed southward along the drive. He gets to the street's edge as the vehicle approaches with windows rolled down and comes to a screeching halt, causing the car behind him to take evasive action and any hope of going unnoticed goes out the window as a bunch of cars start honking at them.

"Get in officer, we have to save Jeanne and her parents!" Carlo hollers with a degree of panic.

"Who?"

"The girl. The one that shot my plans to hell! I am supposed to find you here and then go further south and meet her down at Roosevelt. Come on man!"

Tony jumps in with Mattis, "OK, let's move. The FBI is on my six."

"Mine too. I did not notice the agents repositioned. They must have gotten the heebie jeebies with her acting all funky. She is their real target, but they also want to prove your dog has the gift. So, they set up this elaborate course to make him do something and detect a trap somewhere, and then they are going to take your K-9 officer to run some tests on. Now, I feel like something else is in play here, something from later in the day she came back from."

"You too? The young lady told me Mattis is a time-traveling animal, are you saying something happened this

6

afternoon he came back to fix?"

"No officer, she came back. I am not sure when or where from, but something went wrong with our escape plan. There she is!" He points at her, "That's weird, where are her parents?"

He turns right and stops the car on Roosevelt for her to jump in and looks back to the north across the courtyard. He spots Dan and Lynn. Their faces are red as they struggle through a sea of humanity that seems oblivious to their situation and intent on having a good time. He surveys the field behind them. Two guys running toward them, both with purpose. He decides he needs to use their names, figuring the bureau identified them already so he yells their names and waves his cap in the air. He catches the attention of Dan, who briefly looks up and they lock eyes.

Meanwhile, in the FBI logistics tent, Special Agent Savannah Custos is moving assets around to adjust to their targets scattering all of a sudden and calling out, "Grab team A, control. Are you in your vehicle yet?"

"Grab A here, we are eastbound on Jackson making the turn south on LSD."

"This is Anderson. The girl has stopped at a blue Ford. The animal is in the vehicle, I can see him. I think her parents are about 20 yards to the north, I can't cut them off and we have limited visibility through the crowd."

"Grab A, control, you have about 20 seconds before they are gone. What's your status?"

"South on Lake Shore approaching Balbo."

"Step on it." Custos spins around in her chair, "Where are my damn drones?"

"We are deploying them, ma'am," one agent responds.

"About 5 minutes too late, get on it." Savannah hisses back.

Lynn is gasping, trying to gulp in the air and regain her senses and says, "I feel sick, my stomach is cramping honey, please."

Dan raises his voice, "Honey, you don't have time for that, I'm sorry I have to do this, but we have to go." He looks up and squints at two guys looking directly at them, and although they are wearing sunglasses, he frowns a bit as he turns toward his wife and gives her a big shove on the back side and tucks her head down.

Carlo has one leg out on the street and is half standing, yet still facing them, noting the same two men as well as a fairly obvious government vehicle coming south and says, "Come on man, we have to book it!"

Lynn flies into the back seat with Jeanne, with a certain degree of help from Dan's hand firmly on her right cheek. Dan gets in behind her, Tony closes the door, and they floor it. They take off down Roosevelt and away from the immediate threat, but their pursuer coming down Lake Shore Drive makes the right turn and is now only a couple of hundred yards from them and closing.

The light at Michigan is red but Carlo lays on the horn and hopes someone either hears them or is at least observant enough to understand they are about to be creamed and slow down, if even for a moment. Somehow the hole magically opens and they are able to squirt through. They hear a siren activate on the street as they pass.

"Oh, fantastic!" Carlo says as they barrel towards State Street. "I think we picked up Chicago PD as well. We're going to need a miracle here."

"Did you leave his vest in the park, Tony?" Jeanne asks while motioning at her new furry friend.

"Yes, I took the camera and harness off him, I have his leash tied around him. He's not used to it, but we'll make do."

Mattis seems exceptionally calm given the situation and jumps in the back seat to sit by Jeanne, picking her hand up with his snout wanting a little head rub as they approach the intersection at Clark. Carlo looks ahead and his world slows down a bit as the horror of what he is seeing starts to creep in.

"The bridge is up!" Carlo yells, "Hold on!" The tires squeal as their car uses all its weight to try and stay attached to the ground, but the back end gets loose as they turn south on Clark, and they hit the truck next to them. The sirens are still behind them, but the sound is fading as the gap opens.

They manage to use some of the traffic to make a slight cushion for themselves to work on their escape. "I still have to make it across if we have any chance of escaping from this mess, but we are gaining some distance from them," he says while looking to the right to check if the next bridge is also up.

He finally gets far enough to see and exclaims, "This one is down!" He starts to slow down so he can maneuver around the corner. Tragically, he forgets to look over to the left as he goes into the intersection too fast to react.

Mattis jumps from the floor of the back seat and wedges himself between the window and Jeanne's head as Jeanne looks out toward oncoming traffic.

"Look out!" Jeanne yells as Mattis forms himself into a pad for her head as a pickup coming across on 18th street slams into them at full speed.

The car is launched almost 10 meters to the right and everyone inside who is not buckled down is thrown violently to the left as the truck makes impact. Their worlds flip upside down and the items on the floor linger for a second in front of their faces.

As they flip to the other side and skid along the concrete, the glass and debris act as shrapnel against their faces and bodies. Their vehicle hits another one and finally comes to rest upright after a full roll but facing the opposite direction.

Agent Mahoney pulls up to the scene and jumps on his radio, "Alpha here, I'm on the scene of a major traffic accident at 18th and Clark. The vehicle with our targets on board has been hit by a truck traveling westbound and has rolled over. I Repeat, this is a rollover TA, I'm going in to take a look, but we'll need a couple of medical units rolling to us right away. We have one Chicago PD unit with us on scene."

10

"Mahoney, er, Team A, do not let them take her to any civilian facilities. All of them come to us at the phone store, understand? We are sending agents to take those ambulances."

"Roger that," Mahoney says having already jumped out of his vehicle and is running up to the cars in the mangled mess of metal and rubber. He takes a quick look around, then peers in the window where Mattis' shattered body is positioned between the mangled frame of the car and Jeanne, who looks lifeless.

Mahoney raises his hands and makes wave-like motions with his arms, "Folks please step away, we have units en route." He bends down slightly so he can put his head inside the twisted wreckage and says, "Can anyone hear me? Can anyone speak?"

He gets no response.

Jeanne is barely aware of her thoughts. *This was easier when I was a kid. Why didn't this work? I have to go back again and find Nat this time. We can do it together.*

Mahoney notes the gray matter through the fracture in Carlo's skull and shakes his head. His pulse quickens as a sense of dread fills his mind and body. He touches Jeanne's neck and tries to calm his breathing to make sure he can take a pulse.

Suddenly, he snaps his hand back to his radio and almost screams, "Control, the driver and the dog appear to be deceased, they were struck broadside at full speed. The target is alive, but her pulse is very weak, we're losing her. Rush those ambos! We'll need four, two adult males, and one female in

11

addition to the girl."

"Roger, they are less than a minute out."

Mahoney can hear the sirens as he tries to comfort Jeanne slightly. She opens her eyes to just slits and he says, "Stay with me young lady, you are the key to this whole thing. Come on, don't go to sleep."

Jeanne blinks ever so slowly and looks up at Mahoney, but her eyes start to roll back in her head as she mutters "I'm not asleep, my mind is alive. Again. Again. Find Nat." Her thoughts drift off to her childhood as she tries to concentrate…

Chapter 2

Jeanne and Dan (13 Years Ago)

From the beginning, Jeanne's parents recognized that she was not like all the other children. She was a unique kid, whose exceptional intelligence shone through as she seemed to pick up new things faster than anyone in her age group and appeared to learn concepts quicker than her peers, but her demeanor was vastly different.

She was very quiet. Almost too much so. Her folks always marveled at the time she could spend seemingly captivated by only her thoughts, disconnected from anything in the world and free of distraction. At the same time, she was not maturing as quickly and preferred being by herself.

This led to her spending large amounts of time alone, and her mom and dad worried she'd become completely detached from them as well as the external environment. As she matured, her ability to absorb knowledge like a sponge, grasp complex concepts and demonstrate advanced tactical thinking surprised not just her folks, but all the adults in her life.

They were, however, concerned she was unwilling or unable to socialize like others in her age group and going back to the time when she was an infant and toddler, they don't remember her babbling like a typical baby or smiling at her

13

parents.

Her dad Dan would often remark "Just look at her, you can see the wheels turning inside her head like she's working things out."

Yet she rarely needed to say a word or make a sound, which became a source of stress for her mother Lynn. Frequently, she got discouraged and thought she was doing it all wrong and was being a poor mother to her only daughter.

To her, Jeanne's emotional detachment confirmed Lynn's greatest fears and self-doubts. As Jeanne approached her third birthday, both of them were understandably shocked when their baby girl finally started talking but did so with complete words and thoughts. She showcased a remarkable ability to vocalize and articulate her precise needs and solve problems her parents tested her with.

But, Lynn was especially bothered by the nagging feeling her little girl was not growing up like her friends' kids because she recoiled from physical touch, lacked any desire to play with other children and had very bad reactions that bordered on extreme outbursts when something did not go the way she wanted.

These tantrums usually caught her parents by surprise since they were sudden and seemed to lack a root cause, at least to them. Lynn thought Jeanne needed medical help, but she and Dan chose to raise her without intervention and focused on her strengths during her developmental years.

They fed her obvious interest and ability with books on

14

science and nature because she loved animals. She especially gravitated to the huge beasts found in Africa like hippos, giant cats, the ones she called the painted horses and especially the giraffes.

Jeanne was merely five years old when Dan, picking up on her interest in large animals, introduced her to horses in real life. Hiding behind his purported goal of teaching her about them, his real desire was to frequent the racetrack as often as possible and Jeanne's love of the ponies gave him the perfect chance.

Jeanne became enthralled with these magnificent creatures and relished the times she was walked through the paddock, loosely clutching her daddy's hand. In typical Jeanne fashion, she seldom uttered a word, yet the horses would nuzzle up to her and "talk" to her using some hidden secret language known only to Jeanne and the ponies.

She had an uncanny bond with many of the horses, with some stretching their heads outside their stall to allow her to touch them, while some others would simply gaze at her. She always seemed to be in tune with the temperament of these animals though.

As a five-year-old, Dan breathed easier when it was obvious, to him at least, that the horses calmed her down for days after a visit. So, Dan found other venues that allowed her to pet and ride ponies while learning more and more about them. As the months and years ticked by, her parents found her behavioral issues and tantrums gradually decreased.

15

An unintended bonus manifested in her social skills with other people. Children in her peer group who used to scare her with their loud and demonstrative behavior were now tolerated more and more. The buzzword in the McAlister house became "hoof therapy" because both Dan and Lynn saw the value of the visits with the horses, which made her more like a normal kid.

Of course, anything related to horses was duplicitous as Dan only had a goal of hiding his true desire; to gamble on the ponies. Dan was your typical red-headed Irishman in stature, but he had a mean streak to him carefully shrouded from others. Only Lynn truly understood what monster could be unleashed when he went off half-cocked.

Basically, he was an egotistical jackass who cared only for himself. His charisma, fair complexion and confidence allowed him to skate by just about everywhere except on the highway, where he has been ticketed twice for reckless driving and earned an endless list of moving violations as an aggressive driver, even with his wife and child in the car.

Shaving 2 minutes from a commute was a perfectly good tradeoff when it comes to risking their safety as far as he was concerned, but he still had to repair more than a few vehicles due to his recklessness.

Thanks to his excellent job in technology, he has been able to withstand those costs and still provide for his family. His income was beginning to stretch thin, and family life was getting

16

tense with Dan's gambling losses mounting since Lynn left her engineering career to care for Jeanne after her birth in 2006.

Lynn, by comparison, is a saintly human who possesses patience and can withstand his consistent verbal and mental abuse while maintaining a positive outlook on life. She is always calm even when Dan is in one of his moods and taking his psychological jabs at her body or her lack of income.

He never appreciated her even though she was a very healthy and fit size six with striking hazel eyes and voluntarily left her profession to be a full-time caregiver to a child with some special needs. Her small frame and quirky smile hid the pain she felt on the inside. Just a year after their wedding, she found her mind wandering to the continued despair of knowing she had chosen the wrong path in life and the incorrect partner, but her strength and religious convictions prevented her from simply cutting bait.

She made a deal with herself that if God gave her a son or daughter, she'd soldier forth and be a good wife and the best mother possible. Over time she contributed to building the foundation for the family as a petroleum engineer. Meanwhile, Dan trifled with all his startups until settling into an IT role.

Lynn had a fascination with plants and would often take sanctuary in her garden, where she learned to cultivate many different herbs and vegetables that would grow in their northern climate. Still, her life was one of quiet desperation, spending the formative years of Jeanne's life trying to make a connection that

17

never seemed to come.

Couple that with the challenge of dealing with Dan's open hostility when she dared to deny him an intimate encounter due to a migraine or other perfectly reasonable physical issue. The stress of both the perceived missing bond with her daughter and her husband's constant demands for intimacy piled up and she carried it inside, resorting to counseling when Jeanne was still a toddler.

She persevered to cope with a life that she felt was destined to end in total family failure for her. Still, she remained devoted to her growing girl and eventually was rewarded with the spark of a relationship that began to blossom about the same time she started first grade.

By the time Jeanne was about seven she was a pretty good rider and understood some of the differences between the various breeds, especially quarter horses and thoroughbreds since Dan would take her to the track a couple of times per week and almost every Saturday during the racing season.

She still loved her paddock walks and one day she was intrigued as a handler carried two buckets of feed into a stall. The worker opened the door and walked into the stall while Jeanne lingered in the open doorway. He was prepping the oats and collecting the empty containers when all of a sudden, the guy in the stall next to him dropped his metal buckets and a massive crash rang out.

The horse Jeanne was watching got spooked and made

a move to the door in panic, but instead, he reared up on his hind legs and whinnied loudly, flaring his nose and reaching out in the air with his giant hooves. When he came back to the ground, he pounded his left leg on the dirt and kicked up some hay but was unable to flee. The handler reached out to the gate with his eyes wide and his mouth dropped open, unable to speak.

The door was closed.

He paused for a moment in his confusion, turned to his horse and let his soothing voice calm the animal. He made a mistake not closing the door and realized Jeanne must have closed it, but now all he could do was to try and make sure his horse did not hurt himself with all the nervous energy he had.

He grabbed the horse's bridle and continued talking to the big paint while looking over his shoulder to Jeanne and said, "Little lady, you saved my horse from some nasty trouble. He would have bolted out the door, why did you shut it?"

"It's weird," she said with a quizzical look. "I knew something bad was going to happen."

"Well, thank God for that," he said. Turning to Dan, he gave a quick head nod and the two exchanged a mutual non-verbal look of thanks.

On her eighth birthday, Dan arranged a special paddock visit with a trainer he knew very well, and Jeanne was able to watch a horse being prepped on the morning of a race. She held the water hose as he was bathed and got to sponge one of his legs. She was beyond ecstatic as they returned to the Jockey

Club for the first post of the day.

She had yet to learn what all the words he said to the other regulars meant, but soon enough she got the handle of the jargon. Exacta. Trifecta. Box. Parlay. Her dad was a big gambler and taking her to the track all the time helped him further the habit. One day she blurted out "Three and Five Daddy."

He stopped and asked what she wanted. She repeated and kept repeating "three and five, three and five" almost as if she was in an altered state.

Dan finally said, "I should bet the three and five?"

She was adamant, raising her voice and displaying erratic body movements to near tantrum levels, which was strange because she had not gone through a full meltdown in almost a year. He knelt beside her and put his hand on her shoulder, but she recoiled and screamed, "THREE AND FIVE!!!" in a shriek that made what seemed like the whole club look over at them.

"OK, Jeanne, I'll buy you a ticket," he said, and she immediately calmed within a couple of seconds, her breathing slowing. He looked at the board and his racing form before laughing to himself and shaking his head, because she picked a 40-1 and 20-1 to finish first and second.

Still, he headed over to the cage and along with his bets, he bought her a $2 ticket, walked back to her and gave her the slip. He told her to make sure not to drop it because if she won, she needed it to collect her winnings.

He was secretly scoffing, knowing the chance of that bet

paying off was zip. Still, he wished her good luck and tried to ensure she was calm, nervously looking around to check if any of the regulars were staring at his kid wondering what was going on. His face felt hot and flushed and the air was somehow harder to suck down into his lungs. That tantrum had done a number on *him*.

The bell sounded and the horses broke from the gate. The three horse took the lead and led the field out with a blazing quarter mile. *No way he can hold on to that pace,* he thought to himself as they rounded the first turn. The three was showing no signs of laboring as they hit the stretch and Dan looked down to find his binoculars so he could take a peek and check on the location of the five.

He found the five and his eyes widened as his brain started doing the math. His mouth slowly fell open as he peered through the lenses, his heart rate started to quicken as the horse closed on the favorite, the same horse he bet $50 on to win, but at three to one. For a second the idea of rooting for his bet bounced around in his pride before his inner gambler broke through and he dropped the binoculars and started to yell for the five horse to pass his favorite.

He subconsciously grasped at his chest as pressure built up, but he was far too occupied to care. They hit the line with the five pulling half a head in front of the favorite. "Jiminy Christmas," he yelled out.

One of the regulars blasted back, "Shut up Dan, no one

was stupid enough to bet that exacta you degenerate."

Immediately, another regular pipes up, "Simmer down Mel, didn't you hear the kid yelling three-five right before post? She's a little savant or something."

"Dumb luck," Mel shot back.

The members were all aware of each other's tendencies, and Dan's signature phrase when he hit a big win was heard across the club, but no one would have believed it had it not been for the scene Jeanne made. Hell, he could not even believe it, so he had to check the ticket again to make sure.

Dan had played the ponies as long as he could remember and always said those high-odds exactas were called longshots for a reason. They never happened, and when they did happen it was a boon for the track because no one had the balls to bet high odds and they got to pocket the money. In this case, he didn't quite do the math correctly in his head, but he still wound up with over $1200 on the $2 wager he got for his daughter.

Dan never played it safe and always played $50 exactas. In life, it was the same tale, as he spent his 30-plus years starting and failing at several business ventures, including real estate, app development, and even tried his hand at opening a restaurant before settling in as an engineer at an IT firm on the outskirts of Chestertown, a suburb of Chicago.

Although he was married, his true love was always gambling. His reckless mentality never permits him to just throw $20 on the favorite to win, place, or show, he had to have the exotics. Exactas and Trifectas were his babies, and he researched the races for hours before the bell.

He could not resist the high-risk, big-reward play. His wife never understood the attraction, but they always seemed to pay their bills and have disposable income, so she tolerated his indulgence. Then Jeanne was born, and Lynn asked Dan to cut back on his habit to help support the larger family.

He was able to comply for a while but made up a story about his company having financial problems. He lied and said his salary was cut so he could explain a smaller paycheck when, in actuality, he opened another bank account and diverted $500 per pay period to hit the track just as he had in the past, except now with Jeanne in tow. Knowing the horses had a calming effect on their daughter, Lynn allowed him to continue but had no idea Dan was gambling over a thousand dollars a month.

"How did you get the 3 and 5?" He asked her.

"Because I saw the ending, Daddy," she responded. "Or whatever it was, but you lost all this money and then when we got home, Mom was super mad and she started talking about leaving but I could hear you. That made it so loud in my head I could barely think, then everything got all weird, and then, like magic, the race was going to start, and I told you 3 and 5 would finish first and second."

"So you had a dream about the race before it happened? Like, imaginary or sleepy time?"

"I'm not real sure," she said as she shrugged her shoulders. "It was a strange feeling, but it was like I had seen all

23

of this already." She looked down at the ground and started shuffling her feet against the carpet and wringing her hands together.

"Don't worry!" Dan said, seeing the signs of what was coming. He put his hand on her shoulder to check for a recoil, paused then put his other hand right below her chin to slowly raise her head and said, "You were super lucky today. I don't care how this happened, but it was a very good thing for us."

He paused, and then continued, "Are you ok? Do we need to go to a quiet room?"

She shook her head and took a deep breath, saying nothing while the edges of her lips curved up ever so slightly.

Dan's luck turned around. He hit a trifecta in the eighth and another exacta in the tenth, but his mind was wandering to her tantrum. He paused and thought to himself, *Why did she have it in the first place?* He went through her list of stressors...no sudden changes, nothing was out of the ordinary, no unexpected loud noises or other startling things.

He stared at the racing form, devoid of rational thought, instead thinking about what she sounded like. Pain, confusion, panic, all the things she never really expressed and that's when it finally hit him. It was a raw emotional reaction rather than a typical sensory-based one that sent her into a tizzy. He had yet to witness Jeanne exhibit that much emotion. He shook his head as his eyes darted about the room and muttered, "No way, that can't be."

As he focused on tomorrow's races, he started talking

with some of the others who stayed late. They talked about what almost was in the Jockey Club, but in the end, he did what he does best when he can't understand something. He dismissed it. He labeled his daughter's daydream as a childhood fantasy or a fluke. He had no idea what that cost him.

That $2 bet changed the whole day, and after his other good wins he cleared close to three thousand dollars on that Saturday afternoon, but it could have been the most profitable day of his life had he hit the big one. He had one shining moment that turned his day around, which was not even his.

His stomach rumbled and a flash of heat made him parse his lips slightly as the resentment began to creep in on his proud psyche, but he managed to keep it at bay this time and gave all the credit to Jeanne, his soon-to-be good luck charm.

Four years later, Dan and Lynn were about five years away from paying off their home and being free of a mortgage that was burdensome at times. With gambling losses mounting, the couple had to cut back on a few things like their excessive habit of dining out, their bundle with all the premium movie channels, and a few streaming services, but nothing beyond pure entertainment for them.

After a tough day at work, Dan decided to head down to the Jockey Club to catch the last four races of the day, but he was in a precarious position. They barely had enough to cover the rest of the month's expenses, and he was about to take half that money as his bankroll.

Armed with $500 and a score to settle after a hard day, he opened his racing form and quickly went to work. In the 7th, he spotted a two-year-old moving down in class and using Lasix for the first time.

Everyone will be all over this one, he thought to himself. His experience told him first-time users of this breathing drug significantly outperformed. At 9-1, he was not the favorite, but something did not square. He looked at it twice and tried to figure out if the horse had significant breathing issues or just faded, but he could not detect a pattern requiring Lasix.

The last workout listed for Bully Bondsman was a very fast quarter mile and another showed a good 6-furlong time. It was certainly enough to compete at this level, but why was the horse in the seven-hole going off at 9-1? And why did he need breathing drugs?

No one is taking this one seriously, how is it that I am the smartest guy here? He found the perfect horse to pair up in his exacta and was so sure of himself he threw down a $200 exacta box and his ticket would pay off with the 7 or the 3 finishing first or second. Since it was technically 2 bets, this cost him almost all his bankroll, but he had a winner here. He was sure of it.

The bell sounded, and he casually walked over to a monitor his 7 horse took the early lead, off to the same blazing start he had in his workout. This time, the Lasix helped Bully Bondsman breathe a little easier and he maintained his pace. By the time they reached the final turn, he had nine lengths on second place and was going to win the race going away, but in the pack, Dan's 3 horse, Calypso, had some work to do.

He was pinned on the rail by the 2 and the 5 with nowhere to run. His jockey had him in a bad spot and had to do something fast. As they started down the stretch, Calypso's rider went to his whip, and with a tug, he changed his running lane, forcing the 5 a little wider. They made the hole they needed and were off to the races.

The gap closed to one length, the horses crossed in front of the eighth pole and Dan was screaming at the monitor for his horse. This was the moment he was looking forward to for the last 6 months, he had been losing and losing and losing and this was his big day!

Calypso pulled ahead by a nose as the horses approached the line but missed a step and got off stride. The 2 horses finished strong and they hit the finish line together. It was impossible to tell who came in second.

The tote board had blanks for 2nd and 3rd and beneath the results grid was the red neon light of the word "photo". Dan's heart raced as he began to feel the pain and emptiness in his gut and reached up to his shoulder while telling himself to relax. He started ringing his hands and shook his head to the side to relieve the growing discomfort in his chest.

He needed this race to finish 7-3, it had to, but now his fate was in the hands of the officials examining the photos taken at the line. He was lost in his own emotion for a moment and failed to realize the word "photo" was joined by red neon letters that spelled "inquiry" on the board.

"Jiminy Christmas!" Dan yelped as the photo was shown on the monitor. It was fairly clear to him he had several thousand dollars coming to him as it showed Calypso by a nose for second place. He began celebrating quietly, as it is frowned upon for the pros to show over-the-top exuberance, but this was different.

This time Lynn would be proud of him. He not only paid the mortgage for a couple of months, but he also won enough for their vacation this summer. He was making plans in his head when suddenly over the PA...

"The steward's inquiry has resulted in a disqualification of the 3 horse, Calypso, in race number 7. The 3 has been placed in 5th, behind..." Dan never heard the rest of the announcement.

As track personnel tried to revive Dan, it was apparent he had suffered a massive heart attack. An ambulance was rushed to the scene and CPR was performed on him for 9 minutes as they raced to the hospital. A paramedic removed the ticket from his clenched hand and remarked he should not be playing with money he could not afford to lose, but no one can ever truly understand the mind of a man addicted to gambling.

Back at the McAlister residence, the phone rang, and Lynn answered, talked for a second and Jeanne jumped when her mom shrieked and screamed for her little girl to come down so they could go visit Daddy. At 12, her psyche was getting better, but she did not fully grasp the dire circumstances right away and was throwing a fit when she was being taken away from her tablet.

When they arrived at the hospital, it became clearer for her. She looked across the room as an older man wearing blue scrubs and a paper hat walked over to her mother. The man removed the paper thing on his head and from his chin and put his hand on her mom's shoulder as she began sobbing uncontrollably.

She started to spiral, and in Jeanne's mind, she was overcome with uncontrollable, deafening noise. Her eyes started darting back and forth as the silent, yet debilitating sound paralyzed her, and her thoughts were a time bomb about to go off in her head, but a news story caught her focus.

She was distracted by the television report of a man who collapsed with an apparent heart attack at Remington Downs after his horse was disqualified and a video of the finish of the race was playing. Somehow, without knowing a thing or hearing the conversation, she knew her dad died, but the noise took her deep into the darkness.

For the longest time, Jeanne struggled with her thoughts taking her away in what she could only describe as being loud. Even though it was quiet in the house, when she was stressed or something changed all of a sudden, she'd retreat into her vacuum of thought and could only tell her parents it was really loud.

They, of course, had no understanding of this concept at all. Over time as she grew, they found ways to help her cope and learn how to channel her energy by allowing her to work with horses. She was able to almost comprehend them without a sound and would sense when they were nervous or scared.

Her uncanny ability led to her being called a little horse whisperer by some of the workers at the farms and stables she went to because she had a calming effect on them too. As she got older, she was able to make the correlation between their body language and her classmates' body language, although she could not understand why people never said what they meant.

She interpreted the spoken word very literally and ultimately started to rely on facial cues and body language to try and figure out if someone was playing with her or being mean. As she entered her middle school years, the kids made fun of her differences, as they tend to do. In class, she often said the noise was trying to take her away because she always worried about what people would say.

She always wanted to plan everything out in her day, but things always went wrong and her plans constantly needed changing, and change was her enemy. It stressed her so much, that sometimes the slightest thing set her off, like the time the boy in front of her took the last hamburger.

The lunch lady told her to hold on for a minute, but she was frozen, panicking that the burger was gone. Her breath quickened as she started to get overwhelmed with the noise in her head and she struggled to even function until the new tray of burgers arrived. The noise started to subside, but she was in crisis, her heart beating so fast that she needed some help from a teacher to go through the line.

During times like this, she'd make use of her most important coping device, her noise-canceling headphones. She used them for much more than listening to her music, somehow the music helped her deal with sudden changes. She had no idea how defining and impactful her favorite song *Change* would be later in life.

Chapter 3

Mattis (18 months ago)

Puppies are fantastic little bundles of fun, and Mattis was no different. He had boundless energy and a demeanor that, from a very young age, set him apart from other dogs because he seemed highly protective of his owners and sibling pets in the household.

Mattis was born with jet-black fur, and small brown patches on the base of his paws so he always had the quintessential German shepherd look about him, but his family always saw something else in his eyes. They noticed he had an inquisitive nature and always watched everything around him. Whether it was the kids, the other dogs, or Mom and Dad, his watchful eye always seemed to be engaged, ready to pounce at the first sign something was off.

Once, when Mattis was still a puppy, Sergeant Tony Scott, the K-9 unit supervisor for the City of Austin looked up to see he was sitting at the top of the stairs seemingly barking at nothing. As Tony ascended the beige carpeted steps, he looked up, past the old wooden slats to the landing of the 2nd floor, and realized the little blue gate, usually fixed and locked at the top step, had come ajar, but only slightly.

Worse, their son Preston was standing next to the half

wall near the staircase, about 3 feet away. Was Mattis playfully barking at the boy, or was he alerting Tony to the fact that the latch was open? Tony looked at the gate, then back at Mattis, who barked again, and so he reached over and pulled the gate forward until he felt the click, at which time Mattis immediately dropped his head and went back down the stairs to his blanket and toy rope.

Tony stood at the landing for a moment, cocked his head a little sideways, and gave a glance back to his son before stepping back up and over the bars to pick Preston up. He hugged his little boy and walked him back to his big boy bed, where he put him back down for his nap.

As he came back downstairs, he looked over at Mattis, chewing on his favorite plaything. *No way you just did that,* he thought to himself as a small smile crept up from the corners of his mouth. Distracted, he proceeded to walk into the corner of the wall that separated the family room from the kitchen, wincing at the sharp pain in his shoulder.

Mattis began training with Tony unofficially in 2019 when he was roughly 9 months old. The department typically started new K-9 officers and handlers after their first birthday, but Mattis had already shown exceptional perception and protective skills. Given this, Sgt. Scott started with hand signals and commands a little early with departmental approval.

Mattis was able to train using a handheld clicker that Tony engaged along with treats to further reinforce the behaviors he wanted to see. One day in September, he took Mattis for a short walk with the family through their Barton Creek neighborhood when Mattis did something very uncharacteristic.

It was uncharacteristically warm in Austin for that time of year, and a breeze made for a pleasant feeling for them. As they approached an intersection about half a mile from home, Mattis suddenly pulled the leash hard as Tony's wife Mindy stepped toward the corner of the intersection they were approaching. He threw his body against Preston's stroller, then sat in front of it, barking. Mindy tried to go around him, but he blocked her path. Tony started to command Mattis to move but did not finish the command.

As he gave the command, a Tesla went humming by, completely blowing through the stop sign. The car was speeding at about 45 miles per hour since it was a side street, and Mindy screamed and started to lose her breath. She struggled to breathe as Tony captured the license plate of the vehicle. He turned to try and calm Mindy down as she started shaking.

She instinctively reached to pick up Preston. As she held him tightly against her chest, she started to cry. Tony knew, as she did, that disaster could have struck their family had they been in the crosswalk. The three of them shared a momentary embrace, trying to relax.

Mattis seemed totally on top of it, sitting alertly in front of the stroller with his tongue out, falling a bit on the right side of his face. He looked sharp and proud. Tony leaned over to pick up Mattis, and as he struggled to get the big dog comfortable, Mattis leaned over and started licking Preston's hair, and then Mindy's face. The couple stood motionless, staring at one another.

"What just happened?" Mindy asked as she wiped the tears away and let out a big sniffle as she tried to control her very emotional reaction.

"I think Mattis heard the car coming, but why did he step in the way and stop us?" Tony responded.

"No idea, but I think he's going to be quite the partner when you retire Flash next year, don't you?"

Tony put Mattis back on the sidewalk, leaned his head in toward the pup, looked into his eyes, and said "Yes you will, won't you Mattis? You're such a good boy!" He praised him, petted his head, reached into his pocket, and pulled a piece of dry liver, Mattis' favorite treat.

As Mattis scarfed it down, Tony noticed something. "Did you ever notice this little patch of gray fur on his paw, honey?"

"I don't think so, when did that show up?" she asked.

"No clue, I'm surprised I've never seen it," he said, simply dismissing it.

"Some detective you'll be," Mindy said jokingly, eliciting a smirk and a stare from Tony.

A couple of months later as Mattis approached his 1st birthday, Christmas decorations were up around the Scott house. Young Preston was still too little to understand the idea of the holiday, but he loved staring at the lights on the tree and would frequently be caught playing with the Santa Clauses and ornaments on the tree.

Mindy collected Santas with a very discriminating eye, only selecting friendly-looking ones to adorn their modest home. They all seemed to have a smile and a big white beard, and glasses and some would be fishing, others sitting in their chairs, but her favorite was the one that simply sat on the floor, with a heavy base that almost made it look like a giant old Weeble, one of her first toys in her youth.

One day, that fat little guy of hers was irrevocably altered…

Preston was downstairs playing in his little pen as Tony and Mindy started to make dinner one Saturday night. The Longhorns were playing in the Big XII championship that evening, so they would be entertaining a few friends and watching the game.

Tony cleaned the grill and started the fire for the fajitas he'd be grilling later. He was going in and out as the first couple arrived, bringing some apple cobbler for dessert. Tony opened a bottle of wine and began chatting as Mindy checked on the beans and rice she was making to complement the meat and chicken.

No one noticed Preston slip out of his pen and make the half-crawl, half-walk across the beige shag carpet and tile floor, fixated on his prize. Preston was intent on playing with the fat red weeble Santa at the base of the stairwell.

36

The guys went outside after opening the wine, with Mattis trailing Tony as he always does. Tony's friend Alex popped the top on a couple of beers and the two started sipping on Shiners and thinking about work. Alex, a firefighter, was telling a story about a homeless kid that he'd had to call child protective services about after his house responded to a residential fire which turned out to be nothing more than badly overcooked pot roast.

They were deep in conversation about Austin's growing homeless problems when a sudden shriek cut through the festivities from inside the house. Tony's beer shattered on the floor as it fell and the two men with Mattis following them ran in to see what happened.

They bolted through the kitchen and around the half bar when Tony caught sight of Mindy slumped over on the floor by the base of the stairs. As the guys got closer they observed Preston lying at the bottom of the stairwell, flat on his back on the tile floor with bluish skin. He was still holding the weeble Santa, missing the small bell on the top of his hat.

Alex immediately stepped in to assess his airway, breathing, and pulse. Tony was on the phone with 911 when he noticed Mattis was lying on his back, his eyes completely rolled back in his head as if he was deep asleep.

He had to place the phone on speaker and allow Alex to talk to the 911 operator. He conveyed the critical information to first responders so they would be ready to assist with a child choking. Alex started compressions that comprise the modified

Heimlich maneuver performed on a small kid while they are on their back.

He firmly pressed upward on his lower abdomen, in a frantic attempt to dislodge the object with no success. Mindy was screaming and crying, with Alex's wife Taylor holding her, trying to console the inconsolable mother as she tried to clear the tears from her eyes. They were frozen, and could only look down at Tony and Alex working on Mindy's lifeless son, absolutely powerless to do anything…

Mattis' First Big Jump

Preston was downstairs playing in his little pen as Tony and Mindy decided they'd start making dinner this Saturday evening. It was a huge night since the Longhorns were playing in the Big XII championship after years of absolute futility. They invited a few friends to watch the game, so Tony started the grill and began to prepare the fajitas.

He was going in and out as their first couple arrived bringing apple cobbler, Tony's favorite, for dessert. The ladies opened some wine and the guys retreated to the backyard to nurse some Shiners and talk about the latest happenings on the job.

Mindy was inside working on smashing and refrying some beans and checking on her rice while Alex's wife Taylor was chopping some onions and green peppers she'd cook for the tacos. No one noticed Preston was restless and climbing at the side of his pen, almost ready to make his escape.

38

Outside, Alex was talking about the homeless problems he'd seen on his last shift and Tony agreed, sharing that the city is looking at some passive procedures to try and start cleaning up the encampment under the overpass at a major highway intersection along with others below their big interstate bridges, but they don't have a plan that would not incite a riot among Austin's growing liberal base of citizens.

They were in the middle of a conversation when Mattis suddenly bolted from his lying position and ran through the screen door. He hit it so hard that he physically separated the nylon mesh from the frame of the door, leaving a two-foot hole in the lower left corner, and the latch bent in the housing.

Tony instinctually followed, and after struggling with the now-broken door, asked Alex to watch the grill for a second. Alex is already walking toward the house, and once Tony frees the latch from its injured handle housing, they walk in to find Mattis destroying Mindy's favorite Santa. He's laid out at the base of the stairs, having already ripped the hat off the fat little weeble, and is violently shaking the bell in his mouth.

Mindy yells, "Mattis, NO! What are you doing?"

Tony runs in and commands Mattis, "Drop it." Mattis immediately assumed his pose and dropped the hat. The bell landed on the tile first and gave a sad little clank as it hit the floor. Tony followed that command with "Kennel" as Mattis retreated to his box, calmly walked inside, and sat down.

Something struck Tony as odd, however, because Mattis usually pouts when he was commanded to his crate, but this time he almost proudly pranced over, entered, turned, and sat, looking back at Tony with his ears high and his eyes alert.

Through the commotion, Mindy finds Preston, who escaped from his playpen and was sitting close to the stairwell, shaken up from all the yelling and once she picked him up, he started crying.

Alex took a big breath and exhaled sharply, "Dude," he said in a quivery voice as he turned to Tony, "I've never seen a dog tear through a door and attack a stuffed animal before, what the hell was that?"

Tony tried to piece together what happened. His mind returned to some of the crazy things Mattis had done in the past. He told Alex about some of them like the open baby gate and the time Mattis threw himself in front of the stroller. He goes on to say that just a couple of seconds after that, a car ran the stop sign right next to them, coming out of nowhere.

After hearing all that, Alex clears his throat and swallows hard. He collects himself and says, "So, Preston climbed out of his pen, do you think he was going for the bell that was on the cap of that Santa? But how would Mattis have known from the outside?"

Taylor interjects, "Obviously your dog is psychic."

Alex, annoyed, shoots back "Tay, this is not your astrology stuff, no way an animal can have that foresight gift or whatever you call it."

Taylor immediately comes back with "Well, who's the one who still says 'may the force be with you' and honestly thinks he

40

can save people on the street by channeling his inner strength?" She raises her eyebrows and makes that face that a wife makes when she just won the battle.

"For real Alex? I knew you were a Star Wars geek but really?" Tony laughs.

"Can it, Scooter."

"Seriously, animals have to use emotion and energy to communicate with their humans, they have astrological signs and I firmly believe our pets are tied to us in a way that we can never understand," Taylor explains.

Tony pauses and looks up for a second and says, "I mean, he almost pranced into his kennel and looked proud, like he had done something I trained him to do. He was also expecting a reward based on his body language. Are you suggesting Mattis can sense when something bad is about to happen and can act on that impulse?"

"That's exactly what I am saying," Taylor said, but she smells the tortilla she had on the cast iron skillet burning and runs off to check on it.

Tony went back over to Mattis and gave him a bacon chew while he opened the door and made the hand signal for him to stay, then motioned for him to come and sit next to his right foot using another hand command. "You are going to be one hell of a partner, buddy," he said.

Mattis looked at him and barked.

Mattis was showing great promise as a K-9 officer in training, now in the middle of his 6-month program to become Tony's new companion. Flash, Tony's previous partner was approaching 6 years old and about to be retired, after a career where he apprehended about 30 criminals single-pawedly and assisted in the capture of about 200 other suspects using his superior scent-tracking ability.

He was not specifically a detection dog, but his senses were honed well enough that he could alert on many illegal substances. Flash also lived with Tony and was Mattis' first playmate. Unfortunately, he could not run and play as much as he used to after taking a bullet in the line of duty a year ago. This accelerated his impending promotion to pet doggo.

For the next few months, Tony worked with Mattis on various aspects of his duties including hand signals and verbal commands. Those came pretty easy for him, but Mattis excelled at detection and tracking. With additional training, Mattis was able to detect illicit drugs hidden in a coffee can and placed inside a sealed styrofoam cooler. He was also able to track his partner by scent up to half a mile away, and that distance keeps growing.

In a game Tony called the door-popper, where the rear doors of the squad car are remotely triggered to open using a handheld device that communicates with the car itself, Mattis stays in the vehicle until Tony pops the door open. Then Mattis tries to find him, but Tony makes it progressively harder for him. He's gotten so advanced Tony donned a rubber wind suit, used the water in a stream to mask his track, and deliberately retraced his steps so two scent trails led Mattis in opposite directions.

Every attempt failed. He always got his man. Sure, the first time he did the two-scent path thing, Mattis got confused. It took an extra two minutes, but he still found Tony. All except one time he never found the target, but he found something else instead...

Tony popped the door open one spring day, after meticulously hiding under a natural bridge in a stream about a quarter mile away. What typically took about 3 minutes was taking way longer, so he decided to emerge from the drain and start looking for Mattis.

It did not take long for him to hear the familiar bark, and he found Mattis standing on top of the squad car. Once they caught sight of each other, Mattis bolted off the car in the other direction towards the south, into the trees, pausing at the edge of the foliage to look behind him.

This is an unmistakable sign for Tony. Mattis had a target but wanted confirmation because he was given no command to search. Still, he followed through the brush to a small hut in the woods that had some smoke or steam rising from the top of a smokestack. Tony's first thought is Mattis found a methamphetamine lab or some other lab where they were cooking up a batch of drugs.

He jumps on his shoulder radio for backup, calling in the suspicious building, but Mattis is acting strangely. He pulls at

43

Tony's belt, almost urging him to retreat into the trees. Remembering the uncanny ability Mattis displayed in the past, he read the signals and backed into the tree line.

Mattis proceeded to sprint full out toward the hut, barking. He disrupted the men inside, and the makeshift door opened to reveal a man dressed in lab attire with a gas mask and blue gloves about to level a rifle toward the charging dog, but as Tony grabbed his weapon and took aim to return fire, the rush of incoming air caused a chemical reaction resulting in a massive explosion, surely killing everyone in the little building.

Mattis was thrown a few meters back but sprang up and went to Tony's feet where he sat, motionless. Shrapnel landed all over the small clearing and a thin veil of smoke lingered over the remains of the hut. Immediately, Tony called for a hazmat unit and paramedics for any casualties.

Not knowing much about meth operations, he chose to keep his distance because the two bodies were wearing gas masks. As the haze dissipated, he returned to his cruiser to gather supplies and was able to guide the medics and hazardous materials team.

During the investigation, Tony was asked about what he witnessed and he remarked that the smoke leaving the top of the vent looked yellowish to him. As the team did their initial due diligence, they sounded an alarm and vacated the area, clearing everyone from the scene and calling for some specialized containment units for the remaining cleanup.

As Tony was getting his gear ready to leave the site after

being cleared by the incident commander, he asked one of the responders what happened. The young lady explained she found a chemical in a container that somehow did not explode, and she suspected it was phosphorus.

She further comments that if it reacted violently, it would have killed everything within 100 feet of the blast and released a cloud of gas that caused severe respiratory issues for anyone inhaling it. She goes on to say these guys were idiots who had never done it before and had it all wrong.

"Based on the state of the lab, or what is left of it, and the venting of the yellow gas, they were probably a few minutes away from using the phosphorus. I can't understand why they had so much of it, because that quantity would have triggered a much larger explosion had they not been startled and blown themselves up," she concludes.

Tony looks concerned and says, "Officer...I'm sorry, you don't have a badge on."

"Tamil, Marie Tamil."

"Marie, is this location safe from the explosion had the phosphorus blown?" He pointed downward to mark the spot they stood on.

She answered, "Most certainly not, not without a respirator or other protection. You were north of the blast site, the cloud would have been on you in 60-90 seconds and you would not have known anything was wrong until your chest burned you from the inside out."

Tony blinked, unable to speak. His heart rate quickened.

45

He finally stammered, "My dog. He spooked them into making the mistake. Could he have smelled the problem?"

"Surely he smelled the cook, the prevailing wind brought the scent up here. He's not a drug dog, is he?"

"Not yet, but he has superior detection ability."

"Yeah, that's why he tracked it. I can't tell how much they would have yielded, but he probably took out half a mil of product, and the cooks, of course," Officer Tamil says as she looks over at Mattis.

Tony is still having trouble concentrating. He says, "Thank you. Good work Tamil."

"You guys did the good work here Scott."

He shakes her hand, but he keeps thinking about it, and can't shake the feeling that Mattis somehow did it again.

This time it was way outside the realm of what he thought was possible and his brain could not reconcile it, so he called Alex after his shift. Tony still did not believe in psychic horse hockey but asked if Alex and Taylor would come talk to them that evening.

When they arrived, Tony shared the story of what happened and asked Taylor seriously about psychic connections, animal attachment to their owners, and other metaphysical items he thought were total hogwash, or at least he did mere months before. Alex was already starting to make fun of him.

46

He'd seen Taylor immerse herself in tarot cards, astrology, and spiritual arts to explain things that happened, and to try and tap into what she believed was an inherent human ability to transcend the physical universe and enter a state of transient consciousness. She believed that people could access the experiences of others while in this condition and see the future or the past.

Taylor glared at her husband through all the ribbing and said "You wait, you'll see, Mattis is special. The problem is he can't tell us what he is seeing, what he goes through, and what he feels. But he has a connection to the spirit world somehow."

Alex snorted and covered his face, knowing something was about to be launched in his general direction.

Taylor sneered at him and considered throwing a pillow at him but did not.

Tony sat frozen. He was dumbfounded, wondering what the heck he was doing. He never trusted psychics on the force, he heard of some cases that used them in the past, but he never believed in it. He shook his head and dropped the idea he was forming and politely carried on the conversation.

He listened to Taylor talk about all the things he and Alex made fun of all the while cursing at himself inside his head for allowing the indulgence. At the culmination of the evening, he thanked them for coming and the guys made plans to go out to the gun range that weekend.

Tony thought about that information for weeks, but in the end, he decided it was not for him and went on with his training for the next few months, after which Mattis was officially promoted to K-9 Officer Mattis of the Austin Police Department.

Chapter 4

Natalee (3 months ago)

Natalee sits down at the same empty table she always does, in the same seat she sits at every day, with the same lunch in her brown bag she always has. Coming from the classroom adjacent to the cafeteria always has its privileges. No one would dare sit in that spot even if she was a little late getting out of class, not this late in the school year. Their spots have been established.

The students at McAuliffe High School all knew their places by now and if anyone dared take a place at that table, the regret would be immediate and severe. Looking over the lunchroom at this period reveals the jocks in the corner, with the cheerleaders and drill team closer to the center, but next to the jocks.

The goth kids were in the opposite corner, but only numbered a dozen or so. The math and science geeks had a spot, and the popular ones had their claim to the middle of the room, as they should because they provided the heartbeat of the school and deserved to be the center of attention, at least to them it seemed that way.

Natalee and her circle of friends occupy a table a little off dead center, so of course anyone trying to intrude would instantaneously rue that they tried. Natalee felt a little out of place since she was not considered OG schoolhouse royalty during her first year, but she adapted and has generally been accepted as part of the clique, mostly due to Christina.

"Hey, Nat."

Startled, Natalee looks up, slightly confused because no one calls her that anymore, it was a nickname she shed at the end of the 8th grade at the behest of her friend Emily, who said high school boys would like her if she stopped using her kid name.

"Mind if I sit with you?" asked the tiny woman standing next to her. At barely 5 feet tall, with shoulder-length dirty blonde hair and always dressed like she found her newest attire at a thrift store, Shannon has turned flying under the radar into an art. Given the fact she would rather die than have any manner of attention paid to her, it must be taking all she has to approach this table.

"Uh, sure," Natalee mumbles, "how've you been Shannon? It's been a minute since we've seen each other."

"Well, our third-period classes are right beside each other, so I see *you* every day," she says in a dry way that makes Natalee do a double take. She takes the chair soon to be occupied by McKenzie Shepler.

McKenzie, even though she's incredibly loyal as a friend and impossibly attractive with long flowing brown hair and ice blue eyes, is simply vacuous at times and won't have the good sense to take the next seat, so Natalee is already worrying about the social dynamic.

Natalee's eyes dart around the room, deflecting from her embarrassment. Her former best friend just put her on blast, right in front of God and everybody. She looks back and says, "Right, so, long time…no, um, speak?" It has been a while. Shannon and Natalee used to be super tight years ago, but once they got to high school, they didn't have any classes together and quickly grew apart.

Natalee made new friends, and she…well…didn't. She was certain Shannon wouldn't jive with the people she hangs out with now, so she let her do her own thing for the past three-plus years. She begins to feel bad for not talking to Shannon but decides not to care.

"Yeah," Shannon says quietly and then pauses. She has something to say, but she can't seem to find the words.

After taking a breath deeper than the ocean, she ends the excruciating silence at last. "I'm sorry to bother you, but I need to talk to someone, and I didn't know who else to go to. If you're not busy tonight, do you think maybe--"

"Oh, she's busy alright. Have you not heard about Jack's party? It's going to be the biggest thing of the year," Christina so graciously interrupts, setting her backpack down and sitting down across from Natalee as fabulously as only she can. With her gorgeously curled yet never frizzy chocolate brown hair, perfect sun-kissed complexion, and a wardrobe that would make some movie stars jealous, Christina Sinclair is easily one of the prettiest, most popular, and most powerful girls in school.

Focusing her glorious green eyes directly at Natalee, she says with a conviction no one would dare contest, "You are not missing that party, Natalee." After a few intense, soul-melting moments, she finally releases the glare and turns to Shannon. "Sarah, right?"

"Close enough," Shannon mutters, getting up from McKenzie's seat as she arrives at the table with that unmistakable dazed look plastered on her face. Shannon looks at the ground and repositions her feet so she's not touching any tile lines and fidgets with anything her fingers can touch, then spins around to depart as silently as she arrives.

"Maybe I'll call you this weekend," Natalee says as Shannon walks away, for some reason watching her feet as they quickly carry her across the cafeteria and into the huge herd of hungry high schoolers waiting in line for their food. Natalee wonders for a moment if Shannon heard her, secretly feels a little bad hoping she doesn't, but is not about to go chase her down. She instead takes a bite out of the juicy red delicious apple she's been craving all day.

"What was that all about?" McKenzie asks.

"What was what all about?" inquires Emily as she takes her place next to Christina. Emily Monroe, who is tall, blond, and wears a tad more make-up than necessary, is known not-so-affectionately around school as "Barbie," but she happens to be one of the nicest people in their group.

"I have no idea," Natalee replies, really having none. What could she possibly have wanted? To talk? About what?

They haven't talked in ages and Natalee has changed so much that Shannon doesn't even know her anymore. Natalee ponders to herself *Is she so lonely and desperate that I'm the only person she thinks she can talk to?*

"So about this party," Natalee blurts out in an attempt to end the gossip before it begins, "how many people are going?"

The Party

Thousands. Thousands upon thousands of people are at this party. Or so it felt to Natalee. Bodies everywhere. Bodies dancing, bodies talking, bodies eating, bodies drinking. Bodies doing just about everything bodies do. After a while, Natalee's body decides (unfortunately slightly after about twenty-three other bodies) that she needs to go to the restroom. Standing in the approximately mile-long line for the only downstairs bathroom, she takes out her phone to check the time. 11:03. About two hours until she has to be home. As she's about to put it back in her pocket, it begins to vibrate. *Great*, she says to herself, *it's Dad.*

"Hello?!"

Party music blaring.

"Dad?!"

Partygoers screaming.

"Dad, I can't hear you!"

Party glasses breaking.

She looks back and sees three new people have already lined up behind her. The next girl back makes eye contact with her and shakes her head. "If you leave, you're not getting your spot back," She shouts in Natalee's ear, "and the wait upstairs is longer!"

"Fantastic," she mutters to herself, then screams into her cell "I'll call you back in a few minutes! Sorry!" before hanging up and sliding it into her back pocket. He was going to be pissed, but *she had to go.* Sure enough, her phone almost immediately starts vibrating again, but she ignores it. And she ignores the next call. And the next one.

Her dad is an incredibly persistent person, so she loses count of how many times he calls her until it's finally her turn to relieve herself. She takes a deep breath and steels herself to enter the chaos inside. Surprisingly, the toilet is still in working order. She does her business as quickly as possible, then makes her way outside and across the street.

The cold feels like needles on her bare face and hands. It floods her lungs and they all of a sudden feel heavy. As loud and crowded as it is inside the party, she is completely isolated in the vast frosty space outside.

She gulps down the night, shoving as much of it down into her chest as she can manage, then releases it slowly, watching a small, moist cloud form inches beyond her lips, marveling for a moment at her ability to warm the world, or at least part of McLean, Virginia. Again, she inhales, allowing the frigid air to cleanse her from within her chest, and exhales, dispersing life into the atmosphere.

Her bladder empty and her mind calm, she finally forces

herself to face her father's fury. She takes out her phone and her face contorts as the screen shows eighteen missed calls and three texts, all from her dad. She opens the text messages first to prepare her brain to react to the onslaught.

"Come home IMMEDIATELY!!!"

"The police are here. WE NEED TO TALK."

"You better be on your way back here."

On her way to the house, Natalee has to remind herself several times to breathe. Stress can trigger an episode and she does not want that while driving.

Inhale….

Exhale….

Inhale….

Exhale…

What could she possibly have done wrong? Natalee is not the perfect child, but she hasn't given them any reason to call the police tonight. She told her parents she was at Jack's house with some friends, which was true. She may have strategically left out the part about the party and his folks not being home, but if they suspected illegal activity, why not send the cops *there*?

Hyperventilating by the time she gets home, she pulls into the driveway and tries to sneak inside like she's trying not to wake anyone up as if people aren't waiting for her in the living room, and as if she can avoid whatever's coming. But when she walks in, her footsteps seem to echo like the thunder of a storm rolling in.

Five pairs of eyes turn and rain down on her immediately. First, her father's: dark, distraught, denunciatory. He is confused, he is enraged, and he will not be taking any crap tonight.

Next, the two police officers look up from the book they've been studying and quickly scan her from head to toe, not bothering to hide their attempt to decide within two seconds whether she's guilty of whatever she didn't do.

Her mom remains seated on the couch but turns her blotchy face toward Natalee and lifts her puffy, bloodshot eyes to hers for half an instant before dropping them once again to her feet. She can't bear to look at her, even though she hasn't done anything wrong,

Natalee can't help but feel some guilt. For something. Mothers are quite adept at imposing shame where none exists and her mom is no exception. Finally, two icy blue eyes come crashing down on her. Shocked, she is immobilized by the cold, precise, and unrelenting glare of Dr. Karen Walters, Shannon's mom.

Natalee stands frozen in time, mind racing and unable to utter a word under the immense pressure of the gazes she walked into. She's about to drop into a full-blown panic attack when she is startled by the words, "Sit down." She assumes it belongs to someone in the room and sits down.

"Something very tragic has happened," another voice chokes out. It takes her a while to deduce it must have been her mother's.

The book the police were reading when she came in is

not, in fact, a book, but rather a journal.

Now it is in Natalee's lap.

She looks at the writing. She reads the words.

She turns the pages. And finally, she gets to the last page:

'I haven't talked to the only real friend I've had in years. My mom is never home, and when she is, she treats me like I'm another pAtient. She's kind enough, and she gives me anYthing and everything I could ever need, but sometimes I wonder if she's not as numb as the bodies she performs surgery on. She talks about them as if they're just objects, anyway. She looks inside so many hearts but never understands how anyone feels.

I can't remember the last thing I said to my dad except for an argument. All he does is scream and yell and tell me I don't measure up. Have I no one buT my shadow? But even she leaves me when the sun goes down, and I've been walking in darkness for so long now.

Bones can heal from sticks and stones, but my heart is scarred by words.

Some things are bigger than pride.

What kind of world do we live in, where we allow numbers on a piece of paper to control our lives? So what if I got a B in my first semester of AP Calculus? That doesn't mean I won't get into college. You scream your head ofF at me now, but where were you when I needed help, mister accountant?

So close. I am on the edge of my breaking point. I want so badly to crumble to the floor in pieces. But I can't do it. Giving up only makes it worse. I want to know how much one girl can take.

I haunt myself with thoughts that should never exist. There is no reason for me to be thinking this way. This is not healthy.

I don't know what this thing is, but it comes in the night, and it eats me from the inside out.

Mortality is a gift.

I don't know why it took me so long to realize that I'll never be able to climb out of these holes on my own. All I can do is dig deeper into unnecessary pain and sorrow. There's no getting out without a helper. I know it's been a long time, but I think I'll talk to Nat tomorrow. Maybe she can help liFt me.

Not even a shadow to leave behind…'

Suddenly, the room starts spinning. Up becomes down, down disappears, white is now black, and all other colors seem to whirl around the steady, unyielding eyes of the woman whose daughter took her own life. These people weren't in her house by mistake. She may not have murdered her, but she allowed Shannon Walters to die. "I have to go back," she mutters to herself as her universe collapses.

Chapter 5

Brown Eyed? Girl (4 years ago)

As Dan looks over the racing form for the seventh race, he cannot believe his eyes. A first-time Lasix user is dropping in class and going off at 9-1. He furrows his brow, *What am I missing? This can't be right, can it?* He looks over his form again wondering where the catch is and decides the 7 horse is going to win this one, regardless of what the "smart money" says.

He chooses the 3 horse, Calypso, also dropping in class and although he's not the odds-on favorite, he's close at 3-1. He decides to blow almost his whole bankroll for the day on this one. As he approaches the cage, his phone rings. It's Jeanne calling him and he's got 5 minutes to post, so he answers.

"Dad, the 3 is going to be disqualified. Pick the 2."

"Wait. What? How do you even know where I am?"

"I had another dream, just listen to me, this one was really bad. Please, take the 2 in 2nd, not the 3, OK?"

Dan looks around, but nothing is coming into his head that resembles a coherent thought. Instead, his pulse quickens as he looks at the racing form, then closes it. He reads the tote board one more time and immediately starts shaking his head. Fortunately for him, his mind has other plans.

He remembers the last time this happened, and although

she is not throwing a tantrum in the jockey club this time, the resolve in her voice cuts through him even though the conversation is over the phone. Even though that incident was years ago, she was spot on, so he chooses to trust his daughter and goes against his gut. He walks up to the cage and says, "$200 exacta, 7-2. $300 on 7 to win."

"Sir, are you sure?" the clerk responded.

"Yes, and hurry, they are at the gate!"

"Good luck." And the clerk looks down and shakes her head.

Dan watches in awe as the race unfolds exactly as she said it would, with a photo finish. Nervously, he waits to see the word photo and then starts yelling at the monitor "Inquiry! Come on he got bumped!!"

"Whatever, pal, that run was clean," a bystander said.

Then the board lit up the inquiry sign, and Dan started to believe as he heard the same guy start screaming and cussing profusely at the monitors. How could this be and what events transpired that his daughter knew he was at the track, and further, that he was betting on a horse that was about to be disqualified?

Just then, the announcement rings out that the 3 horse has been placed behind the 5, making the finish 7-2-4-5 and Dan looks at the board to see the final odds.

In his head, he does a little quick math and he estimates his take is going to be $3500. He was close, but a small exacta pool only nets $3200 and he wins another $2700 on his win bet with the 7 horse, so he decides it is time to go home and question Jeanne, who just saved the family house and sent them on vacation with that tip. But how did she do it?

When Dan gets to the house, he gives his wife $4000, grabs a beer out of the fridge, and says "We have a very lucky charm in this house!" as he begins walking up to Jeanne's room.

"Hey, brown-eyed girl!" Dan exclaims but immediately drops the bottle in his hand as she stands up to greet him with a downright ferocious look on her face.

"What the…" Dan looks completely aghast and the color drains from his face.

"Hi Dad, I guess you took my advice," she's about to give him a good whack when she sees his face and the growing pool of liquid on the carpet and says, "Wait, what's wrong?"

"One of your eyes is green. I swear I am not seeing things, one of them is green," he howls.

"You're joking, you know I can't tell when people are sarcastic," she says as she laughs and turns toward her mirror. She pauses, staring at the reflection, and blinks. Twice.

"What?" she stammered. The feelings and the noise started to take her away as her grip on reality weakened, but her dad thwarted the impending eruption with a well-placed question.

"How can this day be any stranger? First, you call me and catch me by surprise just to tell me how to bet on a race you can't see, and that my horse is getting disqualified from a race you don't know about. Then exactly what you said would happen, happened and I got home to celebrate but your eye changed color. So yes, I did take your advice, how are you so sure I did?"

"Because we are not at the hospital watching you die." She said bluntly.

"What?" he mentally flailed for words, "why would you say such a thing, Jeanne?"

"Dad, I had another dream, like the one when I was a kid. It was so real. I dreamt mom got a phone call and we had to go to the hospital. She told me you were at the track and had a heart attack, so the paramedics and doctors tried to save you. In the waiting room, the doctor gave Mom some really bad news, and then A story showed on the television next to me about the race and your heart attack.

It was obvious you died and I got very sad. Then it got really loud and all of a sudden, I woke up and I was back in my room. So, I called you to tell you the horse got disqualified and that this other horse was in second place."

"I am sure glad you did, but I don't think I would have died by missing a bet."

"Well, I am telling you this was real. I saw what happened and could warn you to change it. I don't know how it is even possible, but it did, you better not die dad." She hugged him.

He froze. In the slowest and most awkward hug from a father in the history of hugs, he looked like a robot moving a little at a time and finally hugged her. He had no idea what to do, she did not initiate contact like this.

"OK sweetheart, thank you. I still have some light outside

since I left the track early, so will cut the grass before it gets too dark." With that, he gave her a little peck on top of her strawberry blonde locks and headed down to the garage.

Dan loved yard work, it let him relax and ride the tractor over their 3 acres while he thought about the races, but lately, his thoughts were all about money problems. Those concerns were over for now, but he was still troubled by what his daughter said. After he finished cutting the grass he grabbed his weed eater to sculpt his front walkway.

About 15 minutes later, he felt a little tired and since the light was fading pretty fast he decided to call it a day. He'd handle the rest of the property and trim around Lynn's garden tomorrow. He hung the trimmer on the twin hooks on the wall and did a quick survey to make sure everything in the garage was in its place.

He lost his bearings and felt like his head was swimming as he turned his head. He shook his head and noticed a few beads of sweat fly from the tips of his graying hair and that cleared the sensation for a second, but then he had some discomfort growing in his left arm. *Man, I am getting old*, he thought to himself as he turned off the light and shut the overhead door.

As he made the trek over the path of paving stones that led to the back door and into the kitchen, his pain and dizziness returned, and he struggled to catch his breath. "No friggin' way," he muttered to himself as he thought about his daughter telling him he was going to die today. He went over to the phone and called 9-1-1.

As the ambulance neared their home, Jeanne could hear the siren getting louder and that intuition kicked in again, so she went outside to look for her father, and found him and her mother sitting on the porch. He was slumped over leaning on her shoulder. Jeanne walked up and asked what was going on.

"Remember how you told me I had a heart attack and died?"

"Yeah."

Lynn interrupted, "Hold on a second, did you say your father died?"

"That was before, but I had a deal and was able to call Dad and he changed what he was betting on," Jeanne answered.

"Wait, you did what? Changed what? What's a deal?"

Jeanne shot her dad an annoyed look and said, "Hold on, you never told her about my thing? What did you just take all the credit for being this lucky guy?"

Dan looked up and said, "Not now lucky charm, I am not feeling near well enough to start this argument with you both."

"What's wrong?" Jeanne asked.

"What I was saying, you said I had a heart attack at the track. Well, I believe death will find you when it's your time. I'm not going all Final Destination on you here but what if death is after me and I am supposed to die today? I am worried I am having a heart attack. Whatever was wrong at the track is still

65

wrong with me." Dan tries to explain, but he starts feeling a little dizzy as the ambulance pulls up and the EMTs jump out.

"Hello, my name is Jerry, I am a paramedic for Chester County, what is the emergency?"

"He's having a myocardial infarction, Jerry," Jeanne says.

"Well, how do you know that young lady?"

Jeanne immediately realizes she is wading into dangerous waters, but one of the things about her neurodiversity is that she could not lie, not even close. So she simply says, "I just do."

Jerry tells his partner to grab the EKG leads and they place him on the gurney and roll him back to the ambulance where Melody, Jerry's partner has the machine ready and can hook the leads up to Dan's chest as soon as he is settled in the rig so she starts ripping the paper packaging from the connectors in preparation for use.

As Melody is hooking up and putting the stickers on Dan's chest, shoulders, and torso, Lynn asks what hospital they are going to be transporting him to.

Jerry answers, "We are taking him to Presbyterian in Chestertown. They have a good team and if he is having a heart attack, they have a very good cardiac unit there."

Melody interrupts, "The girl is right. I've got segment elevation in the ST and the T wave is obscured. He is having a heart attack." She hits the microphone on her shoulder, "Dispatch this is Ambo 61, notify Presby Chestertown we're inbound with an approximately 45-year-old male STEMI patient.

66

GCS 15, BP is 90 over 55, pulse 49, and respiration 22 and shallow. ETA 12 minutes."

Jerry is now working quickly to secure the gurney and run back to the front of the rig, but he shouts back at Jeanne, "One day I need to come back and let you explain how you knew your dad was having a heart attack young lady," and with that, he hit the sirens and they took off.

Jeanne began to have a moment, but she reminded herself this could happen and began to calm down enough to remember to run back for her purse while Lynn went inside to collect her keys and other items to take to the hospital and they got in the car for their drive to the hospital.

While on the road for what seemed like an hour, Jeanne thinks about her near freak out and the fact she was able to talk herself down from the noise. She thinks to herself and contorts her face a little bit as she tries to understand how she was able to talk herself down from a meltdown. Why didn't she need help, or her rescue drug? Her thoughts spiral for a moment, but she takes a deep breath as she thinks she is having a remarkable moment of clarity.

This type of stress always got the better of her, but this time she smiled and flapped her hands a couple of times. Her breathing slowed back down, and she closed her eyes. Her smile became more relaxed because this had never happened to her.

Lynn picks up on the hand flapping, and since she'd never seen it before she asks, "What are you doing honey?" and motions with her hands like a bird.

67

"Nothing Mom, just giving myself some stimulation of both sound and touch so I don't go down the rabbit hole again."

"Have you done that in the past?"

"No. The first time, but I feel like it helps."

"Good. I'm going to check on Dad's status, do you need anything? Will you be ok if I leave for a minute or two?"

"Yes Mom, I am fine. Thanks." She puts her headphones back on and loses herself in some music.

Chapter 6

Saving Shannon (3 months ago)

Natalee sits down at the same empty table she always does, in the same seat she sits at every day, with the same brown bag she always has, but this time she does not start on her lunch. She's learned to control her gift, so she chose this place and time to unwind the thing she blamed herself for. This time she scans the cafeteria as it begins to fill with students, looking for any sign of Shannon.

"Hey, Nat."

Natalee jumps. Somehow, even though she is expecting it, she is still surprised by Shannon. "Mind if I sit here for a bit?"

"Sure, go ahead. It's been a while, huh? How have you been?" Natalee tries to sound friendly, but Shannon looks at her with a skeptical expression, suspicious about how nice she is being all of a sudden. After all, they do see each other every day after third period and Natalee never acknowledges her.

Inside her head, Natalee is choosing her words and actions carefully, because do-overs like this are tricky. After ten years of trying and learning this gift, she has some experience to draw on.

Years ago, she'd experience these visions and without warning, fall back through space and time to moments before she or someone close to her made a life-altering mistake or error, but no matter how big the consequences were, she could never jump back more than a day. In the beginning, she was terrified of them. She thought she had dreams of herself dying repeatedly but was never sure if her memories were reality or a dream.

On one fateful day, she convinced herself that her imagination was uncontrollable and was so terrified she'd never be normal she tried taking her own life. Her quirk immediately kicked in and that's when she realized it was triggered by severe, life-altering types of stress.

Once she began searching for patterns, she learned about biorhythms and started down the metaphysical path with horoscopes, but that phase did not last too long. She set out to try and control her responses to these stimuli and over time, she has been able to consciously trigger it, but only when under heavy emotional burdens.

It still triggers without her efforts sometimes. Natalee can't help but think about others who must be going through this but never talk about it. She thinks her biggest fear is to become a lab rat for some crazy researcher trying to unravel the mystery of time travel, so she keeps quiet, never to speak of it out loud.

Out of all her friends, Shannon is the one who always notices when she is discombobulated. Somehow, she always senses the nervousness and confusion that sets in and is always a rock for Natalee, even when her other friends are annoyed.

70

Shannon taught her the power words had to bring clarity and comfort to her confused and crying soul.

With her advice, Natalee began jotting down everything, all her thoughts and feelings as well as the things she hoped were true. Writing helped her clear up the utter chaos that was going on inside the hurricane that was her head. Slowly, the blurred boundaries of time came into focus and she started to remember and then to understand.

Over time, she finally realized what she could do and the thing she considered a curse morphed into a gift. Natalee would never say her life was normal because she didn't believe in anything of the sort. She knew what happened to her was still unexplainable and scary.

For her, life became bearable five years ago because of a friend that she could count on to hold her steady when she was unstable. So now it was time for her to do the same thing for Shannon. She snaps out of her daydream as she hears a voice cut through.

"I see you dyed your hair again," Shannon says, ignoring the initial question. "Bright red is an interesting color for you. I didn't notice after third period. I am not sure I like it Nat, to be honest." All the times she noticed things about Natalee when she jumped, she never noticed the hair.

When Natalee went back, something about her changed at times, and for some reason it was usually her hair. The change did not just affect her roots, it changed her whole head of hair. Natalee never figured out how she could jump a matter of hours and her hair looked like it had been that color for months.

This made things hard to explain at times, especially if someone noticed a color change outside her time loops when she had to go back multiple times to solve the issue. Still, Natalee turned the corners of her mouth ever so slightly, knowing her friends would not have the same courtesy Shannon always had.

Today, she was in no mood for the ridicule that was coming her way, so she appreciated the moment of somebody trying to be nice. She also dreaded her timing, because anyone could notice that her hair changed colors mid-day, as Shannon just did.

"Thanks, I guess?" Natalee says, feigning the urge to roll her eyes. "So what's up?"

"Oh well, uh…I needed to talk to someone, and I didn't know who else to go to. If you're not busy tonight, do you think maybe--"

"Oh, she's busy alright. Have you not heard about Jack's party? It's going to be the biggest one of the year, look at that hair! Upper side pony, when that comes out you know it's time to party!" Christina so graciously interrupts, setting her backpack down and sitting down across the table, fabulously as usual.

Those green eyes are fixed on Natalee and she says, "You are *not* missing that party." After an intense, soul-melting moment, she finally turns to Shannon. "Sarah, right?"

"Close enough," mutters Shannon as she rolls her eyes and begins to rise from the chair.

"You should totally come with me!" Natalee blurts out desperately. Shannon had started to walk away but spun around and locked her skeptical eyes on Natalee as the two green laser beams of Christina's eyes were burning a hole through her from the other direction.

McKenzie approached the chair vacated by Shannon, and Natalee knew without even looking at McKenzie her head would be tilted a little to the left, her nose crinkled, one perfectly groomed eyebrow raised and her pale blue eyes staring blankly ahead, waiting to be filled with information that probably would not make sense to her.

Natalee remained focused, ignoring those two for the moment and staring intently into Shannon's eyes, saying as steadily as she could manage, "Come. To the Party. Tonight. Wear something cute. I'll text you the address later," and finished with a little nod.

Shannon understood that was code for her being dismissed and she shuffled around to face the opposite direction and although uneasy, walked away into the sea of students queued up for lunch.

"Whoa, Natalee, what did you do to your hair?" Emily gasps, taking her assigned place at the table.

"Oh, I thought it was time for a change."

McKenzie is still looking blankly at Natalee waiting for information on why her chair was filled with someone else's

73

body.

Christina narrows her eyes, turning the laser beams up to full power, and says with a voice that could slice through steel, "A little change? You turned your head into a stop sign the day of a huge party and then invited Little-Miss-Who-Knows-Who, who looks like she hasn't spoken to a human being in ages, and you call that a little change?"

She slams her water bottle down, clearly agitated, and continues, "I can't even take you seriously right now. I mean, you look like a clown, that ponytail does not save you!"

"Christina!" Emily exclaims. Only for her and McKenzie to burst out laughing.

"I cannot believe you said that!" McKenzie barely says through her laughter.

"Sorry," Christina says, rolling her eyes to turn off the laser beams. A small, Satisfied smile appeared on her lips at the reaction. "I didn't take my nap in government, so I'm a little bit cranky. But seriously, what was that, are you turning into a pick-me girl all of a sudden?"

"Who'd you invite to the party Natalee?" Asks Emily.

"Oh just this girl Shannon," she shrugs, getting her lunch out and wishing she had packed an orange instead of an apple this time. "We were friends in middle school. She said she needed someone to talk to, and I figured what better place to talk to people than a party?"

"But is she, like, going to follow you around the whole time? Like, she could totally be a stalker," remarks McKenzie.

"Nah," Natalee says thoughtfully. "I'll find her someone to talk to."

Natalee spots her friend Jay and gets up and walks over to him. "Do me a favor tonight, please. Will you talk to Shannon for 10 minutes at the party, and if you are bored out of your mind, you can *politely* leave and go talk to or dance with whoever you want," she says.

"*Whomever,*" he corrects her with a goofy little grin. Jay Gideon, one of the most brilliant kids in the school, never showed off his brains because of the bullying he had to bear in middle school when all the kids thought he was a nerd. His parents moved him out of their DC school and into the McLean area for a fresh start, and he chose to make himself over.

His grades are top-notch, and he's in honors and college prep courses, but he got in as a tutor for the football and lacrosse players and made it into the clique. Now, he makes sure not to show his weakness publicly, except to Natalee, whom he always had a bit of a crush on since they both started high school together almost four years ago.

Natalee hit him on his shoulder, "You're a freakin' nerd, you two will vibe. She needs a little cheering up. Go talk to her about poetry or something."

"Poetry? Seriously?"

"Whatever you want then. Ten minutes is all I ask."

"Fine. Sharon?"

"Shannon."

"Whatever. You're welcome. And you owe me."

"Fine. Thank you, Jay."

The Party. Again.

Jay walks with focused purpose across the crowded room, his gaze fixed on the figure of Shannon, nestled in the corner. Despite this raucous atmosphere, she is withdrawn and has been sitting as alone as one can be in such a crazy environment. She sits, watching everyone while her heart is beating faster than it has in a while and her mind races ahead of her, which causes her eyes to jump about that much quicker.

She makes eye contact with no one, purposefully buried in a sweatshirt that's way too big for her tiny frame. She thinks it makes her look cute for reasons passing understanding. Mentally, she is already starting to fumble for the words she will have to say as she watches Jay come closer and closer.

After what feels like an eternity to her, Jay reaches her and says something that is lost in the cacophony of music, but his body language is transparent. He extends his hand, and with a mixture of suspicion, terror, and curiosity she tentatively accepts his offer. Her eyes dart around the room in search of Natalee, and when their eyes meet, she locks on.

She sends Natalee an accusatory glare, but Natalee smiles back and nods, as if to give permission to Shannon or to encourage her that he is safe, and she should talk to him as he leans against the wall next to her. Jay exudes warmth and tons of intelligence and looks a little quirky, all qualities that belie the fact that Natalie had to resort to blackmail to force him to talk to her.

Natalee felt hope stirring inside of her that they'd make a connection, no matter how small, hang out together all night, exchange numbers, fall in love, and live happily ever after. Or something like that. Natalee gives a smile toward Jay and leaves the scene.

She is in search of Christina, Emily, and McKenzie, her breathing a little less frantic and her mind a little clearer now that the impending drama with Shannon seems to be under control. Upon seeing her hair, which was "fixed" immediately after school by her aunt who owns a salon in town, Christina lets out a visible sigh of relief and a slightly mischievous giggle.

She squeals, "Natalee!" and rushes over to her to give a gentle side hug, as if they had not seen each other in ages. Christina has a way of making people feel special, which is a big reason she is as popular as ever. Emily and McKenzie do the same, though, of course, they are less graceful and only do it because Christina did.

"Dark brown hair, huh?" Emily lets out with a snicker. "Did you ask Christina if you could copy her hair color?"

"No, and I'll probably get beat up for doing it, but I can't help it. I want to be like her. I mean, doesn't everyone?" She is kidding, but only partially due to a deep-seated desire to possess the same magnetism and charisma that oozed out of Christina.

"Very funny," says Christina, rolling her eyes but smiling. "So, did you find that girl a friend?"

"Huh? Oh, yes. Taken care of."

A hunger-induced whine escapes from McKenzie, "I need a snack."

"You're always hungry," Christina snaps. "Seriously, look at you. You've already eaten, what? A thousand chips tonight? Why don't you slow down for a while sweetie?" McKenzie looks down but does not say anything as the weight of those words seems to expand in both volume and mass.

This is not the first time for Christina to imply McKenzie was fat, except she was not. McKenzie has a gorgeous full figure that nearly every guy in school talks about, but compared to Christina, who is radiantly beautiful, though slightly on the thin side, she seems unremarkable at best and dull at worst.

"Let's go dance," suggests Emily, trying to break up the growing, palpable tension. So she and McKenzie grab their boyfriends, and the group heads to the living room to join the giant sweaty mob of dancing teenagers. Christina's boyfriend is away at college, and Natalee's is, well, nonexistent, so they dance with each other, and then with the people around them, and soon find themselves moving with the sway of the crowd.

All these people around them, some they've known for years, some they've never met, become one, joined together as grains of sand in the shallow sea flowing back and forth, driven by the tide of the music. Natalee feels a tap on her shoulder and turns to see Jay standing next to her, a jagged rock disrupting the beauty of the beach.

"What?!" she yells, irritated that her momentary tropical indulgence was interrupted.

Jay's face told her everything she feared before he even opened his mouth, "Glad I finally found you! Your friend left before the ten minutes was up! I tried, I did, but she seemed pretty upset! You might want to call her!"

Natalee is about to head outside to call Shannon when her vision suddenly becomes hazy. Jay soon splits in two, as does everybody else in the room. They split again. And again. Dancers become octopi, limbs flying around in all directions. People are simultaneously getting in line for the bathroom, having another drink, and grabbing food.

The already deafening sounds of the party are exponentially louder. Her senses are blurred. She falls to her knees, clutching her ears and squeezing her eyes shut. Maybe someone trips over her. Maybe someone picks her up and carries her to a chair. Maybe someone drags her outside. She's not sure what happens because everything happens.

She hates it when this thing goes off unexpectedly. Time and space are wadding up around her like a piece of paper with a bad idea written on it in permanent ink. Amid the pandemonium, she realizes that she failed. She is somehow sure Shannon's fate is sealed. Again.

One more time, her bad idea is being tossed out, as worthless as the paper it was written on. This party can't save the friend who saved her. She will have to save her on her own. She focuses all of the energy in her being on getting out a new piece of paper and trying again.

Third Time Through

Natalee sits down at the same empty table she always does, in the same seat she sits in every day, her stomach growling and her head throbbing. She's starving, but the thought of the apple and sandwich in her backpack makes her nauseous. Her senses are taking a while to focus, so she closes her eyes, rubs her temples, and tries to concentrate on what she needs to do.

"Hey, Nat, are you okay?" Shannon is standing next to her with a concerned look on her face.

"Yeah, I'm fine. Just a little headache." She looks up and tries to smile convincingly.

"Oh, well, um...I guess I won't bother you, then. Hope you feel better," she says, starting to walk away.

"No, seriously, I'm fine. Come sit down. What's up?" She is not about to go through this again. Shannon hesitates for a moment, surely trying to talk herself into in.

"I won't bite. It's not a full moon, so you have nothing to worry about." *Did I seriously just say that, what is wrong with me?* Shannon politely feigns a chuckle and sits down across from the table from her, in Christina's chair.

"How've you been Shannon?"

"Alright…. How about you?"

"Are you sure about that?" Natalee challenges.

80

Visibly shaken and surprised, she sits for a moment and breathes. "I've been better, but I've also been worse." She is finally about to respond with substance when Christina appears.

"Hello?" She says it as a question but somehow manages to make it sound more charming than rude. "Sarah, right?" And she plops down next to Shannon as gracefully as anyone has ever plopped in the history of plopping.

"Close enough. I'll get out of your hair," says Shannon, rising.

"Shannon, wait," Natalee pleads. "Come over tonight. It's been too long since we've hung out, and I miss you."

McKenzie arrives at the table, confused as ever, as Christina says, "Natalee Simon, did you forget about Jack's party tonight? It's going to be the biggest one of the year, remember?" She used this tone that she uses with people outside her circle, the condescension hung in the air like a helium balloon with a slow leak.

She continues, "Can it wait? I mean, not trying to dictate your plans or anything, but come on, Natalee, you desperately need to meet some guys. I'm sick of you being single."

She looks at Shannon and says, "I'm sorry. Nothing against you, it's just that this is *very important.*" She turns her eyes back to Natalee as she says the last few words, and they are meant to put the heat on.

After a few seconds which were like minutes, she releases Natalee from her gaze and turns back to Shannon. "Do you mind...?"

81

"*Excuse* me?" Natalee says, probably a bit too loudly. She's hungry, her head hurts, she is responsible for keeping her friend alive, and she is not in the mood to be told what to do by Christina Sinclair.

"Do *you* mind? Yes, I realize that this party is important. Yes, I want to meet some new guys. But you know what? I can live without someone to make out with for a little while longer because my friend nee…I need to talk to a *real* friend," she quickly corrects herself.

That was close.

"Because even though I haven't talked to her in a long time, I am sure she'll still be there for me and listen to me and try to help me, and I would do the same for her. Unlike you. You never care about anybody but yourself." Natalee looks at Shannon. Shannon's head is tilted down, but Natalee can see that her eyes are wide.

"*One*," says Christina, seething as if two holes are about to be melted clear through Natalee's skull from the lasers shooting from her furious eyes. "I'm *trying* to help you. We--you included--have all agreed that you've been single for far too long, and I'm sure it's embarrassing being the only one without a boyfriend."

She rolls her eyes and continues her verbal onslaught, "*Two*, no one would ever want to date you, anyway. You're rude and weird, that black hair looks horrendous on you, and you'd rather hang out with this chick who doesn't even exist than go to the party of a lifetime, and guess what? You don't exist now, either."

"Whoa, what did I miss?" asks Emily, who's been walking up slowly, hearing the ruckus from the table and not wanting to be a part of the drama. She throws Natalee a questioning glance, "What did you *do*?"

"What did *who* do?" Christina's voice is venomous, and she still hasn't blinked, "I don't see anyone."

Emily says nothing.

McKenzie looks around and says nothing.

Shannon glares at Christina but says nothing.

Natalee stands up, looking straight into those poisonous green eyes to show her she's not fearful trying her best to convince herself that she's not afraid. In actuality, she fears for her life. They've seen Christina take revenge. She's usually really sweet to everyone she likes, but Natalee's seen houses, relationships, and reputations sabotaged by this girl who does not like to be crossed.

Most people, for that reason, go out of their way to be nice to her. Natalee had considered herself lucky to be on her good side, and maybe she didn't have to end her friendship with her and subsequently with Emily, McKenzie, and everyone else thought was "important" in high school, but aside from the helpful connections, being "friends" with Christina never really did her any good.

She's stepped on so many people to climb to the top of the social ladder, and now she sits on her self-declared throne and looks down on everybody. She's outwardly beautiful, funny, and charming, and many kids want to be he. She's also self-centered, controlling, and a terrible friend and Natalee wants nothing to do with her. She walks away, wondering if she's been as bad to Shannon as Christina's been to her.

Sitting in Natalee's room, munching on tortilla chips, and looking somewhat comfortable at last, Shannon assures her she hasn't. "It wasn't just you," she says.

"We both kind of drifted apart a long time ago. And I appreciate you standing up for me today. You didn't have to do that. I feel so awful for making you miss the party and making your friends mad at you...."

Natalee stopped counting how many times she's been apologized to but realized *she* was the one who should be sorry. She let this girl, one of the sweetest people she ever met, die twice because she was too selfish to sit down and talk to her. But, of course, Shannon is completely unaware.

"It's not your fault at all," Natalee says. Again. "I've needed to do that for so long--to stand up to Christina. Not enough people do. She thinks she runs the world, and she seems to have the whole school convinced of that.

I thought it was nice being so close to the top, but it's not as glamorous as people think. I mean it kind of is, but *she's* all the glamor. Our job, me, Emily, and McKenzie, was to make her look loved. I feel so stupid for just now realizing that."

"Yeah...." Shannon nods in agreement.

"Hey!" Natalee throws a pillow at her.

84

"Okay, okay, fine. Only a little bit dumb, then. Still smarter than all those other people that'll continue to drool over her all day. And thank God. Not gonna lie, I was a little worried you'd be exactly like that when I came up to you today, rude and self-centered."

She lowered her head and her voice got quiet as she choked back tears, "But I'm so glad she didn't get to you. And the way you defended me...I didn't think anybody cared about me anymore. And after, like, almost four years, for you to throw all that away just to talk to me... How did we ever grow apart, Nat?"

Nat can't look at her. Not that she could if she tried; her tear ducts decide while Shannon's been talking to finally release all of the pressure that's been building up since this day began the first time. All of the lines that had previously bounded her world, those she had used to define popularity and friendship and contentment, suddenly blur before her eyes and wash away.

She is left drowning in a salty sea of chaos. Gasping for air, she desperately reaches out for something solid, something to be sure of. She feels a hand grasp hers, and she clings to it for dear life, her days of being known as Natalee are done.

"Hey, hey, hey," Shannon whispers. Slowly, she pulls Nat out. "I'm here now, okay? I'm right here, and I'm not leaving any time soon. Hey. Talk to me."

Nat thinks to herself, *This is wrong. This is all wrong. I'm the one that's supposed to be saving her. How did this even happen?* The tears flow faster now as she dives back down into misery.

What am I doing? What the heck am I doing? Sitting on the edge of my bed sobbing my eyes out because I'm supposed to be helping the one who's helping me, feeling sorry for myself because I don't know how to reverse the situation back to how it should be, wondering where on earth my true self has wandered off to.

Why have I never noticed she was gone and whether she is here, in this mess that I've created, in this sea of confusion swirling around me, and whether I will find her by diving deeper into this abyss? Why can't I go back to four years ago? Nat tries to trigger her gift to go back to the day before high school started, and her world starts spinning, but she fails.

"You're fine," she hears Shannon whisper.

"I am *not* fine."

"Yes, you are."

Nat wonders *Did I say that out loud?*

"Or you will be if you let yourself. I think you're having another panic attack. I didn't realize you still had those. Listen to me. Just breathe. Come on, deep breath for me."

Nat is scared if she tries to breathe now she never will again. "Come on," Shannon says, no longer whispering. "*Breathe*, Nat!" She is yelling now, but her voice sounds miles away.

"Oof!" Oxygen has never felt so heavy to Nat. "Did you punch me in the stomach?"

"Are you mad?"

86

"Nah...thanks. I guess I needed that."

"Don't mention it. That's what friends are for."

She chuckles despite herself, then sighs. "Oh, God. I don't even... I'm so sorry about that."

"Hey, it's fine," Shannon assures her.

Nat is thinking to herself, *She's so calm. Why can't I be that calm? I'm still struggling to breathe. My heart is still racing. I still can't see what's in front of me perfectly clearly. How do I get where she is? Wait, she's in pain too; enough to make her want to kill herself…*

She shudders. *How do I help her… How do I help us both… How do I… How…*

"Shh. Deep breaths, deep breaths," Shannon reminds her. "I'm here for you, okay? It's okay."

A small silence sits among them, not imposing, not heavy, not tense. It is not between them, nor behind them, nor above, nor below them. It merely perches tranquilly on their souls for a few moments, and flutters away on the gentle breeze of Shannon's next words: "We're okay."

Nat watches them float upward, the words and the silence, linger around them. *We're okay.* And Nat is aware those words shouldn't make a penny of sense because they, the suicidal loner and the hysterical time-traveling drama queen, are so broken.

Somehow, in this moment, her heart doesn't mind. Something deep within her realizes on occasion we need to break to pick ourselves up and put our lives back together even better. It's a slow and excruciating process that need not be rushed.

Moreover, she finally has a friend by her side who is willing to assist her and whom she can help in return, so they never have to be alone again. It hasn't occurred to her until now that she needs Shannon as much as Shannon needs her. They're a hot mess, with their broken faces, broken hearts, and broken lives. But they're okay.

For now.

Chapter 7

Jeanne's Gift, Manipulated (6 weeks ago)

The celebration of a sweet 16 was a happy time for just about everyone that Jeanne went to school with. Many of them were looking forward to graduation in a couple of years. Some at the school were already excited about working and still others wanted a car so they could head to Chicago for the weekend for some good parties.

Jeanne just missed her dad and wanted him to see her take her first drive but that could not happen due to the amount of work travel he had to undertake. In the four years since her father's heart attack, she has never been able to see another vision, or whatever it was.

Even now she did not think about the visions, but always had an uneasy feeling something else she was missing in her life. As she grew, she never questioned the path life laid out for her, even after a bad break up and a boy that strayed, or the C she got on a research paper because someone stole her work and the teacher did not believe her.

Being accused of academic dishonesty sent her into a spiral where she self-sabotaged and gave in to the tantrums more often and ultimately was placed in a special education class at school. Her psyche was at an all-time low, but she finally confided in her mother she needed help, something her dad denied.

They took the opportunity while he was away on business to see a specialist, and about the time she turned 18, she was formally diagnosed as being on the spectrum. In the intervening years, Dan came to grips with his daughter's illness. As a level 1 high-performing kid, she started to understand more about herself, and it helped her try and fit in with the other kids. Her brutal honesty and relatively inflexible ways still caused some tension with her friends though.

From her parents' perspective, they also had some time to learn and help her through the meltdowns, which began to taper off after her diagnosis. She over-analyzed everything, so that gave her the opportunity and the drive to find solutions that worked for her.

This was a time for her to figure out who she was, and what she wanted, and the answer was she had no clue. She was lost and needed a clear path. She was interested in a job at the daycare down the street but the idea of dealing with other kids scared her away.

She found out her hero Lionel Messi, a great Argentinian soccer player was on the spectrum, so she was excited to continue playing in college but tore her knee up pretty badly and has three months of rehab to look forward to. She will have to work her butt off to be awarded the scholarship she thought she'd be able to earn. She spent the entire party remembering the past, self-isolating, and not being fully engaged with others.

She thought about how hard her life was and felt discomfort in the pit of her stomach and her eyes got heavy. She felt some pressure in her throat, her chest got heavy and it was difficult to breathe. Before she realized it, she was frozen in her thoughts again and a single tear escaped down her cheek, the sensation of it breaking the stupor she found herself in.

Something is off, it is getting loud again.

Jeanne's brand of neurodiversity has a great deal to do with an overload of her senses. When her brain starts to race away she can only describe her world as being very loud and when this happens she tries to control her mind…occasionally it works, but most times it doesn't.

This time she looked up at the trees swinging in the wind and rocked herself back and forth at the same pace to try to calm back down. If this fails, she has her noise-canceling headphones she uses that transmit ambient sounds through the bones in her ears to reduce the overall sound level.

They only lived a few blocks away from the old community center where they hosted the party, so after everyone left, she, a couple of friends, and her mother were ready to walk back home when her friend Hannah suggested ice cream on the strip, so they went downtown.

Little Oak is a small town, to be certain, and the 'downtown strip' consisted of Main Street and about 8 little mom-and-pop shops, including a grocery. The ice cream shop is right next to the hardware store, which is getting a new paint job on the front facade.

91

The police force numbers 4 guys, 2 women, five squad cars, and a volunteer fire department of about two dozen men and boys that has a single truck and an ambulance with two paramedics who are on call from the hospital in Chestertown.

As they walk the two blocks to Main Street, Jeanne asks her mom what she should do for work and they talk about being a nanny for the family down the street or maybe getting a job at the library because she loves reading and all things book related, but privately, Lynn is unsure how Jeanne would fit in working with people.

They walk up the road and her mom says, "Hold on a second, I need glue for my scrapbook," and ducked into the hardware store.

"OK Mom, we will walk over to the ice cream shop and buy you some of that cherry pecan you like."

"That sounds good sweetie."

Jeanne heard the bang and realized a guy was running away, but was not aware of what was going on until one of her friends ran into the shop and told her mom was hurt badly.

She was not aware Lynn walked into a robbery at the hardware store. Being the morally unambiguous woman she is, admonished the robber for stealing from others and not having the decency to have a real job.

He responded by looking at her and pulling the trigger. Afterward, the man pulled his hoodie over his head and ran out, leaving his $98 score behind, and took off across the street on foot. When Jeanne arrives, her mom is passed out and is bleeding profusely.

A kind stranger witnessed what happened and grabbed rags to apply pressure to the wound in her shoulder. Lynn struggles to breathe and suddenly goes silent. Jeanne screams for her mom to wake up as the ambulance pulls up to take her to the hospital.

The paramedics control the blood loss and work to stabilize her for transport. Jeanne fears the absolute worst, no way she is going to lose her mother to some idiot in a gray hoodie. The noise starts to take her again and she freezes up in fear because of the uncertainty of the situation that changed in a split second.

It is getting louder and louder when all of a sudden Jeanne clears her mind for a second, lifts her head, looks up at the sky, and lets out a blood-curdling scream that stops people two blocks away as she slips into unconsciousness and goes limp, leaning sideways on Hannah who is startled and grabs her before her head hits the ground.

Jeanne has gone into her abyss once again.

Foiling the Crime

As they approach the hardware store Jeanne all of a sudden stops and has a blank stare on her face. Hannah, who is walking next to her stops and turns around to see Jeanne

93

suddenly take a large gulp of air as if she's been holding her breath underwater for three minutes.

She looks panicked and her eyes dart around frantically as Lynn yells out from 20 feet ahead, "Wait a second, I need some glue for my scrapbook sweetie."

"Wait!" Jeanne screams, "Do not go inside the store." She runs to her mom.

"Why?" Lynn asked.

"A deal just happened again. The same thing with Dad at the track that day, remember? I had another one. Something bad is about to happen here. Stay back." She motions for them to move back from the entrance as she surveys the scene.

Hannah looks at her with a confused expression and asks, "What is a deal?"

"I'll have to tell you about them sometime, but you need to get over there," as she motions across the street.

She grabs two cans of paint from under the scaffolding where two workers had been painting the front of the store and pours out one of them just outside the threshold of the door, then creates a base with those two, finds a third almost full can, opens it and lays it on top of the other two cans she set up as a base about a step away from the pool of white pant she created at the door frame.

She tells her mom and Hannah to go over to the ice cream store and they all run across the street and wait. The first thing they see is a can of paint flying out into the street, then they hear the commotion of the other paint cans with a man screaming obscenities as he picks himself up off the ground, covered in fresh paint.

He takes off down the strip with his paint-covered $98 and the police arrive two minutes later, having been alerted by someone in the store witnessing the robbery happen. Knowing they do not need a detective to track down this criminal mastermind, they simply follow the paint trail to a house four blocks away and find a wet man trying to fit into some clothes hung on the line by the pool in the backyard. Case closed.

Back at the ice cream shop, Jeanne and her friends sit and talk about what happened. How did she know that guy was robbing the hardware store? How come she put paint cans in front? o he'd give away his path as he ran away?

Lots of questions, and Jeanne has no answers. She simply says she had a bad feeling about something bad happening inside the store and wanted everyone to be safe. She is a hero, but the truth is she saved her mom from being shot. Lynn is shaken and thinks to herself, *what if I'd gone in for the glue?*

She starts crying.

In a rare display of physical emotion, Jeanne puts her arm around her mother and says, "Mom, everything is fine now. Nothing happened to you."

At home, Lynn stops. "How did you know? And why did you say that about your dad, it was the same thing when you said you had a dream about him dying. Did you see me die in the store too?" The tears begin to flow again right where the crow's feet stem from her big blue eyes.

"No, mom. A shot rang out, but I was in the ice cream shop with Hannah, and when we looked back to the hardware store, this guy in the gray hoodie came running out with a gun. When we went across the street, you had been shot by the guy in the hoodie and you were bleeding so bad, I kind of froze in panic." She stops, swallows hard, and takes a deep breath.

She breathes in and out to steady herself, and continues, "Then the paramedics came to help. You were going in the ambulance and they were working on you when I lost it. The world got so loud and bright that it was like I was looking directly into the sun. Suddenly I was back on the street and you were like 20 feet away yelling you needed glue. I had to make sure you did not go inside."

"This is the second time something like this has happened, and both times something really bad was about to happen to your father or me, right?"

"Third-time mom. I never said anything about the first one."

"What?"

"The first time was when Dad lost all the house payment money, and I told him what horse would win. He did not believe me, but put a small bet on it anyway and won back everything. He started calling me his good luck charm and his brown-eyed girl after that, but then one of my eyes changed color"

"But he never gambled away the money for our mortgage."

Jeanne was resolute, "he did this time, I was there in this dream thing, but then the daydream stopped and I was back at the beginning of the race."

"Well, he will be back from his business trip on Tuesday, and we will talk about this. I think something strange is happening with you and we need to figure out the...what happened to your eye?"

"Come on Mom, you know I had an eye turn green."

"No, this is different. Look at me!" She grabbed Jeanne's wrist and spun her in for a closer look. "That eye is half brown and half green now. When did that happen?"

"I have no idea," she said as she yanked her arm back from her mother's concerned grasp. "What are you talking about?"

"Look in this mirror." She pulled a compact out of her purse and opened it in front of Jeanne.

As Jeanne looks into the mirror, a strange feeling settles into her. She is feeling the stress of whatever happened to her, and as she peers into her reflection she sees a piece of her mother in the face looking back. She saved her mother but lost a bit of herself in the process, or at least it felt that way to her.

The feeling of something missing in her life is back with a vengeance, and stronger than ever. Something is amiss. She is lost and it's time to figure out what these visions or things are. She does not understand why her eyes are affected when she

97

has a deal, but she makes up her mind it is time to investigate.

As she starts trying to think about who to talk to, the reality of what she is about to say sinks in. Who would believe a teenager who says she can see the future? They will put her in a hospital or worse yet, send her to the psychiatric unit.

Ultimately, she decides to keep quiet and try to experiment on how to make the deals appear, and what she can do to control them so they won't have a grip on her. She goes off to the internet and starts searching for stories like hers.

Tuesday arrives and finally, Jeanne hears the car pull up. She waited and listened. A Door opens, then closes. The trunk closes and the driver leaves. She goes bounding down the steps to the front door as it swings open and he walks in. "Daddy, I am so glad you are home, and I have some super exciting news for you. Did you bring me anything from China?"

Dan spent three weeks overseas setting up a new plant in Hong Kong and has been gone more often than he was home for the last nine months, but he is back for the foreseeable future. Finally, the one person who seems at peace with all this craziness in Jeanne's life is here and she can start to piece together all the things that happened.

She hopes her dad can help figure out what is going on and he will be the one to help set her free from her mental prison. "Hey BG girl, wait a second. What the…?"

"BG still works dad, now it can work for one eye, isn't it cool?"

Lynn walks in and gives him a big hug and a kiss, but Dan wants to all the details. "What happened, you had another deal, didn't you? I need all the deets."

She and Lynn told him all about the event over the weekend, and at first Dan was mad they did not tell him when it all went down, but at that time it was early morning on Sunday for him. They knew he was starting his long trip the next day, so they decided not to worry him about anything. They spent 45 minutes talking about the robbery, the paint, the cops, and the traumatic experience that triggered it.

For Dan, this is a revelation. He takes it all in, and then spends the next few days putting the pieces together like a puzzle. The first time, he was about to lose the house money and she got upset. Then, he was about to die and she was very distressed. The third time, her mother got shot. He detects the pattern.

He has a hard time believing what he is thinking, but he is a gambling man, and being the degenerate he is, he hatches a plan to use his daughter to figure out if his suspicion is correct. He is about to gamble with their livelihood just to find out if this works.

Ricky Vigs

"Jeanne, let's hit the track! It's Saturday and you have no school on Monday."

"Dad, it's raining."

"Sure it is, that only means we have to look for the mudders."

"OK, fine. But you know I always pick the mudders better than you."

Lynn steps in and says "hun, we only have a few hundred bucks in the bank and you don't get paid until Tuesday."

"It's fine," Dan yells, "I have a guy who owes me some money, I will go collect from him on the way over."

"I don't think you two should be going, I don't want us back in a bind. We did so well the last few years, and now we have Jeanne's college to think about"

"So the college fund is on the line, that makes it more exciting then!"

"Wait a second," Jeanne interrupts, "you are using my college money to gamble with? Are you nuts?"

"No, honey, we are using Rick's money, that is what he owes me. We will be fine."

They pull up at Rick's place and it is a dump. Jeanne's eyes are wide and she hesitates getting out of the car. She reassures her but reminds her she needs to stay with him in this part of town. In earlier times, this was an industrial mecca near Chestertown, but now it's a beat-up old shell of its former self.

Rick set up shop inside an old, abandoned mill, and the door lets out a high-pitched squeak as they enter what barely passes for an office. There is a desk all right, but not much else. A light in the corner flickers and glows with a greenish tint that lights up a little filing cabinet and a chair.

The chair is being stressed by a fat guy in a wife beater with a huge coffee stain who looks like he hasn't shaved in a month and smells like he forgot what a shower was. The stale Cheetos all over the floor give the room a little character, but Jeanne is disgusted by what she is seeing.

Her eyes move to the corner of the room behind where the door opened, and a dead rat lying on the floor makes Jeanne jump. Rick walks into the room through the same squeaky door and looks at Jeanne up and down.

"Dan. It's been a long time, pal." Rick says, with an outstretched right hand. To say that Rick is a man of size does not do justice to him. He might weigh 450 pounds on a good day, and his hair is greasy enough to set fire to.

Dan meets his eyes and gives a firm handshake back, "Yes sir, it has been. This is my daughter, Jeanne, I told you I'd bring her down here one day."

"This is the one that saved your ass huh? You told me you had a good luck charm to help you pay off those last two gees. And now, you are putting her to work for the family business, am I right or am I right?" Rick gives a wink to Jeanne and she throws up a little bit in her mouth.

"We got a system today, Rick. I need three grand this time."

"Hey, a degenerate like you ain't good for no three gees. But hey it's your life. I'm giving you this at forty percent. You make good in two weeks or," he turns to Jeanne, "or your dad

101

gets his face rearranged by Tito here. Got it?"

Jeanne is stunned as the sound in the room turns up to 11. No way she's seeing this. Her dad is taking money from a loan shark? Her mind is already racing, trying to figure out how to remove herself from this situation, but her dad is already out the door with the money, beckoning her to follow him.

She's almost frozen as the noise starts to freeze her up. She stands like a statue, her eyes huge and darting around but her knees start to quiver. Dan's heartbeat hastens and he reacts to what's coming next. He runs back over to her and gives her a little shake. "Come on girl, stay with me."

"Maybe she's scared her dad is going to be whacked," Tito says through his laughter, "what, is your kid some sort of freak?" Dan glares at him and turns back to Rick, "You better control your dog or I'll put him down for you."

Tito slings his mass out of the chair and yells, "You don't threaten me who the hell are you?"

Rick steps in, "Relax, you can have your fun with him when he can't pay up."

As they reach the track, the sky is still overcast, but a dampness lingers in the air that exacerbates the heavy feeling Jeanne has in her heart. She has to help her dad make money for the bills and make sure he has enough to pay off the loan shark.

She starts to freak out again as her dad walks up with the racing forms. They check the morning line, just like they have

102

done a thousand times before, but this time, she is too distracted to see anything. All these numbers are gibberish on a page.

She has no idea what to do. In the first race, they find the 2-1 favorite where all the money is going, but a 6-1 choice has some potential and he won a 5-furlong race in sloppy conditions last month. That is Dan's pick. He picks the 4 horse to win and plays an exacta wheel, picking either the 7 or the 1 to finish second. He throws $100 at this one and says, "We will start small."

The race goes exactly as the handicapper planned it and the favorite wins by four lengths. They lose $200 in the second, another $400 in the third and $400 in the fourth. They are almost halfway through the bankroll of mob money when Dan finds a play in the fifth. He has Knightly Shadow, the son of Shadow Fist and Queens Knight.

He says, "We are betting a grand on this race."

"What! You are nuts!" Jeanne screeches.

"No I am not, look at these horses. Knightly Shadow likes mud." He breaks into his best Goodfellas voice and yells, "He's a mudda! His mudda was a mudda, his fadda was a mudda, he's a mudda!"

"You can lay off the fake New York accent Dad." Jeanne rolls her eyes and secretly hopes that he is kidding about betting a thousand dollars on a race. She looks over her shoulder and there is Rick with two more guys. And Tito.

"Danny boy, we got another customer that we need that money for, and he pays better than you, ya punk." Rick calmly says as he walks up with his goons flanking him on either side.

Dan hands the money to Jeanne and says "Bet it all on the 5 horse to win."

"But he is a 10-1 shot."

"Just do it."

Jeanne goes off to make the bet for her dad, with a sense of fear she has never quite experienced before.

"Young lady?" the man in a blue ball cap says.

"Yes?" Jeanne stammers.

"Sorry, you were walking and suddenly just stopped, it looked like you were about to faint right where you stand. It almost looked like you were in a trance," he says.

"I am ok, is this the 5th race still?"

"Why yes it is, but you only have 2 minutes to post. Are you feeling OK?"

"Yes, I am. Thank you for asking sir."

She walks up to the window and says "$400 exacta 2-5. $1400 on 2 to win."

The agent in the cage says, "Honey, where did you get all that money? From your daddy? He is gonna be pissed at you, you're picking a 30-1 shot to win. How old are you?"

She motions to Dan, "That's my dad, he asked me to make the bet while he was talking to his friend." She yelled for Dan, and he gave the motion it was ok to bet, but the agent looked at her.

"Is your dad in trouble? That's Ricky Vigs he's standing with. This is not safe for you young lady."

104

"I am aware, but this win takes him out of our lives," Jeanne says bluntly, and with enough confidence to shut the agent up.

She walks back to her dad and Rick with the tickets and her dad screams, "What are you doing? I said the 5 horse to win, not 2nd in an exacta, and where the hell did this 2 horse come from? He's a gray horse and everyone knows gray horses suck!"

"Don't worry dad, I got it."

"You better pray that horse comes in little lady or we might take our three gees out on you too. Why do you look taller to me?" Rick chuckles as his threat does not have the desired effect.

"I'm the same size I was. Just prepare to leave us alone Rick," Jeanne shoots back with a stone-cold glare that gives Rick a momentary pause.

She turns to Tito, "If we win, you have to go on a diet, tubbo."

Tito squints at her and sneers, "Don't even. I don't care how old you are."

The bell sounds and the 4 horse goes to the lead. As they approach the half mile he has a 5-length lead, with Jeanne's 2 horse and 5 horse a distant second and third. As they round for home, the 4 begins to fade and looks like he is laboring. They start yelling for the 2 and the 5 and at the quarter pole the lead is only 2 lengths and closing.

Knightly Shadow catches him first and pulls into the lead. The 2 horse, Dance Whisperer stalks in third. As they roar down the stretch the unmistakable thunder and slashing of hooves and mud make for a cornucopia of sounds as Knightly Shadow and Dance Whisperer duel for the lead past the eighth pole.

They come to the line and Dance Whisperer is on stride, Knightly Shadow is mid-stride and that makes the difference. "Photo" illuminates on the board, but everyone has the result, it was 2 by a nose with 5 in second.

Jeanne's big bet changed the odds right before post, and other bettors, seeing the shift also threw money on the eventual winner, so Dance Whisperer only went off at 20-1 in the end, but Rick was about to be paid off, and they have $40,000 in their pocket.

Dan hands Rick $3,000 and gives him an extra hundred, "Piss off, Rick."

"You lucky punk. You'll blow through that and be back."

"Don't bet on it."

Rick and Tito turn with their two henchmen in tow and Jeanne howls, "You have to go on that diet now!"

Tito starts to turn back, but Rick puts a hand on his shoulder.

Dan is still wide-eyed and his heart is racing as he turns to look at Jeanne.

"Jiminy Christmas, did you have a vision and change the bet?" Dan asked Jeanne, "That was not what I told you to do."

"I did. Why are you asking?"

"Because I put you in a spot where you thought something really bad was going to happen, and I hoped that would trigger a thing for you."

"You gambled with our lives just to see if I could have a deal? What is wrong with you?"

"Nothing, I figured it out," he said, "you always have these visions when things are getting upsetting for you. Do you remember how you felt?"

"Yes, I got this really weird feeling in the pit of my stomach and it got real loud after the race was over and our horse lost. Rick and his guys took you and were coming for me."

She starts shaking, "We were in a lot of trouble and then I jumped back where I was placing the bet and this guy was looking at me, telling me I looked like I was in a trance."

"OK BG girl, we got it. You have to experience the result to jump. It's not just being stressed."

"Yes, I have to see the bad thing happen, that's what makes it loud and causes the deals, Dad. They happened when I was really scared and something happened to you or mom. I can't believe you would gamble with our lives like that!"

"It's not a chance when you have the result. We can make this work for us, right."

"Isn't that kind of cheating if you are aware of the ending before you bet?"

Dan was momentarily shaken by his daughter's words. His moral code, unflappably devoid of anything resembling a conscience all of a sudden took center stage in his head. Is he about to send his daughter down this path?

Alas, as soon as his better angel tries to step up, his

inner demon hits it in the face. "Nope, it's just playing the hand you're dealt. Rick was right, you do look taller."

Chapter 8

Vic and the Feds (1 month ago)

Special Agent Vic Newsome is glaring at his computer screen, trying to finish up the report he dreaded, but he needs to satisfy his boss, Supervisory Special Agent Mitchell Linkletter. Vic joined the bureau in 2009 and has had a good but not-so-stellar 12-year career that left him desperate to find a way to progress up the ladder.

He works on the FBI logistics team that supports counterterrorism, major crimes, and the behavioral analysis units. He is a glorified order taker, and his job is to make sure resources are where they need to be at the right time.

That's why he needs to nail this. He has something to share, but this case could make him or break him. He has to convince Linkletter and their Assistant Special Agent in Charge that *time travel* is possible.

Two weeks earlier, Vic met his friend at a bar inside the Loop. Less crowded than the joints on Michigan Avenue or Rush Street, they met in a basement bar called "The Underground" where they had been getting together for years whenever they had time. This time, though, was different from the outset as Dan walks in and tells Vic "Drinks are on me tonight pal! I damn near died once, my kid saved me and now she and I hit the big one at the track."

"Shut your pie hole, Danny, you don't have crap to buy anything with"

"I do this time! I have a strange story for you, but you have to keep this quiet because I don't want people thinking my kid is some kind of freak."

"Ok, try me," Vic says, amused but slightly interested in hearing Dan's new tale of woe he is sure he is about to hear.

Vic is a silver-haired military type the FBI loved to have in their ranks. He grew up very poor in the Rio Grande Valley of Texas and his family relocated to Chicago when his dad became a cop. Back then, the cops all had to live in Chicago, so they settled in The Island.

It has gone downhill now, but in his youth, the place was full of police and firefighters, so it was the safest place in the city. Vic grew up to follow his dad into law enforcement, going to DePaul and then making detective in CPD at a young age comparatively speaking. His plump face and overdeveloped biceps give him that look of a bouncer, but his salt and pepper look and fake charm used to draw younger women to him.

Dan was a little jealous back in the day, but those days are gone. He'd often tell the ladies about how he got the scar over his eye while apprehending a serial killer and engaging in a hand-to-hand brawl that landed his partner in the hospital. In reality, he passed out drunk and crashed into his glass end table, but he'd never admit to that.

Vic is a serial womanizer and a classic manipulator who

gets all he can from a woman and then dumps them with no emotion whatsoever. Still, he thinks of himself in a far better light than women see him and he ran short of rizz a long time ago.

He is only able to pull 30 or 40-somethings that approach him and of those, he might close escrow with one or two he did not turn completely off with his drunken rambling about his misspent youth. The only thing that almost works for him is that he can speak Spanish and sound like a Texan.

He gets a lady now and again, but only because of his joint work with the DEA in south Texas that gave him his shot at the bureau. The stories he has from the drug task force make him seem more interesting than he is. Once the truth is out, they leave.

Dan begins his tale, "So, like 4 years ago I was at the track and hit a big bet, but only after Jeanne called me to tell me my original horse was going to be disqualified and I was going to die."

"Wait, what?" Vic stammered, spitting a little of his beer out and getting a glare from the bartender.

"Yeah, she was not with me but somehow knew this was happening."

"How?"

"Well," Dan says, "and you can't tell anyone about this, it happened again with my wife, who was about to walk into a robbery when Jeanne stacked paint cans in front of the hardware store and the schmuck hit the paint and went flying…leaving a trail the cops followed right to him."

Vic is shaking his head at this point. "OK, so your kid is psychic? I don't believe in that crap. I have seen the bureau use these quacks in the past and sometimes they'd get lucky but most of the time it's a wild goose chase. Come on, you expect me to buy this, what's your angle?"

"No angle pal."

"Bullshit. What do you want?"

"Just to tell you the story. We hit a longshot for forty grand, that's why I am buying today."

"You're serious."

"Come on, how long have we known each other, would I lie to you about something like this?"

"Yes, you would," Vic rolled his eyes and gave his head a little shake but Dan kept on.

"I take her to see Ricky Vigs down outside Chestertown."

Vic spits his beer out again.

"Hey buddy, watch your shit! I'll cut your ass off if you do that again," the bartender hollers from the other end of the bar.

"You did *WHAT?*" Vic is visibly thrown and stops for a second to compose his next words. "Are you into this guy, is that what this is about? We've looked into racketeering for a while with this guy and can't make it stick. We even have a CI in his…"

Vic stopped dead and realized he made the mother of all screw-ups for an agent, revealing an active investigation but Dan was so self-absorbed it flew right by him and into left field.

"No, come on. I did borrow three gees but like I said we hit 40 grand as I was standing in front of him and his goons."

112

"Your girl is only 16 or 17, right? How? Why? Man, I knew you were an arrogant ass, but your kid? Holy shit man. Lynn had to be pissed about this."

"She has no idea. So look, I tell Jeanne to put $1800 on the 3rd favorite for me because Rick is hassling me for the money right then. She's stressed about it, but she does this thing where she sees the race and then can go back and do it with the correct result and make things right. So, she saw a longshot winning and my horse in second, and laid down an exacta to win us $40k."

"OK hold on. Back the hell up." Vic is visibly disturbed, and that's saying quite a bit with what he's seen. "So, you take your daughter to a loan shark, take his money, then intentionally put yourself in a dangerous situation hoping that whatever this *thing* is will happen? That's a dick move man. Seriously, even for you."

"It's not like that, I knew it would go down this way."

"Did you? I mean, *really*? I should call CPS on your ass. Your kid is prone to panic attacks and anxiety for Christ's sake."

"I'm telling you she has some kind of gift."

"So she's not psychic, she's a time-traveling superhero now? Come on, we have not been fishing in years, I am not taking the bait. Can we just have some drinks and talk about how bad the Cubs will suck this year?"

"All right. One day, you'll see."

"Sure, sure. Hey, she loves animals, right? We've got a law enforcement K9 showcase and challenge that is going to happen right after school is out next month. Some of the best units in the country are going to be competing. "

Vic starts to think, "The FBI will have their trackers and scent dogs to see who can pick up the most contraband, they'll have a search and rescue course set up, it's going to be a blast. Maybe you'd like to bring her? I'll make sure you have all access if you're up for it."

Vic is acting cool and dismissive, but his wheels are already turning inside that mind of his. He and Dan are alike in one regard, their drive to succeed despite anything in their way. Both men experienced success at the expense of others throughout their lives, but their attitudes are exactly alike.

They cut corners and backstab as needed to reach the brass ring, and Vic is playing along with the bullshit story angle, but he figures that this is an interesting lead for the FBI, and a sensational opportunity like this may earn him a promotion.

Dan thought for a second, "If the crowd won't be too big to trigger her with all the noise, I think she'd like that."

"She handles Remington Downs, doesn't she? The number of people won't be near the same number."

"Right, but she is familiar with the track, this is unknown to her, so it will induce stress, trust me."

"OK, I'll send you the details. Now, what will you bet me I can pull that blonde that just walked in at the end of the bar?"

Dan manages a casual glance. "No way. She's what, 30? Not only is she out of your league pal, she's a completely different sport," he says laughing into his beer, "make sure and walk over like you're carrying suitcases so she sees those guns."

"Don't worry, I got this. Fifty bucks?"

"Bet."

Vic gets up and saunters over in that direction, arms spread out to his side so ridiculously that he looks like a scarecrow in the middle of a cornfield. The girl catches eye contact and gives a little smile, but Dan notices something in her look that makes him laugh as she glances to the door, where an equally attractive woman walks in with brown hair flowing like waves off a ski boat on Lake Michigan.

Vic gets to his prize-to-be and asks her a question Dan can't hear, but he sees her put her hand on his bicep, he chuckles that Vic is laying on the full Tommy Boy workout room routine on this poor girl.

The silky smooth brunette takes a seat on the other side of the blonde, and Dan is about to lose it as he sees Vic obliviously dig himself further into a hole. About that time the brunette catches Dan's eye and gives a knowing smile so Dan pulls out his phone and decides to record as Vic leans against the bar and promptly knocks the bucket of peanuts over and a big clang attracts attention to his ineptitude.

The girls both rise from their seats and embrace as only lovers do and Vic looks over sheepishly, only to see Dan recording him. His fate is sealed. And he knows it.

He calmly saunters back after picking up the silver pail that used to be full, refills it in the peanut trough, and says a pleasant "Nice to meet you," with a cheesy little hand motion that

115

truly displays how weak his game has become and returns to his seat at the bar.

"Well done Tommy Boy," Dan is laughing too hard to even speak.

"I deserve that."

The bartender walks past and casually says, "So, you learn that from, Mystery? I mean, that was smooth. Have a beer to put out those flames," invoking the unmistakable reference to Pete Mitchell.

"Hey, at least you got a free drink out of the deal, but it looks like I am not paying after all!" Dan hoots to Vic's dejected scowl.

His brief memory of the events that led to this report having been rekindled, Vic still glares at his machine as if the paper will write itself. He is unsure about what to do or say to SSA Linkletter, but he is at least prepared with some research he did over the last two weeks. "Link?"

"Yeah Vic"

"You have a couple of minutes? I've got something completely bizarre for you."

"Walk with me," Mitch says as he starts a purposeful stride toward the exit from their bullpen. Mitch is tall, thin, ruthless, and straight to the point, always. It is so rare, that when he manages a smile it's noted on the department calendar.

He is a veteran of the first Desert Storm, pushing 55 now but you'd never realize it by the way he moved and carried himself. He is built like a boxer, cut and toned in all the right places with salt and pepper hair, and dark brown eyes, and although his arms are not as pronounced as Vic's, they create havoc for his suit jackets at times.

Most of the team called him Link, as his marine buddies all called him. Some call him Mitch, but only those who want reassignment use his full name. As they approach the double glass doors with the FBI logo on them, Vic feels the heat of a thousand suns on his face as he is about to either be eviscerated or kick off something that may lead to his own task force for investigative fieldwork.

Mitch looks over and says, "Whaddya got?"

"This is going to sound pretty far out, but listen to me. A buddy of mine has a daughter that I think manifests some kind of temporal abnormality, meaning she can either see the future or return to the past in short bursts."

"Have you been talking to the CTU Vic? Are you yanking my chain too?" Mitch stops and stares directly into Vic's eyes with the intensity of a microwave oven.

"No sir, why?"

"They have it from some LEOs in Texas that they've found something like this manifesting with one of their officers. It sounds henke to me but they are running with it."

"What do they have planned from an investigative perspective?"

"They've created a series of tests that will place the officer in a situation that is impossible to predict and will make it seem like his handler is about to get the bonus."

"Bonus, sir?"

"KIA Vic, you aren't familiar with that phrase? Being killed in action is getting the bonus, work with me here."

"Roger that."

"Anyway, they've concocted this dog and pony show where they've invited select animals and their handlers to the FBI field office for an all-star game of sorts. To me, it's a waste of time and resources on some science fiction bull."

"Yeah, I invited my friend and his daughter to the K-9 show. So, their target is an animal? How the hell did they find out a dog has this?"

"Unknown, but this is not the first they've claimed to have evidence of it. Counter Terrorism has been on this for years and thinks that this dog holds a key. If they can learn about its uncanny ability to find the unfindable, the intelligence generated will be valuable. If you think you have a human subject that also fits this description, I think we're in business. I'm going to add you to Task Force Zulu, be ready for a call from Assistant Special Agent in Charge Alicia Peabody."

"ASAC Peabody, roger that sir."

With that Mitch turns to walk to the elevator. After about three steps he turns and says, "Scratch that, I'll pull the clearance for you, let's go to the briefing...what are you waiting for, you're with me," and Vic hurriedly follows to the lobby.

"Where are we headed?"

Link has his head buried in his phone furiously typing an

118

email. "Task force briefing, that's actually where I am going now. They need our unit to provide some logistical support for the op they have planned. Don't ask, you don't have the clearance yet for all the details, but your information is going to change things. Operations should have your clearance by the time we arrive."

"What should I expect?"

"They'll ask direct questions about the kid. Give direct answers. Tell them what you told me and stick to facts. Leave conjecture at the door. Do that and be ready for them to assign you some intel-gathering activity with your friend."

They arrive at the task force briefing room, Mitch walks in first, Vic holding the door for his supervisor, then he strides in, allowing the big metal and glass door to swing closed behind him.

"This is Special Agent Vic Newsome from my team, he has some information pertinent to the briefing, has access to the subject he'll brief you on, and will be a good addition to the squad. Agent Custos, did you receive my request for his clearance?"

"Yes sir," agent Custos responds. Agent Savannah Custos is fairly new to the bureau, and how she wound up as the logistics officer on this team is up for some debate, but she was a transfer from the CIA where she was stationed in places like Kandahar and Karachi, so she was a steely, no-nonsense woman who was built like a small piece of steel.

Her long hair black hair hid the scars she had on the back

119

of her neck from an unfortunate bout with a suspected terror cell she had taken down from the inside five years previously. After she managed a miraculous escape from the cell and then survived two hits as well as another near miss with a roadside IED, she decided to return to domestic work with the FBI.

She is already highly respected. Many agents find her piercing brown eyes intimidating, knowing what she's been through in her career and miraculously making it through almost unscathed, and having never lost an asset in country. "He has clearance and pulls homeland security 10.4, we are good."

"Good deal. Vic, welcome to the team." Mitch walks around the excessively large black conference table that looks like it could land a small plane with the white striping that runs down the middle and introduces him to ASAC Peabody. "Alicia, meet Vic, he's got some intel you're going to want to hear."

"Pleasure, Agent Newsome," Alicia says while extending her hand for an overly assertive handshake. Alicia Peabody graduated from the Naval Academy in 2012 and went straight into naval intelligence work. She is a pit bull who was in the 6th grade on vacation with her parents eating at the Krispy Kreme donut shop in the base of World Trade #4 when the first plane struck the North Tower on September 11.

That experience should have traumatized her, but instead, it made her resolute that she was going to be one of the ones to catch the bad guys after she witnessed such massive destruction and wave after wave of death while trapped in lower Manhattan. She graduated as the valedictorian of the class of

120

2008 at Cesar Chavez High School outside Phoenix, never really had time for boys, and was appointed to the academy.

She matriculated as one would expect, but she had the intestinal fortitude to beat the crap out of two men who tried to assault her one night, and the legend of her badassery was cemented. To call her a gym rat is an understatement; she has an elliptical in her office and is known to take calls while she exercises.

She simply doesn't care what people think, as evidenced by her plainly styled blonde hair, usually pulled into a simple ponytail that falls past her shoulder blade. Her stare is not as intense as Agent Custos', but her piercing green eyes are so beautiful more than one man has tried to lose themselves in them, but they are always unsuccessful.

Alicia never made time for relationships and simply goes from one night stand to one-night stand, chewing men up and spitting them out with no emotional attachment. "OK people let's begin," she beckons everyone to take their seats and hits the button to automatically lower the conference room blinds and tint the windows.

It's THAT kind of top secret, Vic thinks to himself as the smart room prepares itself.

ASAC Peabody begins the briefing, "Final prep is underway for the exercise, code-named Kilo Niner Tango. Invitations have been sent and RSVPs received from Dallas, Austin, Encino, Denver, Helena, DuPage, St. Louis, Birmingham, and Raleigh. Our target is K9 officer Mattis of the Austin Police

Department. His handler Tony Scott has been informed that he will be one of the select dogs performing a search and rescue operation.

We will conduct the op in two phases. The dog's vest will be equipped with monitoring chips and a GoPro to record his movements. Our strike point for S&R exercise 1 will be at the location where Sgt. Scott's scent will be tracked to, where the dog will be trapped in netting. The strike point for S&R 2 will be immediately following the obstacle course and will consist of a simulated attack where his handler is abducted.

The objective is to determine if Mattis can detect both these events before they engage. This may seem like we are creating an elaborate plan around a dog that we can simply pick up, but we want to document the anomaly in action, so to speak, hence the additional gamesmanship. Special Agent Newsome, I understand you have new information?"

"Yes ma'am. I was about to brief SSA Linkletter on this. An old friend of mine shared a story of his daughter who has some manner of, in his opinion, the ability to travel forward or backward through time in short bursts. He claims she saved his life once and the story was compelling because she was not with him where the event took place, yet she had details that were impossible to have in real-time.

A second event happened a few weeks ago where she again spontaneously showed the ability to intervene in what was about to happen in their immediate future. She changed their intended action to compensate for the undesirable result. It sounds like this is what you are trying to confirm through the K9 unit's behavior."

"Vic," Alicia begins, "what kind of activity was your friend engaged in?"

"Horse Racing ma'am."

"Do you have any other details?"

"Yes, his daughter was placed in a position of high stress to trigger the episode."

"Anomaly."

"Pardon?"

"This is a biological anomaly. Savannah, read him in, please."

"Sure." Savannah briefs the room, "We have conducted information and intelligence gathering to attempt and find more of these instances where people act in unnatural ways, or foil crimes before they happen after learning of Officer Mattis.

We've uncovered a case in New York that dates back to September 11. A passenger on a plane suddenly lost consciousness and woke up screaming 'They are going to kill us all!' That passenger was subdued but the captain decided to cancel taxiing and return to the gate.

Immediately, 4 passengers became irate and fled from the aircraft as soon as it reached the gate. Later, box cutters and documents implicating them in the attacks were found on the plane. The man on United 23 that morning was identified as Ira Wannamaker, 73 of Queens. He died of a heart attack almost immediately after the event.

Interviews with his family revealed a pattern of uncanny events that led us to believe he knew the attack was imminent. We found he could turn his biological rhythm back. Much of this information comes from the CIA, who seems to have opened a case file on Wannamaker shortly after the terrorist attacks.

His wife told them Ira swore her to secrecy that he could see things that happened an hour before they happened. We believe this anomaly is limited to, at most, a single circadian rhythm, or 24 hours. Based on notes on Wannamaker, we think he only had a weak diurnal anomaly, so he could only move in time that was either day, or night, but not both.

Even though this was over twenty years ago, we were able to obtain the autopsy and samples of DNA after an interagency task force discovered his decommissioned records at Langley. A thorough analysis in post-mortem revealed that, for his age, Mr. Wannamaker had an exceptionally high number of stem cells present in his cerebrospinal fluid.

Secondary analysis in Quantico revealed his DNA had numerous mutations but the most pronounced was at the time of death, his ASPM gene protein expression was off the charts. For those of you, like me, who have no idea what ASPM is, it is a gene responsible for brain development at an early age.

We believe he suffered from Periventricular Nodular Heterotopia or PVNH. This normally makes an individual prone to disorders such as epilepsy or autism spectrum disorder, even though Mr. Wannamaker did not exhibit symptoms of those conditions.

Another puzzling fact is one of the DNA mutations controlled heart rhythm and cellular regeneration and he could not have survived more than a matter of moments with this mutation. It is certainly responsible for his heart attack, but the question is how this gene could spontaneously mutate and cause sudden death.

Further study will be required to ascertain whether the combination of the abnormal ASPM with PVNH is responsible for the anomaly and what if any biological changes can be attributed to the anomaly. Our goal is to find others who possess this anomaly and study them to determine if any threat to national security exists or if this phenomenon can be reproduced, and potentially harnessed."

"Can we move things along please?" A voice comes through on the speakerphone Vic never realized was active. Alicia picks back up, "Yes sir. Vic, SAC Sanumo is on the line, I apologize for not giving you that information. Special Agent, given this new information we may want to expand the op to include the girl, can we have her attend this event at the same time?"

"I already invited them, she loves animals. I told them they could have an all-access pass to see the animals behind the scenes."

"Good thinking, let's make this happen. Mahoney, Richardson let's develop some contingency plans on how to pick up the girl." She turns back to Vic and gives a nod of approval, "Thank you, everyone."

"Alicia, please video call me when you return to your office," Sanumo says as the meeting is breaking up, and he disconnects.

As Alicia enters her office, she secures it and makes the video connection. On the other end looking back at her is the silver-haired and very foreboding look of Special Agent in Charge and assistant to the Deputy Director Brett Lucas Sanumo.

SAC Sanumo is one of the few old-timers who get away with facial hair at the bureau, with a nearly white goatee that covers the scars on his chin he received in the field doing wet work for the CIA. His chiseled appearance comes from a daily workout regimen that sets the tone for the rest of his day.

He is a no-nonsense leader with little tolerance for mediocrity and no ethical or moral backbone to speak of. Rumor has it he sanctioned hits on United States citizens as a part of an operation following the capture and elimination of Osama Bin Laden, but this information is highly classified. His jacket is filled with redacted information, black bag work, and a history that, to put it mildly, strains the belief that people like this are still in the service of the government.

He is as ruthless as he is driven, and his career is, in his mind, about to get better as this opportunity will make him the obvious candidate as the next choice when the Deputy Director

126

retires at the end of the year. "SAC Sanumo, what can I do for you?"

"We have a human subject of the investigation. You have my authorization to use all necessary force to bring her in."

"Sir, this won't require that." She looks away for a second and thinks, *This man creeps me out, how can he be completely emotionless?*

His face barely moves, "I don't care. Get her in. Test her. Take tissue and brain samples, I want to be on top of this thing and push funding for a program that you'll be my hand-picked leader for. You read me?"

"Yes sir."

"Good, stop at nothing Alicia. This operation now depends on the girl," pausing as he takes a breath and looks through the camera, through the monitor as he stares directly into Peabody's soul and says, "And you."

Alicia disconnects and immediately exhales. She thinks to herself, *Finally. This devil of a man is going to trust me. I have to find this girl.* She immediately calls for a full workup on the girl given the information Vic shared, she is taking no chances on this operation and she has a month to prepare.

Meanwhile, back in Quantico, Sanumo picks up a burner phone and dials. On the other end of the call, he hears silence but Sanumo speaks anyway, "Echelon November One Four go secure." He hears the click and continues, "I think we've found one or more candidates that possess the anomaly that blew our op in 2001. Make arrangements to set up labs and secure sites within 50 miles of Chicago and Langley. We're going to use this to our advantage this time and finally have the castle."

Chapter 9

Brett (20 years ago)

Brett is awake early this Tuesday, another start to a great fall day with his normal workout routine, stretches, yoga, some weights, and bike. He is a small piece of iron, a little over 6 feet tall, with brown hair and brown eyes, growing a beard recently to cover some scars he received on the job during an altercation he did not expect.

He is in a secure room at his safe house as the clock chimes, signifying 4 am in Virginia. *Three hours,* he thinks to himself as he picks up a secure satellite phone to communicate with his assets. "Zodiac this is Dagger," he says as the line is secured, "sitrep."

His team leader responds, "Zodiac is in position outside the apiary. Our bird is on schedule, with no delays. We'll be making our approach in 55 minutes."

"Contact Jasmine when you're inside and near the birds, give the go/no go at that time and wait for further instructions."

"Roger. Zodiac Out."

After another hour passes, he receives the text confirmation his team is at the bird and will be boarding soon. He dials the phone one last time and waits for the call to be connected.

The commander picks up, "Hal's Hardware, how can I help?"

"I believe I may have the wrong number, I am sorry."

"There are no wrong numbers, friend."

Hearing the code phrase, Brett says, "Go secure."

"Zodiac is Secure."

"Zodiac, you are cleared. The target is modified to the temple. I repeat, the temple. All high-value targets are present. The foliage is off-site as planned, but Ricky Ricardo, Big Shot, and his right hand are all en route for a briefing, and once the eggs start breaking, they'll shelter in place. Dive in the middle of the temple, understood?"

"Roger that."

"Your families will be taken care of, you are the true warriors of Allah."

"Allahu Akbar."

A short time later, Brett picks up the phone again, verifying for the third time that his handler, their section chief, the deputy and director of the CIA were en route from Langley to The White House for a joint chiefs meeting with the Vice President at the head of the table, but the President will be running the call from Air Force One.

After receiving confirmation, he is set to invoke the cleanup protocol for his assets currently boarding United flight 23 from JFK. "Nighthawk, this is Dagger. Leave the tree and break the eggs at all four nests, repeat, break the eggs, and sanitize all four flocks, the condor is about to fly."

He paused for a moment to reflect on how he's gotten to this position. Brett is back stateside after several successful operations abroad and has been acclimating to life back in the US over the past six months. It's been a long road planning and covering their chatter, but his opportunity is almost coming to fruition.

He'd spent the last few years overseas infiltrating and executing several key political targets in the Middle East, but his allegiance to the CIA was eclipsed by his commitment to himself, so when he learned of the elaborate plan for September 11, 2001, the opportunity to set up a promotional fast track appeared.

He was aware of the strike points for all four planes, so he simply added a fifth one to hit either the White House or Camp David, depending on the schedule for POTUS and the CIA Director on that day.

Over the last six months, he'd spent all his capital with treasury, justice, and the NSA to put together and confirm the joint chiefs meeting scheduled for 10:00 this morning.

As news of New York starts to leak out, he checks his satellite tracking. Everything is on time, except for one plane that is delayed. That one is going to The Pentagon, so he's not overly concerned. A few moments later, his sat phone chirps, informing him United 23 left the gate and is taxiing.

He calls his team in Washington and makes some plans to be the on-call chief for CIA operations as soon as word comes in that the leadership of the agency has been killed. His secret plans are known only to him, his staff are unwitting accomplices.

News of the attack in New York starts to gain traction, the President is informed and the FAA is talking about grounding all aircraft. Brett takes up a position on the patio of his house that looks back toward where he expects to see smoke rising from the horizon in about an hour. Instead, his phone rings. It's the handler he has for his team on United 23. "Jasmine here. Code 99 abort."

"Give me a sitrep, Jasmine," Brett says, overwhelmed with anger.

"A passenger on the flight went nuts. He started spewing all kinds of garbage about seeing the people on board kill the pilots and take over the bird. The disturbance happened during the taxi and the pilot went back to the gate at 9:25. The ground stop came down 17 minutes later. The assets are off the plane and I have them, we're headed back to the drive-in."

Brett is steaming, "What do you have on the passenger?"

Jasmine answers, "They got a name. Ira Wannamaker. His wife called his name because as soon as he got them to turn around the guy had a heart attack. Our assets bolted as soon as they opened the jet bridge. Our man on the ramp signaled that the police and feds had taken the aircraft and found the box cutters. The whole thing is fubar Sanumo."

"No names Jasmine!" Brett roars on the sat phone, "Get them back to base, it's time for emergency sanitation. Do what needs to be done to ensure no one ever finds them."

Brett contacts his planning team to inform them the op

132

failed. He retreats to the interior of the safe house to plan his next set of moves. His career in the CIA has been primarily in the area of wet work, but he had other plans to move ahead which involved taking his promotions by force.

Handlers and section chiefs are killed every day around the agency. It's a danger that goes with the profession. He uses his connections to obtain clearance to head to JFK and board the plane, eventually taking custody of Ira Wannamaker's body for an autopsy and other study.

He became obsessed with understanding how this old man was able to foil his plan, and he set about interviewing the family. He opened a new operation using his Middle East position as a smoke screen so he could operate domestically.

Brett decides right then and there that his days as a wet boy are over. He needed more operational work and it's clear to him he'll have to rise in stature at the agency. Over the following months and years, he gathers all the information he can on Wannamaker and delves into the theories or temporal displacement, time travel and genetic abnormalities in an effort to understand what opportunities there may be for him to progress in his career and is prepared to sacrifice everything to succeed.

His plan ultimately leads him away from the CIA since the clandestine nature of the agency did not allow him to adequately build alliances and gather information. He turns his sights to the FBI to continue looking for others who are certain to exist and hold the key to harnessing whatever is inside the head of the deceased Ira Wannamaker. Using the guise of a domestic threat allows him to establish a team and begin work on his life's work. He wants whatever the old man had and will stop at nothing to find it.

Chapter 10

Natalee's Ordeal (2 months ago)

In the grand scheme of things, McLean is a big town outside Washington, DC that still has a small-town vibe; people are all up in each other's business, relationships are common knowledge, and gossip is a fact, or at least as far as the town was concerned.

It did not take long for the falling out Nat had with Christina to make the rounds. As prom season approached, though, Nat and Christina made up and the circle of friends began to allow Shannon access, within reason.

At lunch, Nat splits time between tables, and on rare occasions, they'd tolerate Shannon sitting with them, but only when they could all get help from the eager-to-please smart girl who was more than happy to let them cheat on a test if it meant she gained acceptance into the club. She never *really* would.

It is a normal day when all of a sudden, Christina bounds up and plants herself in the chair next to Nat, as gracefully as ever, "Hey Natalee, Zach Almeida wants to talk to you."

"The captain of the Lacrosse team? I barely even know him."

"Well, try and get to know him, he's coming over."

Zach walks up with the unmistakable bravado of a man-child who thinks he is one of the kings of the world, "Hi Natalee."

"Hey, Zach. By the way, I am going by Nat now."

"OK, Nat. I am having a little party at my place this weekend, the 'rents will be out of town visiting my uncle Anthony, maybe you can come?"

"I am not sure, I have plans Saturday with a friend who…"

"Who can make it a night without you, Natalee," Christina famously interrupts, annoyed.

"Tell your friend she can come too. But I'd like you to be there. It's just some of the guys on the team and a few other friends." Zach continues, unfazed by Christina's interruption.

"I'll be there." McKenzie blurts out, standing and waiting for Christina to vacate her normal chair, as if she could not simply sit in Christina's usual spot.

"Be where?" Almost on cue, Emily arrives to take her spot at the table.

"Zach's party," McKenzie says with a blank look on her face as she works out where she should sit.

"Can I dress up? I like glitter and sparkly dresses." Nat says,

"I like baking and things that smell like winter!" McKenzie interrupts. Again.

Nat rolls her eyes and says, "OK. Send me your address and I'll be there," ignoring McKenzie again as she is already thinking about how Shannon will react. They got past the suicide thing and have gotten back to being besties in the last month, but there is still tension between Christina and others in the

136

group.

The dynamic is such that they would rather not have the inconvenience of an outsider potentially taking their social standing down a notch by simply being seen with them. Still, Christina was being uncharacteristically chill about the whole situation.

The embarrassment and the gossip died down pretty quickly because, after all, it was Christina. Something bothered Nat that no retribution ever came, and they made up quickly after what was a brazen show of force toward one of the queens of the school.

"Awesome, what's your number?" She gives it to him, and Zach sends his info to Nat, then saunters off to be with his crew.

Another Party

One of the best things about Northern Virginia in the spring is all the cherry blossoms. Zach's house had a bunch of them scattered all over, even though they were the tattered old blooms carried on the whims of the wind and gathering along the base of the fence and trees. Tonight was a cool windy night, so the leftover blooms made a chaotic yet beautiful pattern on the yard and sidewalk that snaked up to the front of Zach's house.

Nat promised Shannon they'd still catch the last few episodes of their latest binge after the party. Therefore, she planned on simply dropping in, staying the requisite amount of time to take some Insta shots in, and then slipping away after an hour or two.

"Nat!!" Zach yells from across the room. She looks around wondering where the raucous behavior is, notices that hardly anyone is dancing, and only a low buzz of noise is present. She squints a little and starts to squirm a bit as Zach approaches with a blue solo cup in each hand.

"Most of the team is not here yet, we're just kind of chilln'. Want to start with some beer pong? We can team up."

"OK, sure," she says, taking a drink from the cup Zach gave her. *Blue Moon, OMG did he raid his dad's beer stash?'* she thinks to herself. Over the next 20 minutes, she and Zach have an incredible time completely demolishing two other couples as they start making a bit of a connection.

He's cuter than I remember. "I need another drink, but this is the last one, I have to drive home." She says.

Zach saunters away to fetch another beer for her as the music and crowd both begin to approach their customary levels. He comes back and kind of blurts out, "Here you go. Look, I suck at this stuff, but how'd you like to go to prom with me? I know it's late, but my folks have a lady that can make you a killer dress."

"Wait, what?" She chokes on her beer.

"I'm serious. It is sudden, but not gonna lie, I've been

138

lowkey crushin' on you for a while, and when you did that thing with Christina I was like blown away."

"Yeah," Nat looks down at the floor, "not my finest hour."

"No, it was totally dope. You got noticed that day for all the right reasons."

"Well, thanks," and now she is completely swept up in thought. *Does he really like me? Wait, is this even real? Why do I feel like this after only two beers?'* She stammers out, "I think I was more scared about what people thought."

"Don't be." He puts a hand on her shoulder, right by her ear, slowly curls his fingers around the back of her neck, and looks dead straight into her eyes. She's looking at his lips, then back up to his eyes, then his lips again.

Is this happening? Screw it. and Nat leans in.

"Wow," Zach says, after having his tongue assaulted by Nat's. "Let's find a corner somewhere."

Nat is feeling the rush of emotion, a rush of something else and the room starts to become a little foggy. *Shit, I have not done this in a long time. Wait, what am I doing? Why…*

The rest of the night is a completely blank space to her.

The Morning After

Nat wakes up in her bed, her phone chirping. She looks at her phone. 4%, she forgot to charge it, but she answered.

"Hello."

"Nat, I've been worried about you all night. I tried to talk to Emily and Mackenzie and they all said you had left the party and no one knew where you went."

"I suppose I came home, but I don't remember driving home."

"Did you drink that much? You can always call me."

"Yeah, I guess so. My head is killing me." Nat notices that she has a lacrosse tee on, and she sits up in bed, also realizing she has no underwear on.

"Wait, something is wrong. I don't have any underwear and I am wearing someone else's shirt." Nat's mind is drifting as she starts to sit up in bed only to feel a sharp pain. "Oh, Shannon, I hurt down there."

"I'll be right there, just stay there."

Shannon rushes over to Nat's house on this beautiful Sunday morning. Birds are singing and it's another gorgeous spring morning, if not a bit chilly. "Nat," she asks as she enters the room, "are you ok?"

Nat is crying. "No. Look."

"NAT!" Shannon yelps and points at the blood stain on her mattress. "What happened?"

"I am not sure, it's all a blur, but I think I had sex with Zach Almeida."

"No. Jesus, that guy's gone through all the cheerleaders and most of the drill team by now."

"He asked me to prom."

"What? What about Jennifer?"

140

"Huh?"

"Even I know that he asked Jennifer to prom like two weeks ago, it was on Insta and TikTok."

"Shit. Really? Then what, why?"

Just then the phone chirps again. Then both their phones chirp. Then again. And again. "Now what?" Shannon says as she opens her phone and about three seconds later she drops it and screams.

"What?, *WHAT?*" Nat yells, reaching for her phone.

"Don't!" Shannon says, grabbing for it. Too late.

The first message is from Christina, simply saying: *Did you think everything was cool? No one does that to me.* Nat could not believe her eyes as message after message popped in, some asking what she did, others asking if she was ok.

Then the video came. Multiple guys. At the same time. They were having their way with her and she was motionless. One of the voices in the video says, "She told me she wanted to go through the whole team in one night, we need the others."

Her face went cold, "Those bastards drugged me. I remember starting to feel off during beer pong, but I don't remember anything after that. I woke up here. Did they bring me back here thinking I would not figure out that my insides got taken apart last night?"

"We need to go to the hospital. We need to call the police too."

"Hold on, I need you to look at this." She flips her phone around so Shannon can see it.

141

"That *bitch*! I'm going to kill her."

"No." Nat is fully red-faced and pissed. "Look, you are not going to understand this, and I have never told anyone about this, but I can redo my life when I mess up. We don't need the cops, I can fix this before it happens"

Shannon looks at her with wide eyes and her mouth agape in disbelief, but all she can manage is a quiet and very breathy, "What?"

"The panic attacks, the ones that you see and no one else does? Well, they are not panic attacks, they are me bouncing back into my previous life after seeing or doing something wrong. To you, it looks like me having a seizure or a panic attack.

To me, I'm just moving through the fabric of time back into a place where I can fix something. I don't know what will happen to me in this timeline when I leave, but I am going back to last night and I'm going to deal with them. Let's try something. I am going to pass out or something. Go home and write in your journal what happened to me. Maybe somehow, you'll remember or I can see it."

"Nat, wait. What's going to happen?"

"I don't know."

"I am scared, Nat. Don't do this."

"I have to." Nat's world started shrinking again, another day that was being wadded up and discarded, this time stained with her bad decisions and bonds of trust that were broken. This time, though, she was in complete control.

142

Shannon watches in disbelief as Nat's eyes kind of roll back in her head, her body shakes for a second, then collapses into the bed under its weight, as if she just passed out, but Shannon completely freaks out because her friend was lying there. She was barely breathing and about to die, or so it seemed.

Shannon is one of the smartest people in the class, she loves physics and math and she is an avid reader too, so even though this goes into the realm of science fiction for her, she is somehow able to suppress her panic, and knows she'd see Nat again.

"Go kick their ass girl," Shannon said through her tears as she kissed her bestie on the forehead and started to prepare mentally as Nat took her final breath, but never got a chance. She was instantly back in her bedroom on that beautiful morning, with no recollection of her being with Nat or anything being amiss.

Nat's Vengeance

Nat calmly walks over to her dad after their breakfast on Saturday, which is more like a brunch but they always eat late on Saturdays. "Hey Dad, is Uncle Pete on duty tonight?"

"I don't know sweetheart. Why do you need him?" Steve asks. Steve Simon is a burly heap of a man a little less than six feet tall, balding, and as round as a bowling ball. Dad bod somehow does not cut it. The odd thing is his legs are toned and small, but that beer belly is a work of art.

Steve is a big volunteer at the high school, and when he is not there, he works at home all day, trading crypto and day trading stocks with his play money, as he calls it, an inheritance from an aunt who lived in DC and left all her nieces and nephews $250,000. He's made some, and lost some, but is worried that his nearly one-million-dollar fortune was being vacuumed into the void that is Ethereum.

He lost thirty percent in the last 2 weeks and is deathly afraid crypto winter is setting in again. His wife, Nat's stepmother Shay, is a little younger than he and still looks as radiant as the day they were married. A little bit of gray started to dot the landscape of beautiful jet-black hair that would lay down just barely below her shoulders, and her impossibly clear complexion always irked Nat.

Shay never uses any creams while Nat has to use 5 different things every day or the red little face devils would pop up in what seems like hours. She is also gifted with bright blue eyes to offset the dark skin tones and hair to make quite the package.

She and Steve met about 2 years after Nat's mom died of a freak case of breast cancer found just days before her mom's 33rd birthday. Nat was only 11 when she passed away after battling the disease for only 14 months. Nat could not go back that far, she tried.

"So, this is going to sound odd, but my friends are going

to do something illegal. I don't know what to do so I want to see Uncle Pete."

"Is it Christina? I've told you for the last couple of years not to trust her. I've seen her do some horrible things to kids in this town trying to hold on to her little kingdom. She doesn't care about anyone but herself."

"Why do you have to go there immediately?"

He throws up both hands, "She's your friend, but I am up there volunteering a lot of my time. Teachers and administrators talk. She's a mean, catty girl. And you verbally bitch slapped her in front of everyone."

"Yeah, I know."

"So?"

"What? Oh, I don't want to speak to you about this, Dad. I need Uncle Pete."

"OK, I'll call him."

Nat went upstairs to contemplate what she was going to do. She thought about what Shannon was going through in the last timeline. Strange as it is, she'd never thought about what others thought or did after she left it.

Did she wake up and live life out with her mistakes? Did anything change? Would she be able to tell later? All those questions bounced around in her brain clanking like old shoes in a dryer when all of a sudden, "Hey Nat, Pete says he is off duty today. He's coming over."

"OK dad, thanks."

"So, you going to tell me what's up now."

"NO-uh!" Nat said in the typical leave me alone dad inflection where everything gets the 'uh' at the end, regardless of how the word actually ends.

"Fine, but I will sit in when Pete gets here. 10 minutes."

"Uncle Pete!" Nat sort of squeals as she opens the door for him. Pete Simon is a typical cop. Six foot two, 240 pounds of what looks like all upper body. Big arms, a big torso, and a little bitty bald head on top of a tree stump-looking neck. With the jet-black goatee, he looks formidable for anyone, let alone a kid trying to boost a game from Walmart. She hugs him as best she can and escorts him inside.

"Hey bro," Steve greets his brother with their customary grip as if they are air-arm wrestling. "She's got something for you, and I am betting her prima donna ex-bestie Christina Sinclair is at the center of it."

"OK, cop mode then. What do you have for me, Natalee?"

"It's Nat again Uncle Pete. My old friends made me change it for their purpose. I like Nat. So it's just Nat."

"Ok, Nat. What's going on?"

"So, I got into a fight with Christina while I was trying to save a friend a few weeks ago, but she's been all nice and made up with me. The problem is she's a vindictive bitch who would never let something like this go. She is planning something, and it's going to end badly for me unless you help me as a police officer."

146

"This sounds serious, but I need to back up. Who did you rescue and from what? Was Christina hurting her too?"

"No, she was going through personal issues and I wanted to-- look, it's not important, that all worked out fine." She dang near spilled a secret that was not hers to tell.

"So, this boy Zach Almeida has all of a sudden been trying to be nice to me and make me like him. I think Christina and he will try and let my guard down at a party tonight so he can drug me and then his lacrosse team is going to run train on me."

"Run what?"

"Uncle Pete, you have to know what that is! When a bunch of guys have sex with the same girl, usually without consent."

"Oh, No!" Steve barks out. "Who is this little shithead again?"

"Dad, he's doing what Christina told him to, I swear it."

"Ok, how do you know that Nat?" Pete asks.

"Look, I can't tell you, I just do."

"Well, I can't just haul a kid in for what he is *going* to do. I have to catch him in the act, or there has to be evidence."

"He's a dumb jock. He's going to make a deal of greeting me at the door at the party to gain my trust, come with me, and search him when he gets to the door."

Pete is slowly shaking his head with a bit of a frown on his face, and says, "Well, honey it does not work that way either. I need to have probable cause to enter a residence and search a

147

person without their consent, and if he has GHB or some other date rape drug on him, he won't give permission."

"What about my word, does that count?"

"Do you have proof of this?"

"Not really."

"Come on Nat, work with me here. Don't you have some kind of proof this is happening, something you heard, something you saw, anything?"

Picking up on the signals he was throwing down, she sat up "Oh, yes Uncle Pete. There was this text message from him on her phone she did not know I saw. He asked when he should do it."

"That's what I need. The problem is that's hearsay. I wish you had a screenshot of it."

"Wait, I can get her password, Christina's. It's her XChat account, that's what she uses to keep things on the down low. She forgot she gave me access a while ago. Hold on." As she messes with her phone Steve and Pete look at each other with a knowing glance, they are going to take this kid down.

"Here it is. Will This work?" She shows Pete an IM exchange:

QueenSinc: *I need your help with something that has to stay on the DL.*

BigStickBoi: *KK, sup?*

QueenSinc: *It's Natalee. She needs to understand her place.*

BigStickBoi: *Ooh ya, I heard about that. Want to talk at school?*

QueenSinc: *KK. Do you still have liquid X?*

"Well, it's not concrete, but I think that's good enough to establish they have something planned, and if we combine it with your hearsay, I have a judge that will grant the warrant. Send me that. When is the thing tonight?"

"Nine."

"It's Saturday, but I'll push one of the sex crime detectives to see Judge Babish and draw up a warrant, then I can go with you and execute it. We're not lucky enough that he's having the party at his house are we?"

"Yes, he is."

"OK, well. The next question is how much do you want to be hated at school? This will be a house full of minors in possession. You want a full raid, or just me to take him down without drawing a crowd?"

"Quiet. Can I get him to follow me outside? I only need to wink at him and he'll think he's getting some in the car."

"You're terrible, kid. Just like your uncle, that's some shit I would pull. Consider it done. Now, if there is nothing on him, the game is over."

"He's a moron, he'll have it in his pocket and try to dose

me during beer pong."

"How do you know that?"

"Not important."

"You're hiding something, I can tell. Like that time you told me to take Pepper out of the yard right before the neighbor's dog got loose, or that time your dad told me about when you screamed at him and made him change lanes and the car in the next lane had a blowout right after and would have taken your car with it as it crashed? I've only been a detective for a few weeks, but you sound like you have something going on that I dare say borders on the metaphysical."

"Uncle Pete, please just don't ask."

"Ok. I'll see you at 9 at the house. Send me the address when you can, I'll need it for the warrant."

"I'll see you out, bro," Steve says as they stand up. As they walk outside toward the car he asks, "Do you think this will work? It's not exactly sophisticated by your standard."

"Neither is the piece of shit delinquent. He won't know what hit him. I just hope he has the substance on him. Liquid X is basically GHB, the most popular date rape agent out there. Kids used to use Rohypnol back in our day but they changed the drug so it turns blue in liquid so they quit using it."

"Can you pin this on Christina?"

"That IM chain is thin. But I can use it to flip him and he will implicate her. He's technically done nothing except conspire to commit a crime. Christina is running the game, I can lock her up, as long as his folks don't cause issues and lawyer up

150

immediately."

"What do his parents have to do with it?"

"If he's under 18, a parent or guardian has to be there when we question him."

"He may be 18, he is a senior. All right bud. Take care."

Chapter 11

Mattis and The Bank (1 month ago)

The weather is starting to show signs of warming up as spring takes hold in Texas, and Mattis is training hard for the showcase he will be a part of in a matter of weeks up in Chicago. Between the training and his patrols, Tony is spent. The FBI taking an interest in Mattis is not helping matters, as he always feels like he has to be on his toes, ready for anything.

All he wants to do is jam in the garage like he used to. When he was a kid, he grew up idolizing Neal Peart as the best drummer in the world, but as he got older and Neil passed away, he got into punk rock and picked up a new favorite drummer in Andy Hurley of Fall Out Boy.

He used to put his headphones on and drum to the songs, picturing himself playing before a crowd and he even started a band once with a couple of detectives, but 'Swift Justice' never went anywhere except for a single gig at The Texas Showdown near the University of Texas campus. Music is nowhere in sight as he gets ready for some urban detection training that is a patrol outside the state capitol where a protest is being held by a large group of Gen Z students.

It is pretty rare to see K9 officers out in public except in airports, but in the case of large gatherings, the officers search for any explosives on or near the capitol grounds and provide protection for their handlers if the need arises. Tony and Mattis are just finishing a perimeter sweep as the crowd is starting to gather, so he takes Mattis to a designated staging point off the northwest corner of the grounds near the Reagan Office Building.

Protests are nothing new, but there is more tension with young people these days coupled with a series of laws being passed students are not in agreement with, Tony and Mattis remain vigilant and check in with their incident commander. "241 on station."

There is a mix of police and Texas Rangers on the scene this spectacularly sunny day. For spring, it is a little on the warm side, with the temperature getting close to 85 at the one o'clock hour. The sun is high in the sky, beating down on everyone so Sgt. Scott is hoping the heat will cut the protest short, but with rising temperatures come rising tempers.

The officers downtown are concentrated on the North and East parts of the grounds and are not particularly paying attention elsewhere, focused primarily on the crowd. No one notices a blue van two blocks away as it moves south on Guadalupe makes the turn and stops in front of Moody Bank. Three men in suits exit the vehicle one by one and the driver continues west.

The men pause slightly to raise the bandanas over their faces and open their suit jackets to expose AR-15-style rifles as they storm the bank lobby. The first of the attackers enters, shouting "Everyone down," he points his rifle at the teller line, "If you touch the alarm you die, little man," staring intently at the first young teller in his view.

He is a 20-something blonde kid wearing a name tag with "Will" emblazoned on it. In an athletic move, the first attacker jumps on the teller line and stands over the tellers as he tosses a bag down to them, "Give me your first and second drawers. No bait money. No dye packs."

"Come on fat man," the second attacker now has the branch manager in his clutches, "let's go to the vault, get your double custody," he says knowingly.

"My what?"

"Come on big boy, you can't access the vault by yourself, get your other half of the key combo, now!" As the assailant speaks it's obvious they've cased the bank and are aware of the procedures this bank uses to make sure the vault money is not accessible by any single person.

The bank manager lowers his head, but they have him beaten, so it is pointless to try and resist. He calls his assistant over, "Emily, I am sorry, we need your A key, please. Just give me the key, you don't have to go in with us."

"No, she's going in with us, come here lady," the attacker beckoned, "now!"

"Please, you don't need her, I swear on my life to you," the manager said. The bank manager is in his late forties and looks like the late former President William Taft. He is rotund, with a light mustache that is disheveled and longer than it should be and he's balding a bit up top but is dressed impeccably with a silver suit and patent leather shoes that look like a pair of mob shoes with their black and white tones and wing tips.

"Yes, Roger," Emily answers sheepishly. Emily Irons is a young assistant manager, recently promoted to the position after excelling as a salesperson and as a teller in the branch. She is a confident woman who looks like a model with long flowing brown hair, perfect skin, brown eyes, and high, pronounced cheeks. She has a slender neckline and is wearing a skirt that is a size too small.

For the past two weeks, she's been trying to pull one of her commercial customers and this skirt accentuates the perfect little bubbles she has on her backside. Today, though, her hands are shaking and she's wondering if she'll make it through to see that customer.

"Come on, let's move it." The second attacker yells.

"Two thirty," The third man hollers. They've timed the potential response, given the protest outside the men feel the cops are distracted and as long as there is no alarm, they can slip out unnoticed.

It is a bad idea to hit the vault because it takes time. Payroll is dropping this weekend, and their inside person told them $1.9 million is in the vault waiting to be sent to satellite branches, so they took the added risk. "Two fifteen," as the two managers reach the outer door of the vault and open the gate to go inside. "Two minutes."

The first attacker shouts again, "All the top drawers and

everything in the 2nd drawers!" He looks away from Will after collecting the money from him but in his peripheral view, he sees Will reach for something.

He spins around and shouts, "What did you reach for?! WH

?!!" Will recoils back against the wall and has his hands near his face, shaking violently.

"One thirty! Did he hit it?"

"Did you hit the alarm you little punk? Did you?" Will is shaking his head but it doesn't matter as the assailant puts his rifle barrel to Will's chest and makes a motion like he is going to shoot, but does not.

A woman screams at a decibel level louder than a jet engine which startles the gunman and he spins around. As he does, he applies a little too much pressure on the semi-automatic weapon and it discharges, blowing Will's right shoulder apart and spraying blood all over the wall and window.

People in the lobby start screaming, and a couple make a break for the entrance. The third robber, having entered sloppily and stepped too far inside, is too busy looking at his watch and does not notice until he hears the door open. He levels his rifle at the door and carelessly fires a shot into the door, shattering the window. Now there is chaos in the street as well, "One minute!" He yells, unfazed.

The workers in the vault hear the shot and go down quickly while the gunman pulls a duffel from his backpack, helps himself to all the large bills he can fit in his backpack, and then fills the duffel. He mutters to himself, "You idiots." He slings his backpack over his shoulder, grabs the duffel, and exits the vault.

He locks the shiny silver vault door on his way out, trapping Emily and Roger inside, and tosses the key into a large plant outside the main doors of the vault. "What the *HELL*!" he screams at the other two. "Are you morons done?"

At this point, the assailant behind the teller line jumps back over the counter with his backpack somewhat full and the three prepare to back out of the lobby of the branch as the blue van makes the full trip around the one-way streets surrounding the bank and pulls back up in front almost exactly three minutes after leaving the men at the front door.

Two blocks away, Mattis heard the gunfire and pulled on his leash. Tony, recognizing it's a robbery, begins running the short two blocks toward the bank, Mattis leading him on leash. As they pass Lavaca Street, the first of the robbers exit the bank and Tony realizes he is outgunned.

Three men with assault rifles against him with a nine-millimeter handgun. He also has no cover except for a parked car outside the hotel valet stand about 20 feet to his left, across the street. He sprints over and goes for his weapon, gets behind the car, and commands Mattis to remain by his side, which he does.

The first man, seeing Sgt. Scott immediately opens fire. At a distance of about 150 feet, he hits the car Tony is behind, but there is no immediate danger. Tony peeks out from behind the Tesla that took a bullet or three for him, levels his weapon, and fires two shots, one of which hits the shooter in the shoulder, spinning him around and dropping him to the ground.

The other two shooters open fire, but one stops to help his fallen comrade to his feet and into the van. Tony commands Mattis to strike, even though it's a huge risk, and starts across the street behind his dog to potentially take the other two shooters. He fails to notice the driver's window rolled down and he never heard the shot that took him down in the middle of 15th street.

Mattis the Hero

Tony and Mattis finish their sweep and take up a position in their assigned location, "241 in position," Tony radios in. Mattis is sitting at his feet as usual, alert as always to his surroundings. Suddenly and without warning, Mattis slumps to the ground.

Tony, startled, drops his leash for a moment as Mattis regains his senses and immediately bolts to the west. Tony is yelling his sit command, "Bleib, BLEIB! *MATTIS!! Nein! NEIN!!*" but Mattis is on a mission, Tony is in full sprint at this point. A bystander sees the commotion and immediately pulls out his phone to see what will happen to the dog.

A blue van approaches 15th Street, coming south on Guadalupe Street. It stops in second position at the red light, waiting for the vehicle in front of it to clear, but Mattis reaches the intersection, and cars stop as an incredible scene plays out.

Mattis jumps on a silver Honda in the second lane and in stride, leaps at the blue van, flying through the open window and connecting with his teeth on the face of the driver. Mattis has half his body outside the window while he has the man gripped in the vice of a jaw by the neck.

Panicked, the driver floors it, hitting the old truck in front of him and careening over the curb. The vehicle takes out a street lamp as it cuts the corner in front of the bank, and Mattis releases his grip on the man, falling to the pavement and rolling for about 10 feet as the van had already reached a speed of about 25 miles per hour.

"241 Officer needs assistance, at 15th and Guadalupe. The suspect is in a blue Econoline van headed west on 15th street, turning north on Nueces." Tony gets to Mattis, who is standing and barking at the van as it turns out of sight.

"Mattis. Sitz." Mattis sits at his feet like nothing happened, even though his snout is covered in the blood of the driver of the van. "Mattis, what did you just do?"

Tony hears activity on the radio, "205. Suspect located, driving erratically eastbound on MLK."

"He's going for 35," says another voice.

"147. TA at Brazos and MLK. Four white males, heavily armed!" screams a third.

The City of Austin Police routinely set up command posts near the capitol for days with large rallies, and this was no different. The staging area is a parking area three blocks north,

159

on Brazos Street, so the assailants drive into a cluster of police.

The driver passes out from blood loss because Mattis hit paydirt on his flying attack and punctured the carotid artery on the left side of the man's neck. As the van slows, it hits a vehicle stopped at the intersection.

The remaining men jump out, carrying their rifles, but realize they are outnumbered almost immediately as they see the units converging from the north and the unit trailing them from the west. One of the gunmen raises his weapon and is put down almost immediately.

Inside the van, police find backpacks, schematics, and notes about who the manager and assistant managers are at a bank on 15th Street. It is obvious to them that they intended to rob the bank, but the crime was foiled when the superdog took a header through the window of the van.

Tony leashes Mattis and listens to the units on the scene as they report what they find. Tony turns to Mattis and asks, "Did you know those men were going to hit the bank?" Mattis could not understand him, but he was still surprised when Mattis responded with a single bark.

Once the shock wears off, he notices a slight limp in his left hind leg. They stop so he can examine it, but he freezes when he realizes that Mattis' hind leg is now silver from the hip down. The black and brown socks are gone. *What the hell?* he thinks to himself.

Just then a bystander walks up to Tony and says "Dude, that was fire. Your dog totally blitzed that van. I got it on video,

160

want to see it?"

"Nah, I saw it in real time."

"What's your name dude, I need to send this to KVUE."

"Sgt. Tony Scott. Those men were about to rob that bank."

"How the hell did your dog know that?"

"I have no idea, but he's done stuff like this before. Look, I need to go and report all this."

The Media Responds

Tony and Mattis are at the downtown precinct writing up a report and waiting for the incident commander to arrive when they hear on the TV, "Thank you for tuning in to KVUE news at 5, I'm Kate Clark. We begin in downtown Austin where police were involved in an altercation that you'll only see on KVUE. We go to Reginald Mann, on the scene."

"Hey, turn that up!" someone shouts.

"Scooter, your dog is about to be famous," another voice says.

Great, he thinks to himself, *I don't need this going into next month in Chicago, it's going to make for a circus.*

"Thanks, Kate, I am standing in front of the downtown branch of Moody Bank, where earlier today 4 men in a blue van were about to commit a robbery according to police. A bystander recorded the interaction between one of Austin's K9 officers and

161

the van as it approached the bank and before we show this, some viewers may find these images disturbing."

Tony watched in disbelief as Mattis ran through the intersection, jumped on a car between him and the van, then used that car as leverage to launch himself through the open driver's side window and attack the driver of the van. The van took off and he did not realize Mattis hit the pavement hard, and this was likely the source of his minor limp.

"Authorities confirm they detained two suspects, also noting officers killed one man who attempted to open fire with an assault rifle, and the K9 unit killed the driver of the van, who has yet to be identified. Sources inside the Austin PD have confirmed that the K9 officer is named Mattis and has a distinguished career, is credited with 9 captures, and is responsible for over 200 kilograms of drug seizures in his short career. The bystander who uploaded this video to TikTok told me his video has already been viewed two hundred thousand times since he uploaded it just two hours ago."

"Reggie, is there any indication the suspects were easily identifiable, how did the K9 unit know to do that extraordinary action to thwart the robbery?"

"Kate I spoke with several observers, one of whom did not want to be identified who told me that he spoke to the officer who appeared to be the dog's handler who indicated this is not the first time his K9 officer has done something extraordinary, almost as if he knew something was about to take place."

Over the next two days, the TikTok and other videos

garnered millions of views, and soon Mattis received awards from the American Kennel Club, the Austin PD, and the FBI leaked he was invited to the K9 skills competition in Chicago at the end of May. The FBI also put out a call for people to send in other stories of persons or pets acting fantastically to stop crimes from happening before they actually do.

On the other side of the world, a deceptively frail-looking older gentleman is reading his newspaper. His hands are wrinkled, his face dark and leathery, but his eyes are sharp as a hawk. He is reading a Filipino account of the events that happened halfway across the world, and he opens his tablet to find a video of the incident.

The man squints at his screen, his brown eyes narrowed by the glare of the sun off the screen. He wipes his long gray hair from his face as he sees the actions Mattis takes and also notices the assailants have done nothing to identify themselves. "Finally." He says to himself, "Someone else that shares the gift."

He puts his tablet down, folds his newspaper, and begins to think about how he'd be making his way to America, the country of his birth. Barely five minutes earlier, he was breathing a little heavily because the air felt like a wet biscuit trying to invade his lungs. Now he does not even notice as his heart rate quickens and his mind starts to race, thinking about travel plans. He breathes a little easier and a slight smile crosses his face as he remembers his lost comrades.

Many years ago, he and a group of others who shared

the same gift worked together to try and fight the terrible governmental corruption and high crime that was a fact of life in East Asia. His group, called The Order, was responsible for taking down several of the most corrupt Chinese businessmen as well as some local street thugs who insisted on making the lives of ordinary people in their neighborhoods as chaotic as possible. One by one, his former mates passed on as genetic abnormalities got the better of them.

He snaps back to his current surroundings and realizes that this day that started as another hot day in the dry season is now almost bearable. He's searched the world for someone else who displayed this rare gift of foresight so stunning it could not be explained but he never expected to find it manifesting in an animal. The more he thinks about it and watches the video again and again, listening to eyewitness accounts and news reports, he is certain Mattis has the gift.

Growing up with the same gift has taught him many lessons over time, and the fact he said goodbye to over a dozen other people who also had it made him respect the power and unpredictable nature of it. He's worked hard during his lifetime to understand it and has learned to control it with great accuracy.

He suspects there has to be more in the world who share this gift. With that, he quietly resolves to make his way to the US on his quest to make contact with Mattis and continue his search for others who share the gift of time manipulation.

Chapter 12

Nat, Christina, and The Revelation (One Month Ago)

Nat stares at the blue numbers on the dashboard of her car, lost in the thought this may be the last night of her high school social life. In 5 minutes her uncle will show up and they will ruin the life of a boy who has no idea they are coming for him. *8:56,* she thinks to herself as the blue numbers merge in front of her eyes into a glowing mass of light reminding her of her reputation going down in a blaze of glory.

This is such a bad idea. Everyone will hate me for this, her mind is starting to run away with scary and unsettling thoughts as she lets fear and doubt overwhelm her resolve. *8:57. I can still get out of this.* She sees headlights in the distance.

What are you doing, Nat? The headlights are a little closer as her heartbeat quickens and her throat tightens. *8.58. Last chance. This is my last chance.* The headlights stop and turn off in front of her, about 50 feet away.

The top-heavy figure of her Uncle Pete exits the driver's side and starts walking towards her. *8:59. You can do this. You didn't come back to let them get away with what they did to you. But they didn't do it, they haven't done it, yet. I don't remember it but I felt it. The video and the blood, they have to pay.* The argument inside her mind is raging, when all of a sudden…

Uncle Pete knocks on the window, looking at her.

"Nat, are you ok?" Uncle Pete is standing outside her window.

9:01. I just lost two minutes. Where did they go? Am I losing it? She opens the door and the blue night light keeping her sane suddenly winks out of existence. "Hi, Uncle Pete. I'm sorry, I don't know what to do. Everyone is going to hate that I did this, and I'm going to be frozen out. I'll go from A-list to D-list overnight."

"Look, we don't have to do this, but from what you are telling me they will simply try and do you the next chance they have. They are going to try and ruin your life by any means they can, so there is nothing that should stop you from striking first."

"You think?"

"Yes Natal, er, Nat. You are strong and you have an edge. You know what they are going to do before they do it. That gives you the advantage."

"Yeah, if they do something awful, I can always fix it." She stops dead in mid-thought because as she got lost in her feelings, she just admitted her secret to her uncle. *Please don't notice. PLEASE.*

"What are you saying, Nat?"

She stammers and struggles for the words, her world almost starts to collapse around her as she immediately wants to take the last 5 minutes as a redo, but at the last second, "You know Uncle Pete, I go like, from zero to legitimately thinking I'm a wizard within like two drinks. I can fix it."

"Well, we're fixing something right now, no booze required. You're about to cut the head off the snake. Maybe you can step in as the next queen bee."

"You mixed metaphors, Uncle Pete. No way I want that. Let's just see what happens here." She starts to walk up the sidewalk to approach the house, and as she gets to the porch the door opens. *Wait, something is different here.*

"I thought that was you, who's this dude, your dad?" Zach is laughing with a couple of friends when he sizes up Pete and realizes the dude is big. Like, real big. "Wait, you're not Natalee's dad."

"No, I'm not, son." He goes to the pocket of his sport coat, "Zach Almeida, I have a warrant to search you and this premises."

Zach turns to run when he feels the iron-clad grasp around his left wrist, but it's too late, his momentum is already too far ahead of him and he twists down in a heap, to which some people on the porch start laughing. "Get off me!" he hollers.

"Son, we can do this the hard way or the easy way; now get up." Pete pulls him up, still holding his left arm, now behind him as he nudges him against the brick column in front of the porch. "You have anything sharp, guns, knives, anything I should know about that may hurt me?"

"No. Come on man, what did this bitch tell you?"

Pete starts to pat him down and pulls his wallet from his back pocket and tosses it on the ground. He goes to the front

167

pocket and feels an edge. "What's this? I don't think you're happy to see me." He instructs Zach to empty his pockets.

Zach instead tries to bolt inside the house but the word is out that a cop is at the front door and the mass of humanity fleeing the party knocks him back off the top step, right into the waiting hands of Uncle Pete.

"Bad choice son." Pete has him on the ground now and just sits on him as he struggles. "Stay down, stop resisting, you want to go to jail?" That calms him for a second, long enough for Pete to pull out his radio. "1 Baker 9, I need backup to roll immediately to 4114 Mason Dr. I am executing a search warrant and need some assistance."

Zach can't hear the response but something sneaks into his little brain and he starts squirming again, trying to escape from the hold of this man mountain that has him pretty much pinned against the grass. "Natalee, I swear, this was not my idea."

Nat interrupts, "I told you."

"Son, I need to tell you right now you have the right to remain silent, anything you say can and will be used against you in a court of law. You also have the right to an attorney, if you cannot afford an attorney, one will be appointed on your behalf, do you understand these rights?"

"Get off me, man!"

"Do you understand?"

"Yeah, just get off me. I'll give you what you're looking for. It's in my left front pocket."

168

"Dumb jock, just like I said Uncle Pete."

"Your uncle's a *COP?*"

"Damn straight I am, and you were about to do something stupid. How old are you son?"

"Eighteen."

"Good, so do you want to tell me what this is?" Pete is holding a small plastic tube filled with liquid.

"It's liquid X. I got it from Nat. She said we were going to party tonight, I was going to ask her to prom."

"You lying sack-"

"Nat, calm down," Pete interrupts. "Do you expect me to believe this?" I've got the IM you had with Christina Sinclair where she asked you if you had this liquid X.

The blood drained from Zach's face and he clammed up. "I'm not saying anything else. I need my dad; he'll call our lawyer. My uncle is a bigwig with the government, so you can kiss my ass butterball."

"Aren't you funny, little man? I hope you don't have a scholarship next year, cuz if you don't play some ball with me right here, right now, I guarantee you that your life is over. You give me something and we can work something out to keep you out of jail tonight."

A squad car pulls up and two officers dismount their vehicle and walk up to Pete. "Whatcha got rook? And what the hell are you doing executing a warrant without backup?"

"Detective rook to you Vermillion. The eighteen-year-old male was found with GHB, based on evidence he intended to

169

sexually assault a female subject. He's under arrest for possession of an illegal substance and conspiracy to commit sexual assault. Let's get him to the precinct so he can tell us what happened and save himself a night in jail."

By now a crowd has gathered, and there is enough light from camera phones to illuminate a stadium in Zach's front yard. There is some muttering in the crowd of kids and a voice shouts, "You bitch, are you so insecure you're going after us now because you *used to* be popular?"

The two officers are already leading Zach to their car when Pete turns around and faces the crowd, "Do I need to check IDs here? How many of you want an MIP on your record? Let's see them." The kids scatter.

He turns to Nat, "Let's take you home." They both turn and walk to Nat's car. She is shaking like a dog at the vet. "You need me to drive you?"

"No, I'll be ok, I just need a second."

"Ok, I am going to the station and we'll try to flip Zach before he completely lawyers up. We've got a pretty thin case on Christina, but we've got him nailed."

"Thank you, Uncle Pete."

He gives her a peck on the forehead and says, "You were real strong to do this. I'm proud of you. So is your dad."

She starts crying.

Pete has Zach in the box, he figures he's only got a few minutes before the kid lawyers up, so he hits him with the full-court press. "Look kid, I don't want you. I want the one who had you do the dirty work. I've talked to the DA, and we're willing to take these charges down to disorderly conduct, a misdemeanor, you'll get a ticket and a court date and you're out of here."

He slides a coke over to Zach and sits. In a quiet, emotional tone, he says, "More importantly, your college never has to be made aware of anything. Just give me a statement about how you came to be in possession and what you were instructed to do."

Zach puts his head down; he's giving it some real thought. Just then the door opens, "Detective, a word."

Pete steps outside to speak with Detective Sergeant Al Morris, "Pete, you can't make that promise, it's Saturday the DA hasn't been advised of jack."

"I know Al, just give me some leeway, we've got the lynchpin dead to rights and all it takes is a statement from the kid. I haven't even processed him yet…no one needs eyes on this. I'll make him a CI."

"All right Pete, but you have 10 minutes. Once the kid's parents walk in, all hell will break loose and we'll have to hit him with the whole smash."

Pete goes back in, "Zachary. I've got some bad news for you. We just picked up Christina who rolled over on you, and said this was all your idea take revenge on Nat for what she did."

"No freaking way, man. That bitch is the one who set this all up. She even paid for the keg. I am not going down for her. I'll tell you whatever you need."

"Not whatever I need, son. I want the truth; can you write that down for me?" He slides a pen and paper over to Zach's side of the table and says, "I can help you if you help me here."

Zach squirms for a second, his eyes narrow and he breathes out through his nose for what seems like 3 minutes before he finally looks up at Pete and says, "OK." Zach writes what can only be described as an epic tale of despair and explains how just two days after the blowup in the cafeteria, Christina came to him with this plan.

She wanted him to drug her and then the entire Lacrosse team would have sex with Natalee, but he'd tell them she wanted to 'do the whole team' in one night. That's why he had invited most of the team and also why hardly any girlfriends were invited.

To keep deniability, Christina and her friends were all going to say they went, but right before the party, Christina told them all to go to a different party. Zach was planning on doing exactly as she asked. He set up beer pong to play against one of the few couples at the party, and he planned on putting the GHB in one of the cups closest to her she'd drink.

But, he never got to do it because the officer came in and arrested him after finding the liquid on him. He also wrote that Christina wanted some of it to be on camera so she could engineer the takedown of Natalee via social media that would end her.

He ended the confession with a note that shocks Pete, the fact that Christina plans to do something else to implicate Natalee in a cheating scandal in an attempt to have her academic credit and her future scholarship revoked.

"She's a piece of work, why would you hitch your wagon to this girl?" Pete asks Zach.

"You don't get it, do you? Christina runs the social order of the school. If you're on her bad side, nothing will go right for you. The athletes have it a little different because we can let our on-field performance build our reputation, but all it takes is for her to make up some crap about you acting inappropriately and you're kicked off the team."

He bangs his hand on the table, hard, and continues, "And she's done it. She will do it. You better promise me this won't kill me."

"If this even gets to trial, it won't be until after the school year is over, and you'll be on to college by then. High school is only important while you're in high school. Soon enough, you'll understand this crap does not matter. Look, this won't help you right now, but my wife was the captain of the cheer team in high school, I was a year older than her but I wasn't one of the popular kids, I was a band dork."

Zach chuckles, managing to find a little humor in the events of the night.

Pete goes on, "You know what, we met in college one

day by mistake. She was lost, I helped her, and we started talking like nothing ever happened in high school. The whole social order went out the window. We started dating that year and got married the day after she graduated. We're still married now. That's how much crap this is. You'll be fine Zach, I got you."

He turns around and walks out, but turns as he does and says, "I'm serious Zach, you gave me information to save my niece a shit ton of pain and suffering, you'll be ok. I'll make sure of it. Thank you for your help today son."

"Yes, sir."

Pete lets his sergeant read over the confession and they get the arrest warrant for Christina. Pete calls Nat to let her know the good news, "Nat, we got him to roll over on her, and he gave us a signed note. Did you know that she was going to pin a cheating thing on you?"

"No, I didn't. Zach tell you that?"

"Yep. That surprised me. The girl is a menace."

"Uncle Pete, can you make it so they arrest her at school? I want her to burn now, I don't care anymore."

"Way ahead of you, I am pulling a string to have a judge issue the warrant tomorrow and I'll be the one to serve it at school on Monday. We'll do it at the end of a period so the perp walk happens as the kids are all in the hallways. I know what it's like to be mistreated in high school. Time for some payback. Imagine all the videos that will hit Instagram and TikTok on Monday."

"You're the best Uncle ever!"

174

Natalee hangs up the phone and goes back to her TikTok, she scrolls by a stupid cat video, then one where an inner tube hits a dog and sends him flying into the pond. She makes it through the activist videos about reproductive rights and people making fun of politicians.

Bored, she turns in her chair and a video arrives on her for you page with a caption of '*Hero dog takes down bank robbers before the robbery'* and something inside her tells her she needs to watch it. She watches it in disbelief, and at the end, the creator adds the question to his handler at the end, where he says his dog has done some incredible things before that could not quite be explained.

She puts her phone down. *How can this be, a dog has this thing? No way.* She decides to look on YouTube to see if she can find more, and she does. Video after video with commentary about the original incident. She finds another where the FBI is asking people for help in identifying others who have a psychic connection and can predict events like this.

Good luck with that, she thinks to herself, *there is no way that's not a science experiment waiting to happen.* Her curiosity gets the better of her and she decides to google the psychic police dog and finds a wealth of videos and other information, along with a story the FBI is hosting a big K9 event in Chicago in May around Memorial Day.

Her senses tingle. Something is up. *The FBI is going to kidnap this dog!* She wants to go to Chicago and warn his handler but doesn't have a clue how she could do that without

175

implicating herself as one of the people the FBI was looking for. Her mind is going in circles as she plans how she can slip away around Memorial Day to go to Chicago to find Mattis.

Her mind clears and she pauses, *why wouldn't the FBI just take the dog, under the guise that they want to work with another agency? Wait, they want to find people like me too, and are using this to cast a net.*

Her resolve is set. She thought about calling the Austin Police, but she wants to meet Mattis, so she is going to go to Chicago and it's time she uses this thing she has to do some good for other people. She starts looking for places to stay and more importantly, how her parents are not going to find out.

She decides to enlist Shannon in her plan and is already planning a story about spending the weekend with her and her family as they head to Norfolk for the festivities in and around the naval yard.

Chapter 13

Windy City (Day 0)

Memorial Day weekend is a festive time for the city of Chicago, as it is across the nation. It is a time to honor and remember the brave men and women who gave the ultimate sacrifice in order to ensure the American way of life for the entire city and the whole nation, regardless of race or ethnic heritage.

Many services of remembrance are held nationwide, and this year, the Chicago PD and the FBI also put together a skills competition on Memorial Day weekend for officers who go unheralded throughout their careers. The first annual Paws and Shields competition is starting at 2 pm local time and some of the invitees have started to arrive in Grant Park in downtown Chicago to witness and in some cases, participate in the festivities.

The FBI was kind enough to book them a suite at the Blackstone, just across the street from Grant Park, so Tony decided to take a jog through the park to first, familiarize himself with the layout of the grounds and second, make mental notes on where to find some of this famous Italian beef he's heard so much about.

The sun was already up, shining high over Lake Michigan, but even for late May, this was an uncharacteristically cool morning. Tony shivers a bit as they walk outside, his smoke breath floating up and back into his face with the wind off the lake.

"Well, buddy, they say it's going to be a great day today, but it's cold as hell right now. Mattis, Foos," Tony commands, to which Mattis immediately takes up position on his left to heel, keeping pace with his every move. As they cross the street towards the park, they pass in front of a green city bench where an older man is seated, wearing a blue shirt with a picture of the Shedd Aquarium emblazoned on it.

Mattis slows, takes a few sniffs, and sits down, motionless. Tony, puzzled, stops and apologetically greets the man. "Good morning sir, I apologize for my partner here, he seems to be picking up a scent that he is trained to detect."

"Well, officer, the substance he is smelling is perfectly legal here in Illinois." He pauses to look at Mattis as he stands up and continues, "Is this the legendary canine officer Mattis? I recognize him from the television. May I?" He reaches his hand ever so slightly towards Mattis.

"He's off duty, of course."

"Thank you. Mattis, I have been quite impressed with you young man. You display a very rare gift." As he speaks to Mattis, his tail starts to dart back and forth as he rises from his sitting position to sample the odor of the old man's outstretched hand.

Mattis licks the man's hand, then stands on his hind legs and places both his front paws on the man's chest, forcing him to lose his balance and fall back into a seated position on the

178

bench. Mattis seems to almost recognize the man and whimpers ever so slightly.

"Mattis, Platz." Tony commands.

"It's all right Sergeant, he doesn't have to go down."

"It's the training, sir, I have to make sure he is following commands."

"Of course you do, you don't want another repeat of the bank robbery."

How does he know all this? GREAT, another crazy stalking a dog. Tony thinks to himself as the old man gets up from his bench once again.

"Sergeant Scott, it is a pleasure to meet you, I'll be seeing you soon at the competition."

"Thank you, sir," he says, realizing that the man's hand is outstretched for a handshake but he is distracted by the man's left eye, which looks almost white with a cloudy look. He breaks his gaze, shakes the man's hand, and says, "Call me Tony, and you are?"

"Just an old man who enjoys finding gifted people and animals." With that, he turns and crosses the street toward the Chicago Hilton.

Tony starts jogging with Mattis, having given the heel command again, and looks at Mattis, as if he can understand, "That was a little strange buddy. I think you may have a bit of a stalker." Mattis runs alongside Tony, but he keeps looking back over his shoulder like something is distracting him.

After a few seconds, the distraction seems to be gone and Mattis is focused on the trail ahead as it winds through the park. Tony has a fleeting thought, *How did that guy know my name? TV maybe?* As they approach the venue where the detection competition is, they are still setting up temporary bleachers and getting the various placements ready.

Tony takes a mental inventory of the obstacles. A car, some barrels, and other objects scattered about, most likely to be used as hiding places for the contraband. As they cross Columbus and move closer to Grant Park proper, he notices that fencing has been erected the length of the park, stretching for over half a mile by his estimation.

That must be the search course, Tony thinks to himself. "Are you ready for that buddy? You're going to have to find me on the other end of the fountain or start from up there and come this way. It's a little bit of a cheat fencing you in, but we don't want you run over on Lake Shore Drive."

He's petting Mattis on top of the head and scratching behind his ears as he looks to the south and notices a tent at the far end of the field. He wonders why they'd set up logistics way out of the way but dismisses it.

Inside the tent, Assistant Special Agent in Charge Peabody is making final preparations with Agents Newsome and Custos. "Vic, you are being stationed north of Buckingham Fountain where we'll be simulating the grab on the animal. Keep your eye on the officer and make sure he's out of the line of sight

180

for the grab team to do their thing."

She turns to Custos, "Savannah, you'll be coordinating logistics from right here. Grab teams A, B, and C are all deployed and in plain clothes as planned. We have Chicago PD to provide extraction of the grab teams if anything goes sideways. Search and Rescue up first, then we transition to detection if needed on Columbus."

She picks up a clipboard and faces the group, "We've got the kid and her folks at the Chicago Hilton and an asset is on them feeding on-site intel until grab team C makes contact. Savannah, do a com check with the asset at eleven hundred, code name Huck. All right people, any questions or are we good to go?"

"Good to go, Alicia," Vic says.

"I'm ready ma'am," Savannah responds.

The team gets up and quietly files out, everyone headed to their destinations after the remaining members change into their street clothes. Savannah stays behind with ASAC Peabody. "You know this won't work, right?"

"Which part?"

"Any of it."

"This is the second time you've alluded to this Savannah, tell me what's on your mind."

"This dog and this kid have a temporal distortion within their ability. The grab teams might as well have signs that say, 'we're going to kidnap you.' on them. They'll go through the experience and then simply jump backward to thwart the

181

activity."

"I'm counting on it. I'm also counting on them displaying some noticeable change about themselves. The K9 unit had a white paw show up according to his handler last time. Who knows what happens to the girl? We found over 200 mutations on the subject we found in 2001. Something will be noticeable, and if not, the sheer coincidence they avoid at least three different attempts that are total and complete surprises will tell us all we need to know."

"Then how do you plan on getting them in?"

"Easy. We offer them jobs."

"What?"

"Get them in under false pretenses so they come in willingly. This thing can't go back more than a day, so we tell them we'll be running a little test, but instead, sedate them so they sleep that amount of time. Then they are ours."

"I see. That's not the most ethical thing, Alicia."

"We're talking about national security, Agent Custos. I've seen your jacket, and I don't think I need you growing a conscience now, but I understand what you're saying. Believe me, I realize the tactics are morally indefensible, but they are absolutely necessary. There will be others who manifest this anomaly. Do you want China to figure it out first? Or Russia?"

"No ma'am. But I have a question."

"Go ahead."

"Is that you talking or is that SAC Sanumo?"

"Is there a difference, Custos?"

"Damn straight there is a difference. I heard things about him in the agency, or at least the stories. He'd rather kill a friendly than admit wrongdoing. Do you have any idea how many war crimes that shit bag is responsible for? He'd sell out his mother if there was profit in it for him."

"You need to close your mouth before you get yourself in a jam, Special Agent. Let's keep our eye on the ball. You gave me an idea. Let's accelerate the sedation. Muster grab team C on comms."

Jeanne and her parents are getting ready to leave their downtown hotel which overlooks the park and Lake Michigan, make the short walk across Michigan Avenue, and see the sights and sounds of this new event. Jeanne is prepared with her noise-canceling headphones in the chance she suffers an auditory overload with the ambient noise.

As they exit the hotel, they walk past a gentleman on the sidewalk who catches Jeanne's eye. A strong sense of déjà vu comes over her and she fixes her gaze on him. The man is medium height and slender, wearing a Cubs hat and sunglasses but Jeanne somehow feels she has seen him before. She smiles at him. "Hello."

Dan snaps his head around, he'd very rarely seen Jeanne initiate a conversation outside of forced communication at home or school, and never with someone she would consider a stranger. "Jeanne?"

"It's ok Mr. McAlister, I mean your daughter no harm."

"How do you know my…do I know you?"

"We've never been officially introduced, I work at Jeanne's school, that's probably how she recognized me."

"Oh, erm, I'm sorry. I'm Dan."

"Yes sir, I've seen you there, usually after this little one has an outburst of some sort. I've seen gifted kids come through time and time again, but yours is special," he looks over at Jeanne who is only a few inches shorter than he is now, "this one has so much potential locked inside her and all she needs to do is have a breakthrough and learn to control her gifts."

"We've been working on that, haven't we Jeanne?"

"We have a dad."

The old man nods in agreement, "Good. Are you here for the dogs today? That's why I am here."

"We are," Jeanne says, "my dad's friend works for the FBI and he got us some personal invitations so we can meet the dogs up close. I can't wait. First, we are going to have lunch. I want pizza."

"Let me guess, you guys are going to Giordano's up the street there," he says, motioning to the north, "yummy stuff."

"Yep! It's my absolute favorite. We're fortunate we get lunch paid for because we are VIP guests." Jeanne goes on to say, while Dan is dumbfounded she is carrying on a normal conversation with what he still thinks is a stranger, or close to it.

"Well, you guys better get going then, very nice to see you, Jeanne." He pats her on the head, then extends his hand to Dan, "Pleasure to meet you in person Dan."

"Great to meet you as well." They shake hands and part, going in opposite directions.

"What does he do at the school, baby girl?"

"I don't know. I've never seen him at the school."

"Are you sure, he said he works there?"

"Well, maybe he knows me. He does look familiar to me, but he feels more familiar than he looks. It's like he's been with me for a long, long time. I can't explain it."

Dan makes a mental note to not let Jeanne out of his sight as Lynn walks out of the lobby and onto the sidewalk. "It's crisp this morning, isn't it? That cold front dropped the temperature overnight," she says, "are we ready to get some pizza?"

She looks at Jeanne and tries to tickle her a bit, but Jeanne recoils at the touch. Lynn looks a little disappointed and curls the edges of her lips, but she smiles and says, "They should be open by the time we walk up there. I need a good pie."

Jeanne senses her mom's dismay and hugs her, "It's ok Mom, I just have to do this kind of thing on my terms."

Lynn chokes back a tear as Dan's jaw drops. Displays of emotion from Jeanne are so rare and initiation of physical touch, although a little more common, is still a surprise to him. She has empathy, her gift has shown that more than anything, but things like this show how fragile the family is emotionally. As Dan and Lynn compose themselves, Lynn says, "Are we ready for lunch? Who's hungry?" and they walk off to the pizza place.

As it approaches noon, Mattis and Tony are walking into the park when they are stopped by a young lady who asks for a selfie with Mattis. Tony agrees, and while she has his back to them getting ready to snap the picture she says, "Officer, don't show any emotion, but the FBI will try and take your dog because of the gift he has. Be super careful, ok?"

Mattis jumps on the girl's back as she takes the picture, and Tony has to admonish him, "Mattis, get down! That's the second time you've jumped on someone today."

He turns his attention back to the young girl and says, "I am sorry about him jumping on you, but young lady, why would you say such a thing?"

"It is safer that I don't tell you how I know, just watch your back. I'll try and help you if I can, good luck." Nat turns to walk away and leaves Tony a little confused.

After a second, Tony continues towards the check-in area as he is a little shaken up at what the girl told him, but his instincts are not telling him there is any danger as they arrive at the logistics tent so Mattis can be fitted with his camera and unbeknownst to Tony, a GPS tracking beacon.

There are several other dogs there for the competition and Tony makes small talk with some of the other handlers, making friends with a couple and being surprised at how talkative the FBI handler is. To him, the FBI has always been a bunch of stiffs, total blowhards that don't do any actual police work, they just give orders to the ones that do. "How are we doing here, agent..."

"Custos, sergeant."

"South American?"

"Yes sir, my family hails from Peru."

Just then, Mattis jumps up and places his paws on her chest.

Tony barks at his dog, "Mattis, what are you doing? I am so sorry, that's the third time he's done that today, my apologies."

"Not a problem, hello Mattis," Savannah says.

Tony, returning to the earlier part of the conversation says, "I thought you had some Peruvian in you. We have a large block of population from Peru on the east side of Austin and Lima is our sister city."

"I didn't know that Sergeant Scott."

Ain't this a live one, Tony thinks to himself as Savannah goes on outfitting Mattis.

"I am placing his body cam on his harness, here," motioning to a clip that extends upward from the center of his harness, right between his shoulders at a height of about 4 inches, "do you think that will be a hindrance to him at all? We don't have any tight quarters in the search or detection courses." Mattis scooches up to her and licks her face and she withdraws a bit.

"I think that will be fine Agent Custos. Tell me, do you ever have any fun? You look all business to me?"

"We don't have fun on duty in this agency, Scott."

"Well, it does not appear everyone shares that sentiment,

your handler over there is quite the barrel of fun."

"K9 is a little different. Counter Terrorism is a little more by the book."

"A little?" Tony says, laughing.

Savannah sends him a glare, "I've been in country with guys like you. I hope you are as good as they were. You're up for meet and greet in pen two." She motions to a series of makeshift cages with numbers on them.

Tony finds it vague but disturbing. He gives a little nod and as Savannah walks away he can't help but fixate for a second on her toned and very noticeable glutes stretching the sides of her pantsuit ever so slightly to reveal the perfect curves in the perfect places for him. *Damn, I think she likes me.*

Having all but forgotten the conversation with Nat merely 15 minutes ago, Tony ushers Mattis into pen 2, and shortly thereafter he starts to see some civilians with families walking around outside the logistics tent. Savannah comes outside with another agent to greet the gathering group of people and checks their identification against some list she has on a clipboard.

As she goes one by one, she hands them a lanyard with a pass affixed to it with a green border and a logo of the skills competition. As they begin to line up, they will be starting at pen 1 and moving down the line, so he'll see them next. "You ready buddy? Time to meet a bunch of people," he says to Mattis as one family comes walking closer, leaving pen 1.

Mattis is completely uninterested in the family that walks up. He just sits at the edge of the pen as they approach, meet Tony, shake hands, and walk off. Tony has a picture of Mattis with a paw print on it to give to each family as they pass, along with a pin for the Austin PD.

As the families pass, one by one, one last family is speaking to Savannah and they start walking to pen 1. Mattis becomes agitated immediately and starts running back and forth in the pen along the fence separating him from the civilians, whimpering.

Tony commands, "Mattis, Sitzen." Mattis walks up to the fence and sits, but he is fixated on the family that is late. As they leave pen 1 and start walking toward Mattis, his tail starts to brush the ground and he starts to make a high-pitched whine. "Hello there, I am Sergeant Scott of the Austin PD and this is Mattis, my K9 officer."

"Hello Officer Scott," Dan says, extending a hand to shake.

Mattis barks.

"Well, hello to you too, Officer Mattis," Dan says, slightly startled.

Lynn shakes Tony's hand as well and they introduce themselves as Jeanne goes straight for Mattis.

"Can I pet him?" Jeanne blurts out.

"Of course, but please don't make sudden movements near his face, just extend your hand below his nose. He won't make any sudden movements and is very well trained." As Tony

189

says that Mattis is still seated as commanded. Tony opens the door to the enclosure and Jeanne moves suddenly in front of her dad and enters the enclosure first.

Mattis immediately goes to his feet, gives her a sniff on the hand, and rises on his hind feet, placing his paws on her shoulders and begins licking her all over her face."

"Honey, wait," Dan is lunging for her at the same time Tony is entering the enclosure to reprimand Mattis. Dan turns to Tony and says, "She is neurodiverse, sudden physical contact usually startles her, but she has a way with animals," as he is saying that he notices she's not startled in the least and hugs the dog back.

"Like I said, she loves animals. She does this with horses back home, somehow she can almost talk to them. The stable hands all call her a horse whisperer."

"Mattis, Platz. What is with you today?" Mattis recoils at Tony's command and lays down but is crying, obviously wanting to see more of his new friend. Jeanne leans down and gets on her knees right next to Mattis and he begins licking her again, and she is giggling like her parents have never seen.

"I like this dog, mom. Can we have one just like it?"

Mattis barks again. Right in her ear. She jumps, and Tony says, "I'm sorry young lady, he seems to be jumpy today. He keeps doing that to people today. We're going to work on that next week."

"Honey, are you ok?" Lynn says in a concerned voice. That startled jump is usually followed by an immediate tantrum of

190

overstimulation. Instead, Jeanne starts waving her hands on either side of her face, almost like a bird flapping its wings.

Lynn, clearly worried, says, "Honey why are doing that flapping again?"

"I've started to realize when I am stressed I can flap my hands, and hear it, feel it, and see it and my senses start to return to normal so I don't freak out like I used to."

"Ok, have you been doing that long? I've never seen you do that before. Mom seems to have seen it though," Dan says.

"No Dad, I did it before, but just started doing more at the pizza place when you were getting the pizza, it was getting loud and this helped me concentrate. This dog is special. I need a dog like this."

Dan looks at Tony and shrugs, "I have no idea what she means, does your dog have the ability to be emotional support or a therapy dog?"

"No, we've never tried that. He does have the ability to anticipate things, did you see him on the news a while back? He foiled a bank robbery before it happened."

Dan's wheels were already turning. "It sounds like your partner here is gifted with the gift of foresight. My daughter has a similar ability."

"I firmly believe everyone on the spectrum has something beyond our comprehension. Their brains are wired so magically that the body is not yet advanced enough to handle all the information it brings. It's like a computer that has a processor that's too fast, the computer just shuts down for no reason after being overloaded so many times. She'll find her path, so will you…try and use it to make her incredible."

"Thank you so much officer," Lynn shakes Tony's hand. "It sounds like you know a little bit about neurodiversity."

"I do, only because I have a nephew on the spectrum who has a photographic memory. He can tell us we had a conversation on April 29 three years ago and tell us what the conversation was about. It's really amazing. Conversely, he can't stand a touch, is aggressive toward other children, and has a speech development issue that holds him back in school. I think his brain is just too good at one thing and it short circuits the normal pathways."

He looks at Jeanne and kneels on one knee next to her. "Young lady, I know you are destined for great things, you find your thing and make yourself the best version of *you* that you can be." He slowly reaches his hand out toward hers, but stops short, allowing her to take his hand.

"Thank you, sergeant. I am going to root for Mattis today to win all the things."

"We'll try and make you proud."

Jeanne shuffles over to the exit with her parents and Mattis, still lying down, whimpers, barks, and then lowers his head into the grass, almost looking like he's pouting. "Mattis, what's wrong boy?"

Mattis looks back at Tony, but then just drops his eyes and lets out a long sigh. Tony is puzzled. He's not seen Mattis look depressed after a human interaction before. "Maybe she's a dog whisperer too Mattis."

    Mattis looks up and barks.

Chapter 14

Kilo Niner Tango (Day 0)

The horn sounds and the first dog, from Canada, starts on the search and rescue. It's really just the door popper game he's trained Mattis on for the last two years. The announcer is commenting on the dog's progress and showing him on the monitors as well as the big screen they have for the spectators. They are separating the scent from the subject, and it throws the first dog for a complete loop.

The order of the competitors is randomized, so it's unknown when Mattis will be up, and for which competition. The staging area is closer to the search and rescue course so the action is clear to him, but not on the detection course. Just then, an agent appears to tell him he and Mattis will be next up on the search and rescue course. "All right buddy, it's your time to shine!" He gives Mattis' favorite toy a jingle to prepare him for a search. The toy is Mattis' reward for a job well done and he gets a few minutes of playtime every time he searches successfully.

"Ready grab teams A and C, the first exercise begins in 2 minutes." Agent Savannah Custos says into her headset as she peers into a series of CCTV monitors trained on the spectators, the grounds, and the strike points for the operation about to kick off.

194

"K9 Mattis is taking position. Take the scent marker to the netting area and arm the net. Escort team, take the officer to the number 4 rescue position."

"Roger that. Grab team A in position. Net armed."

"Grab team C standing by, in position at the VIP seating area."

Dan, Lynn, and Jeanne are in the VIP area, a small section of chairs with a better vantage point on a platform that overlooks the search and rescue course. Jeanne is intent on watching Mattis, so they are ready for the next search run, which the announcer says is Mattis. Jeanne says, "Dad, how is the dog supposed to know not to go for the scent and find the person hiding?"

"They aren't. This is meant to find dogs that have a special sense and can continue searching even after they find the scent of their handler. So far, the first three dogs all got confused."

"Well, it's not fair. They send the handlers across the fountain from where their clothes are. No wonder the dogs are confused. Mattis will get it right though."

"Maybe so," Lynn says.

They hear the announcer count down to the start of the run and the gate flies open. Mattis picks up the scent immediately and sprints toward the north end of the park in about a minute and a half. Here, he loses the trail ever so slightly but picks it up on the other side of a large walkway.

They masked the scent by not marking anything on the

separating walkway. Mattis picked up the few steps Tony had taken getting in position and was off to the races again. He reached the fountain in 2 minutes and 27 seconds where he deviated substantially further to the left than the other K9 officers.

"Grab team A, the subject is approaching the grab area, are we secure, the netting is obscured from view?" Savannah asks.

"Affirmative team leader. Netting is ready for the subject. We have eyes on."

"Grab team C, be ready if subject two leaves the seating area. We have to be prepared for anything."

"Roger, in position."

"All units, operation is a go, I repeat, operation is a go. Chicago PD is prepared for the extraction of the animal if possible, make the call when he is secured and they will mobilize. The girl goes on ambo 21 when ready." ASAC Peabody is on the channel now and communicating with the team.

Tony is in position, he can barely hear the PA from where he is, but he heard the count, so his watch is active. He looks down at it, *three minutes and 10 seconds, he has to be getting close.*

Mattis catches a strong scent trail and sprints into a bank of trees to a clothed dummy lying in a small clearing amidst the trees. He runs over to it, catches the scent, but looks around for a moment because although the scent is strong, he does not see

196

or smell Tony.

Just then, *SNAP!* The ground below Mattis seems to move all at once and he is ensnared in netting that fell from above. As he struggles, he gets more intertwined in the netting, but he suddenly goes completely still. A dart hits him in the torso, but nothing happens. No movement. Nothing.

Back in the VIP area, the monitor has gone out on Mattis' camera, so no one can see what is going on. Jeanne all of a sudden screams, "No! Mattis is in trouble!" and she bolts from her seat before Lynn or Dan can reach out to stop her.

Both drop their drinks and give chase, but Jeanne has already turned the corner and started down the walkway to the ground level. As she reaches the ground level, a man suddenly comes around the corner to go up the ramp and she runs right into him, bouncing off him like a doll and falling to the ground.

"Jeanne!" Lynn shrieks as Jeanne hits her head hard on the ground. "Dan, call 911."

The man who Jeanne ran into is hunched over her, "Young lady, are you ok? Can you hear me?" He reaches into the pocket of his coat but his hand emerges, empty, and he claps his hands right above Jeanne's face.

Lynn gets to her daughter and kneels next to her. She puts her hand on her head and notices a small amount of blood on her left arm, "Did she hit you here?" pointing to the spot on her arm and motioning to the man.

"I don't know ma'am, she just ran right into me."

197

"JEANNE!! *JEANNE!* Baby, please wake up."

Two agents show up and one radios in, "Ambo 21, we need you at the VIP area right now. Ramp to the second level, northeast corner."

After what seems like only seconds, two paramedics roll a gurney up to the scene. They quickly assess Jeanne, she's unconscious, but breathing. "She appears stable, are you the parents?"

"Yes."

"All right, we are going to transport her to the hospital. This agent here will follow us if you need a ride." They start strapping her on the gurney and within seconds they have her on the bed and moving.

"Once again, I am sorry, but I can take you to the hospital, my vehicle is just over here," as he motions a little bit to the north, where a blue Ford is sitting on the grass next to the road.

"Can I go with her?" Lynn asks.

"Unfortunately there is no room in the ambulance because there is always an agent since this is an FBI activity where she was injured. We assure you; Agent Richardson will be right behind us, and you'll be in his vehicle." They are already loading her in the ambulance and the couple start sprinting to the car with Richardson.

"Control, Grab team A, we have the animal. Proceeding to point charlie. No police intervention is needed."

"Control, Grab team C, we have the girl in ambo 21.

Parents are following in Richardson's sedan. Prepare traffic intervention at Balbo west of Columbus."

"Roger grab teams, acknowledged, both subjects have been secured." Savannah turns to her commander and nods.

Then, she keys the transmitter again, "Grab team B, stand down. Prepare the story and leak it to the news outlet closest to the incident with the girl."

Tony is annoyed. He's been waiting for over 5 minutes, no way Mattis takes this long. He decides to stand up and walk toward the course when he is stopped by a plain clothes agent who says, "Sergeant, your dog suffered an injury on the course. Our medics have him and have rushed him to the FBI's veterinary team."

"What happened?"

"He appears to have lost his footing and slipped down an embankment. He looks like he may have fractured a leg in his fall."

"No! This was supposed to be fun and games. How could this happen?"

"Don't worry officer, we are headed down there to see him as soon as a unit is free. We also had a young girl fall from the bleachers at the same time, which used the medical resources we had for this side of the park."

The crowd is oblivious to all this, and a routine announcement gets everyone focused on the next dog running the search course. Meanwhile, as Richardson gets ready to turn left on Balbo, he is cut off in traffic by another vehicle and hits the curb. "Dammit man, watch where you are going," Richardson shouts as he exits the car.

The other driver speeds off and Dan yells, "Forget about that let's go to the hospital, which one are they taking her to?"

The Old Man

"Ready grab teams A and C, the first exercise begins in 2 minutes," Savannah says into her headset as she looks at the bank of CCTV monitors trained on the spectators, the grounds, and the strike points for the operation. "K9 Mattis is taking position. Take the scent marker to the netting area and arm the net. Escort team, take the officer to the number 4 rescue position."

"Roger that. Grab team A in position. Net armed."

"Grab team C standing by, in position at the VIP area."

Tony arrives at the staging area where he is to wait for Mattis to find him, but he finds things looking a little strange. There are no agents there with him to catalog the score or validate that he did not call out to Mattis to guide him.

He looks around but there is no surveillance, no equipment or anything, but the announcer says, "3,2,1…," from way in the distance so he starts the timer on his watch.

Mattis is making excellent time through the first obstacle at Balbo, where the path crosses the park, separating the two sections from one another. He picks the scent back up on the other side of the street and sprints to the west of the fountain where he is picking up a strong scent. Suddenly, he stops.

"Control this is grab team A, we have eyes on the subject, but he's stopped and is looking at the scented garments, he may have the true scent."

"Grab team A control, can you trigger the net?"

"Negative, he is not in the drop zone. Wait, he is approaching the net trigger mechanism. Control he's disabled the net."

"Roger that team A, allow him to find the handler." Savannah turns around to talk to Alicia directly, "Ma'am, you were right about the animal detecting the trap before he got there."

Alicia nods, concern starting to show on her face.

As Mattis approached the heavy foliage, his camera went black to the spectators in the area. Jeanne, fearing something was dreadfully wrong, yells, "No! Mattis is in trouble!" and bolts from her chair, so quickly that Dan and Lynn are caught flat-footed.

They leap up to give chase, but she's already turned the corner and is headed down the ramp to the ground level. As she gets to the bottom of the ramp, a jogger runs by from her right and collides with a man who is about to start up the ramp. The collision is hard, and the men roll a few feet to her left.

The man who was jogging gets up and yells at the other

man on the ground, "Watch where you are going pal," as he places an object in his pocket. Jeanne stops for a second which allows her parents to catch up to her.

"Isn't that the guy we met in front of the hotel this morning?" Lynn asks.

"Cubs cap, sunglasses, I think so," Dan says, but Jeanne is running again, this time following the jogger disrupted the kidnapping attempt no one was aware of.

"Jeanne, wait!" Dan yells.

"Come on Dad, that's the guy who has something to do with this," Jeanne yells back as the man in the Cubs cap turns around ever so slightly, revealing the Shedd Aquarium graphic on his shirt.

"Control this is grab team C. Richardson is down. The girl is running away to the north. Should we pursue?"

"Negative team C. What is her location now?"

"She is going north along Columbus approaching Balbo with her parents following behind her. The man who made contact with Richardson appears to be the person they are chasing."

"Grab team B, control. Be on the lookout for four individuals running north near Balbo and Columbus, two males and two females."

"Grab team B here, we see them, but we are on the other side of the park, moving to engage."

"Is this guy they are chasing involved?" ASAC Peabody says to Savannah in the command tent. "This was supposed to be an easy snatch and grab."

"Unknown ma'am, this subject came out of nowhere."

"Pull up CCTV," Peabody says, raising her voice slightly to the agents on the surveillance monitors.

"We have all eyes on, there is no coverage on that side of Columbus as it was a pedestrian zone and isolated from the events," Savannah says with a more concerned tone.

"Damn. Come on Savannah, get me something."

"Yes ma'am, I am trying. Grab team B report."

"They've ducked behind some trees control, we're about a quarter mile away. We've lost visual."

"McAlisters, come quickly!" The old man shouts. As they catch the man, he uncovers a small car that has been hidden in the trees off Columbus. "I don't have time to explain, but she is in danger," and he motions to Jeanne. "We've got to put Scott and Mattis in here too, so you three jump in the back."

And they were off, just like that, going north and swinging around to Lake Shore Drive. He picks up his phone and dials, "Sergeant Scott, this is the man you met in front of the hotel who connected with Mattis. I don't have time to explain but your K9 officer is in danger. Meet me at the corner of Jackson and Lake Shore. I am in a blue sedan with Michigan plates. You'll have to breach the fence, but it's temporary fencing, it should come apart at the seams."

They speed over to the corner, where three men are running across the grove of trees, but Mattis and Tony are already slipping through the break in the fence. The man pulls up to them and says as they open the door, "Ditch the vest on the dog, they're tracking him."

Tony looks back at the man for a fast second, then unbuckles the harness from Mattis and leaves it on the ground as they hop into the vehicle and zoom down Lake Shore Drive to the south.

Tony turns to the driver and says, "What on earth just happened? This whole thing was cloogy, there was no agent presence where I was, what do you know and how did you get my number?"

"Relax Sergeant. I got your number when we met, you just don't remember on this timeline. I'll explain all this to you on the way. We're going to a safe place. Once the cops are activated, they'll be on you. Do you have any valuables at your hotels, and what does cloogy mean?"

"Nothing but clothes for us," Dan says.

"My police laptop is in my room, and cloogy just means out of the ordinary in a bad way, like clunky," Tony says.

"Did the FBI set up your room for you?"

"Yes." They all say.

"Too risky for you to go. I can retrieve it for you. Look, this is going to be difficult for you to hear, but Jeanne, you and Mattis have a genetic difference that allows you to control your biorhythms. Have you ever noticed strange things happen when you are mad or upset, maybe when you are in an emergency you seem to know what is about to happen?"

"Yes, that's exactly what happens to her," Dan says.

"It would explain what happens with Mattis, too." Tony says, "He recently foiled a bank robbery before it happened, and it's not the first time he's done something like that."

"That's how I found you, Tony. It's a condition that is very rare. I thought I was the only one for many years until I met others. They all passed on to the next plane after jumping back in time, one by one, until I was the only one left in Asia. The FBI is calling it the Circadian Anomaly. Whatever it is called, I've learned to control it.

I am sure that they've found out about you somehow Jeanne and sent teams of men to kidnap you. My guess is they want to test you until they can control it."

"Why, who would do that?" Lynn says loudly as Jeanne begins to hyperventilate in the back seat. "Jeanne, use your words, come on baby it's ok."

"First rule of government overreach; if you can't explain it, and it looks like it can be used to your advantage, take it over before someone else can make something useful from it. They want to see if they can use it to predict terror attacks, win wars, or tell them what to eat for dinner. Who knows exactly, but whatever they want, they won't stop until they track you down now. They don't have a clue about me, I live in The Philippines."

"But you are American, I can hear the accent," Tony says.

"Yes, I am."

"What do you mean you can control it?" Dan asks.

205

"Don't play coy Daniel. We both know that you learned to use it for yourself."

"Wait, what?" Jeanne and her mom both say in unison.

"Dan, did you not tell them you are using your daughter to win money at the track by forcing her to think something horrible will happen if she does not jump back in time to tell you who wins the race?"

Lynn hits Dan. Hard. "You pompous jackass. You put our daughter in harm's way just to win a bet?"

"Honey, it was not a chance, it was a certainty. Wait, how do you know about that?"

"I've been lurking around the FBI after they publicized this event. They had to be trying to invent some way to explain a disappearance in a way that you would not question them. I've been through this day three times to be in the right place to overhear their plans, but I wanted to find you first. All I have is an agent named Newsome they say found the girl, but they've been on the dog for longer than that."

He looks at Dan through the rearview mirror, "What you are doing is dangerous Dan. When we go back, sometimes we don't fully understand the risks and don't have a good reason we are going back. We also don't have the exact time and place to jump to and all that means we may have to jump again. Every time we jump, it stresses our body greatly. When that happens, more stress causes our DNA to mutate sometimes. It does not happen every time, and usually, the more stress, the bigger the change. Have you noticed physical or mental changes after an episode?"

"My eyes have turned different colors twice," Jeanne says.

"Mattis has two parts with gray fur on him that shouldn't be there," Tony says.

"Well, this is exactly what I mean. Those are just cosmetic changes; the big ones are the ones that kill you almost instantly. I've seen someone collapse moments after they reintegrated into the timeline and one less than an hour after. It's not something you can jump back and fix."

He looks at Jeanne, "Young lady, it's how you'll die most likely. Sorry for the crap news, but we can go to my rental house and debrief on our next steps." The old man looks determined as he gets to a highway and makes his way out of the loop westward to Naperville.

Dan is seething. He told his friend about this in confidence and now they just tried to kidnap his daughter. "Don't jump back honey, I'll deal with Vic."

"Vic told them? That sack of-", but Lynn is interrupted by Tony.

"Lynn, it's ok. I am afraid I outed my partner months ago after he did this a series of times. He's been psychic ever since he was a puppy." He looks at Mattis, "It's ok boy, I have no idea where we can go, but they are going to want you."

In the meantime, back at the park, the chatter is still going on the radio, "Control, grab B, we've lost them, they appear to have had a vehicle stashed in the woods along Columbus. They went east on Jackson; my guess is they hit Lake Shore and went south."

"Vehicle description?"

"Dark blue sedan. May have been a Toyota or a Ford, but we were not close enough to ascertain plates or the make and model."

Savannah slams her headset down. "We lost them." She picks up the headset again, remembering something else, "Grab team A, where are the animal and handler?"

"Control, we lost sight of the dog, we've been searching the wooded area and backtracked to the control point but they have both left the location. There is a fence breach on the north side, near Jackson."

"Keep looking grab A. Dammit! Newhouse, where the hell are you?

"Newsome, control. I am on station, north side of the fountain."

"And you did not see the grab team OR the animal? What kind of station did you make for yourself?"

"I was trying to remain concealed, control. I had the animal before he disabled the trap, but the order was to allow the animal to find the trainer. I was on him but he must have moved his location without authorization."

"Come on, Agent Newton, you have to be better than that!"

"Newsome."

"Whatever!" She slams the headset down again; this time a little plastic piece goes flying into Agent Peabody's hair. "Ma'am all units have lost contact with their marks."

"What happened Savannah, aside from you displaying extraordinary people skills as a net control?" ASAC Peabody asks, annoyed.

"The girl and her parents escaped in a vehicle driven by the man who disabled our grab agent. The dog and handler are unaccounted for but breached the fence in roughly the same direction as the girl fled."

"They can't be in this together, can they?"

"Doubtful ma'am, an escape to the north is logical, but we'll keep looking."

"Any public impact?"

"Negative. The op was not compromised."

"It was, but it did not go public. Let's pack it up. Give your awards and let's shut it down." Alicia turns and exits the tent, trying to appear frustrated but this exercise was all about proving the anomaly was real. Her bosses would understand that and give her a wider berth now.

The guy who disabled the grab agent bothered her though, where did he come from and how did he know something was going down? Through her furrowed brow and gaze that could disable many electronic devices, it hits her. They may have just seen a third anomalous subject who knew to take action to disable the grab.

Could the anomaly be genetic? Maybe an uncle or other

family member? She refused to believe this was just some uninvolved third party in the right place at the right time, her gut told her something was up. She flipped around on the tips of her right foot with such crispness a marine would be proud and walked back inside, "Savannah, bring up all the CCTV footage in and around the grandstand and VIP area where this guy who took out Richardson was. He has to be in on it, let's try and ID him."

"Yes ma'am. I'll take care of it."

Peabody's phone rings. "Yes sir, this is Peabody."

"You disappoint me, Alicia."

"How so, *Brett?*"

A hush falls over the room as Alicia walks into the adjacent room and closes the door. Savannah lowers her head and says softly to the others, "The great and powerful Oz has been keeping tabs on us."

"Oz?" One of the other tactical agents asks.

"SAC Sanumo. He's the overseer. Alicia is running this task force for him. Has no one informed you he's the real driver here? Don't mention it again. He's ruthless, just do your jobs and don't give him a reason to can your ass."

That same hush falls over the room again as they digest what Savannah says.

"The girl and the dog both escaped your grasp, why did you not just take them when you had the chance?"

"How do we explain that in front of a hundred people? Oh, a dog and a girl happened to faint at the same time, and we happened to be ready with transports and personnel? Give me some credit Sanumo, we've thought this scenario through. This was not designed to capture them; just prove they can elude an event. We have them on surveillance and track them down." An uneasiness fills her stomach because they don't have them on the CCTV yet.

Although upset, his voice remains cold and calculated as he enunciates very clearly, "Don't fail me again. I don't think you'd like it if I needed to take command of this operation. Then I would not need you." The line clicks. Three beeps tell her the call is over. She swallows, hard.

Chapter 15

The Safe House (Day 0)

Dan is irritated at this point. He is a bit of a control freak and as competitive as they come, but this guy seemed to have all the answers and to him, held all the cards. As a gambler this was not acceptable to him, so he needed more information, "Hey, what is your name, you've been pretty cagey with us."

"Better you do not know my name, that way they can't pry the information out of you later." The old man tells Dan.

"How do we know you are not military or government?"

"Be real man, do you honestly think this is all a ruse?"

"Yes. I don't know who to trust." Dan looks out the window in a huff and the car gets quiet.

Mattis moved from the front seat to the back and made a space for himself on the floorboard between Jeanne's and Dan's legs and is now nuzzling Jeanne as if to comfort her. His big brown puppy dog eyes are transfixed on hers, and they almost seem to be having a conversation without making a sound.

Dan shatters the silence as stupidly as only he can, "Jeanne that dog has a crush on you."

"He knows," the old man remarks. "He senses that you have the gift. Dogs are wondrous creatures. I've never heard of an animal with the gift, he must be amazing Officer Scott."

"Yes, he is," Tony says, "the more I think about it, the more I think he's saved my child from hazards multiple times. Either falling down the stairs, choking, wandering out an open door, and probably other things we have not noticed. Do you think he can control his gift too?"

"No. Controlling the gift requires a higher form of reasoning that an animal will not possess. My guess is he may be able to jump back only short distances and only to fix the things that went wrong right in front of him. We all have different strengths and can jump back by different amounts of time. The government knows this exists, Dan, and this is why I am being guarded with you. They just tried a coordinated kidnapping without a lot of fanfare. Someone in charge has a good grasp on what they are doing."

Inquisitive now, Dan asks, "Why do you say that?"

"They coordinated their attack and tried to hit them with a tranquilizer or some other drug. If they can sedate us longer than our ability to jump back, then they have us. I don't know exactly what they tried to do with the dog, but my guess is he figured it out and jumped back. They should have shot him with a sleeping dart. They won't be as sloppy the next time, or he was not the primary target."

"That's ridiculous, chief. You're saying the FBI tried to take them both at the same time?" Dan says.

Tony breaks his silence, "They handled us weirdly. There was no handler assigned to track the time, there was no presence anywhere close to me, but there were a bunch of

213

people in the woods where they placed the decoy scent. That's why I said it was cloogy back there, meaning it was all haphazard, chaotic, and just wrong. My assumption is they tried to take him there, but he got out of trouble."

He pauses for a second to breathe, lowering his voice, "As a law enforcement officer, I'd agree a human target is vastly superior to Mattis. They can't interview Mattis, all they can do is make him a blood sample machine and look for some kind of blood marker or DNA error that tells them he is different. If they take him, we will never see him again. What's worse is they could theoretically pull rank on the department. For now, I can pull off reporting that an attempt was made to take Mattis, and we left the scene for safety."

"That won't fly for long, Tony," Dan says.

"Agreed. If we're not back in the hotel by tonight, I'll hear about it."

"OK, let's head back to my place and we can plan out the next steps," the old man says.

As they arrive at the rental property the old man has booked, they all exit the vehicle, but Mattis is acting oddly. His limp in his left hind leg is back and seems to be more pronounced than it was after the bank robbery. Tony looks over and says, "Mattis what's up bud? The chaos makes you hurt yourself?"

"What's different about him?" The old man asks.

"His limp, he had it one other time when he jumped in that van to stop the bank robbery, but it went away after a day or two. It's worse now, but I don't think he's suffered trauma."

"He probably jumped back and this change affected his legs or back."

"How can you possibly...old man?" Dan almost shouts.

"Look, I've been around this a long time. I've seen people lose their sight, lose a limb, change every aspect of their physical appearance, and even change their voice. There is absolutely nothing off the table when it comes to this, it can change your DNA. If it changes the wrong strand in the wrong place, then you manifest changes that are too severe to survive."

Dan continues, "OK, you've seen this. How many times will it take to be fatal for someone?"

"No way to tell. I met a man named Zhang who went back for his first jump and passed on to the next plane. Well, it was the first jump since he became part of The Order."

"The what?" Tony asked.

"The Order. We just called it that. It was a group of extraordinary men and women who possessed the gift."

"The order of what?" Dan jumped in but trailed off realizing he had not heard a peep from Jeanne in some time.

"Nothing. Just The Order."

Dan is looking around, his eyes squinting and the veins in his forehead start to be a little more pronounced as he starts breathing a little faster, "Where are Jeanne and Mattis?"

"They went outside in the backyard," Tony said, "nothing to worry about."

"OK, good deal," Dan stammers and takes a long breath

followed by an even longer sigh as Lynn puts her hand on his shoulder, sensing the tension. "Sorry to interrupt you there, chief."

"I was done. We just called ourselves The Order. It seemed better than 'a bunch of people who can time travel when they are pissed off or stressed out' right?"

Everyone chuckles. "Let's plan out how to retrieve your stuff officer," the old man starts, "you say you have your laptop in there, and I'd assume the carrying crate for your dog?"

"Yes sir. What do you have in mind?"

"Simple. This team did not look too sophisticated, so I'll simply show up as housekeeping for the evening turn-down service. I don't know about getting the crate, but I can snag the laptop. You think the FBI will be on the room?"

"I would be."

"Good then, I'll go for the laptop and if I can manage, I will get the dog hardware out."

The Fallout

"OK people, SAC Sanumo is on speaker, patched in at his request. Newsome, Mahoney, Richardson, what the hell?" ASAC Peabody begins the debrief.

"Ma'am?" Vic says

"You were on the cop." She turns to Mahoney, "You two were on the girl. Someone explain how we lost both *and* got an agent neutralized."

Vic begins, "Alicia, we were on them. The plan for the dog was flawed from the start, I made known that unless you tranquilize the animal, he'll be able to do that thing and anticipate what is about to happen. Have you ever seen a dog disable a trap before? I have not. Now, the girl had help. The person who disabled our agent is the key to this. He knew what was going down. This is another one of *them*."

"What are you saying Vic, we have a third anomaly?"

"Vic," Sanumo interrupts. "Do you expect me to believe that after looking for years for someone to show this anomaly, we find three in a matter of 90 days? One of which purposefully puts himself in our crosshairs?"

"That's exactly what I am saying. Hearing my friend talk about his daughter, she sees what will happen, jumps back in time, and undoes what is about to be done. The dog, to me, sounds like he can do the same. He randomly jumps in a van full of guys about to pull a bank job? Come on, two plus two is four. He went back to disable the trap. This was a tactical error, but the op was blown from the start since we did not know the unidentified subject before the event."

"OK Vic, let's entertain this for a moment," Alicia begins and turns to Savannah, "Savannah any hits on the CCTV footage you requested? We may be able to track the movements of this unsub."

Savannah addresses the room, "Yes ma'am, we have him lingering around our trailer for a time, he may have overheard us say something that would make sense to him his second time through the scenario. Assuming he also has the anomaly, he likely tracked us using the same information we had. My guess is he was here for the animal but deviated when he realized the child was the primary target."

She brings up a map of the area, "His movements were simple, near our command center, then with the crowd, back to command, and then to the VIP area where he took the grab team's sleep agent and used it against them. This is a learning experience that these people will be very difficult to track and apprehend. I agree with Newsome, I think a sleep agent and extended sedation is the way to go."

"Hey, you know my name kid. I thought your company types were all about honing your memory and social skills."

"Don't knock the company, Newsome. You may not live to regret it." Sanumo lets that statement linger and then issues a diabolical-sounding laugh.

She looks at Vic and slyly says, "Well, today it seems you are valuable enough for me to remember, but SAC Sanumo gives me a good reason to not commit your name to memory."

Sanumo laughs again.

"Nice." Vic blankly says as he thinks, *Was that a flirt? A professional flirt?*

As Vic gets distracted and pleased with himself that his manhood is wearing down the lovely Savannah, he is deep in thought about what his next cheesy move will be when he is blasted by Alicia, "Newsome, why were you not on the cop, if we

218

are talking about tactical errors here?" Vic's temporary ability to revel in his charm is immediately crushed.

"I was on the cop until the call was made to allow the dog to find the handler. I chose to stay hidden to track the animal once he arrived, but the cop changed his position with no authorization."

Alicia retorts, "Seems to me we had no one there to authorize him. When we do this again, we'll need to make sure we have 100% eyes on at all times with these anomalous individuals. In the meantime, we need a BOLO on the cop and our unsub. We have a good picture so let's use Chicago's finest on this one. We can track him and the dog for sure when they return to duty, but I'd like to take care of this here. I don't want to call Baker in the San Antonio field office unless I have to. Are we on the hotel Savannah?"

"Yes ma'am. We have a grab team and a sneak and peek at the hotel to try and reacquire the animal when he reenters the hotel with the APD officer. We also have a second grab team across the hall from their room with surveillance to see anyone coming and going from the room. The sneak and peek went in and Officer Scott's equipment is still in the room, as is the kennel so we feel confident they will return. We placed a tracker on his laptop and his laptop bag as well as the dog crate. We will reacquire them. Given Vic's assessment, we'll send tranquilizer darts over to them."

The whole group is startled when the doorbell rings. "Who on earth could that be?" Dan asks.

"No idea, but I can check. You guys make yourself scarce. Tony, you have your weapon?" The old man says.

"Of course. Want me to check it?"

"No. You are not supposed to be here."

The old man rises as the rest of the group retreats to the kitchen and slowly approaches the door with skepticism and is slightly relieved to see a young woman standing at the door. *She must be lost or selling something,* he thinks to himself. As he opens the door, the young lady turns around to face the door, revealing her perfect complexion under a bunch of dirty blond hair with a gray streak in it. "Can I help you, young lady?"

"Hi, I don't have time to explain this to you, but you all are in danger."

"I'm sorry young lady, I am renting this unit alone, there is no one else here."

"Where is the dog?" She says.

"I'm sorry?"

"The dog sir, the dog they tried to take, the one that I saw you pick up, and the one in here now."

"I think you need to leave, little lady, you are mistaken."

Mattis barks twice from the backyard, trying to paw at the back door.

"That dog," the girl says bluntly, "look I don't have time for this, they are going to try and take him again, this time they will be smarter about it and they will turn him into a damn science experiment."

"And just how do you know that?"

"Because I've spent the last 12 years of my life avoiding becoming one myself. If they knew about me, they'd be after me too."

The old man stood there in shock. He thinks about going back to see where she came from and who she is but decides there is a more intriguing option. "Let me guess, your hair changes when you go back."

It's her turn to be astonished, "Yeah, um… wait how do you know that?"

"Because I am one of the time travelers. Aren't you miss?"

She looks at him skeptically, afraid to answer, about to decide if this is a trick, and just lets out a "what?"

"You have the gift of time jumping, don't you? What's your name?"

"No, I'll tell you mine if you tell me yours."

"You don't want to know my name young lady."

"Because you have been running all your life hoping not to be found? Well, I found you, and if I found you, they can find you. Who are you?"

"Fine, they call me Carlo. My birth name was Carlos, but when I unified and led The Order, Carlo means strong in The Philippines, so the group dropped the s. Call me Carlo."

"Carlo, is it very good to meet you," She extends her hand to shake his, "is there any way I can be off the street now? I don't think either one of us wants to be seen right now. Good work with the agent, it took me a couple of jumps so I didn't lose you as you sped off."

"Yes, of course, come in," he is looking puzzled, "fascinating you've learned at such a young age to control it."

"Oh, it is an illusion. There are times it controls me."

"That will be the case well beyond adulthood, there are times I still involuntarily jump, and I hate it every time it happens. What do yours feel like?"

"Mine feels like my life is a bad story written on paper and the paper gets wadded up and thrown away. My senses all jumble up, my directions are off, I lose my bearings and then bam, it's over."

"Interesting how it manifests differently for different people. Mine looks like a halo of light, sort of like a bad migraine. When I decide to go back, it's not as bad because I visualize where I am going back to, but the light is still there."

"What part of you changes Carlo?"

"I am missing a toe. I have pain in my joints now that will never go away. I have had multiple colored eyes, fingernails grow oddly, too many to count. You?"

"My hair does something, well, sometimes...and I have two crooked toes."

Carlo nods in understanding as the rest walk into the room, the formerly silent Lynn is overcome with emotion and

222

hugs the girl. "I am so happy to meet someone my daughter's age who has this too. I hear you talk about it, and you are special. My daughter has it, and we've noticed her eyes change colors, but she has not had many episodes. She's unique so we always thought she was just different."

"Ooooh," the young girl coos, "can I meet her, and the dog too?"

"Wait, how are you familiar with Mattis?" Tony asks.

"I saw him on the news, and I read about this 'dog challenge' put on by the FBI and it's obvious to me they want him just to experiment on him. I've been hiding my gift for years hoping it would go away or I could grow out of it. So far, I've been able to lay low. I am taking a risk coming here, but I had to warn you. As it turns out, I did not have to do anything, well, almost. I jumped a couple of times, but the second time through Carlo here jumped that guy and all hell broke loose. I was actually after the dog but jumped to the wrong place and time. I realized after that happened more was up, but I decided to follow you instead."

"Your name is Carlo old man?" Dan almost yells, annoyed as only he can be when he feels like he is not in control of something.

"Yes. I am sorry Dan; I did not know who to trust and I did not want you to be forced to say my name. Besides, Carlo is not my given name, so it is ok."

Lynn looks over as Jeanne is coming in, and says, "Jeanne, look, we have another young lady your age who has the same thing you have. I think you two should be together and maybe you can help each other. Would you like a drink or anything young lady, I am so glad you are here."

Jeanne stops for a second as she walks in, rolls her eyes in a very sly way, and says, "Oh, mother is mothering again."

Dan turns to the young lady as Jeanne and Mattis come back into the room. Mattis jumps on the girl's shoulders as Tony commands him to sit, a command which he ignores. "Tony, I think the dog knows when he meets one of them," Dan says plainly.

Tony responds, "I think so, he was enamored with Jeanne too. Wait, you were the one who tried to warn me that the FBI wanted my dog. You're a jumper too?"

Carlo grunts, "I hope you don't plan on being a detective."

Dan roars with laughter.

"Hi Mattis, I've been looking for you," the girl says staring deep into Mattis' eyes as he licks her face, "I came here to warn your daddy about the coming danger."

"You have the deals too?" Jeanne asks.

"What's a deal?" The girl asks back with a curious look.

"You see bad things and can go back and fix them?"

"Well then, yes, I guess I do. You must be Jeanne."

"Yes, I am." Jeanne walks over and gets close to the girl.

Suddenly, Jeanne hugs her. Lynn's jaw drops and Dan smiles. Neither says a word, but their demeanor says it all. They are pleased to see Jeanne show an emotional reaction that is both appropriate and timely. Jeanne smiles, the girl smiles back, steps back, and clears the gray hair from in front of her eyes, "I'm Natalee. I came out here to help save the dog, but now I feel like we all need to make ourselves safer than we are now."

Chapter 16

Savannah and Vic (Day +1)

Savannah stares intently at her notepad. She's never been good at jotting notes down, she's more of a doer. Her mind is wandering back to her days in Kandahar. The night terrors have finally dissipated but the nightmares still come. She does not remember anything about the incident that got her captured, she just remembers the bomb going off and then waking up three days later.

She thinks about the beatings she survived, the warlord who abused her, and how she was able to find the opening she needed to escape from their hold. She avoided the hits they sent later and was able to take the assassins by surprise when they showed up.

Those events made a name for her as being unhittable in the CIA, but under the iron exterior was a soft woman who wanted a partner in her life but never prioritized love. She'd much rather be running an asset in country now, but it was not worth it to her to sacrifice her mental health. The FBI is a cakewalk by comparison, but this op has her stumped.

She knows exactly what happened, a third target entered the playing field with the ability to jump in and out of the timeline, so there was no way for them to anticipate what was about to happen. Her heart raced as she started scribbling ideas to prove to Agent Peabody and Sanumo that she was ready to attain the Supervisory Special Agent rank.

She wrote down all the reasons for them not to hold the last tactical meltdown against her. She kept getting distracted and flashed back to the op. She had tactical command of the team and yet they failed. Her mind would not let go, she started to feel numb and she saw spots in her field of vision. She shut her eyes winced, and finally snapped out of the spiral.

They need to widen the search and include Interpol and other worldwide agencies. It was possible the notoriety of the animal and his exploits attracted someone with the anomaly to try and make contact. *Maybe that's it. We should stage a second attempt that would draw him out.* She starts drawing out a plan of action that includes Newsome trying to approach his friend one more time.

She shakes her head. *They will be on to us.* They'd have to set up surveillance on the kid, her family, and any friends. They'd have to strike by complete surprise or she'd just go back and wiggle out of trouble.

She picks up her phone and calls Vic, "Newsome, look I think we can make another run, but we'll need intel on their residence and intel on their daily activities."

"Ok Custos, what do you have in mind? Want me to approach the family?"

"No, my expectation is the family will approach you and it will not be a pretty sight. They have to suspect you were the source of the information."

"Yeah, the thought crossed my mind, but I am going to play it off like I was talking about this girl that had a gift and had no idea what the bureau did and talk about some agent trying to make a name for himself."

"That can be plan B. What we need is a basic snatch-and-grab to approach by stealth knowing the family will be on guard. We also need to plan for the contingency the unsub will convince the family their residence is unsafe and may try to bait us to show our hand."

"We need to play the long game and wait them out, I am talking weeks."

"Yes, they need to feel things are going back to normal."

"No, I am wrong. They won't do that Savannah. I know Dan, he's a control freak and won't let us get close to her again."

"All right, you have a history with the family, let's brainstorm likely places they may flee to and try to anticipate."

"Roger that. See you tomorrow, well, later this morning."

"I'm not done yet, Vic. I've been jotting some notes, and if they are working together they will be much harder to stop since we have to take both by surprise and neutralize them immediately. We still don't have great intelligence about this anomaly, so we're speculating that keeping them sedated for 24 hours will be enough."

Vic suddenly is a little confused on the other end, "Savannah, are you saying we may have different time skip durations? I mean we only have anecdotal evidence from family on the gentleman from 2001. What information do you have on this?"

"I don't have anything other than a hunch. That's why I want to test them and figure out if we can detect the genetic defect responsible for this ability and then figure out if we have strength differences between the two. I don't care too much about the dog anymore, we don't have that genome mapped to the degree we can understand it."

"Interesting theory, but I don't want to think about whether one of these people can jump back more than a day."

"I'm not talking about that, I think it's clear no one can do more than a day, but our biorhythms are on different cycles. It stands to reason that someone can only be able to jump a matter of hours, while others up to a whole day. As it is, it seems the Wannamaker gentleman had a history but never jumped outside either day or night, which places him closer to 12 hours. Seems like a sleep cycle may reset the anomaly. Again, that's just a theory."

"OK, I see what you're getting at. That's why sedation is the key, first they won't be able to jump back during the grab, and they won't be able to get back when they wake up either. Maybe we can use the threat of harm to the dad to bait Jeanne." He pauses for a second, then, "Never mind, he's never going to allow that. He's manipulating her anomaly right now."

"Right. We've got to coordinate a grab somehow. We'll need more intel on their movements. Did we ever get an ID on the vehicle?"

"No ma'am. We tried traffic cams, but the guy was smart."

"So we've got bupkis then Vic."

"I'm afraid so."

"OK. We've got some work to do. Let's expand the facial recognition and I'll reach out to an old handler and use their resources, as well as the NSA."

"Be careful Savannah. Peabody doesn't share with the other boys and girls."

"I am aware. It's not her, it's Sanumo. I've heard of him from back in the agency, he was an old head as I was getting started but talk about not sharing. I can't prove it, no one can, but that guy killed someone on his own team for screwing up an op, then handled it himself and scored all the points with the brass."

Vic pauses, "Shiiiit. Ruthless sucker, that one."

"You have no idea. Just don't take anything to drink from him directly."

"What?"

Savannah pauses, thinking about her words carefully, "He uses poison like no one I've ever seen or heard about. Silent, deadly, and somehow never harms himself in the process because he'll drink with you."

"How the hell does he pull that off?"

"No one knows, but the guy is a world-class psychopath, and he's in charge of a whole division of the FBI. Go figure."

Jeanne, Nat, and Mattis have been in the bedroom for hours as the sun sinks below the horizon. They are talking, comparing notes on when they've jumped, and Nat started to explain how she started to control her jumping ability.

"For me, it started when I was about 10, or at least that is the earliest I can remember something weird happening with time. For a long time, I did not know I was traveling back to fix something. It was only a minor fender bender that my mother had, but I guess it startled me so much that I jumped back and warned my mom that it was about to happen."

She takes a long breath, thinking, then says "Oddly enough, the hair color changes only started manifesting later in my life as I started to know what I was doing, sort of, and jumped back for longer periods."

She asks Jeanne, "What's the longest time you've been able to travel back?"

"I don't know, maybe a few hours. The longest one was when my dad had a heart attack. We were at the hospital for hours and when I heard he died and that he had a heart attack at the track, I was able to go back and tell him who would win. So, maybe 6 hours. Maybe."

Nat says back, "Wow, you saved your dad, that's dope. I've been able to do 12 hours regularly, but when I do that long a jump, my hair usually changes. A few months ago I had to save a friend from suicide. I kept getting the night wrong and had to go back from morning to lunchtime three times before I finally fixed it. It was totes messed up though, I was a bad friend to her and if I could have gone back years to undo everything I did, I would have."

"You're in high school now, do you have lots of friends? My friends were not really my friends, one of them tried to have me raped after I made her look bad, but I went back and got her arrested, so I know where I went wrong in High School. I picked friends based on popularity, but that was all a lie."

"Seriously Natalee? Your friend tried to have you--"

"Yeah, the worst part is I remember bits and pieces, and remember the pain I woke up with the next day, but not the actual event. That one was a big jump too, like 22 hours. I so got her back though; she never saw it coming and the queen of the school went to jail. The best part was when they did the perp walk right in front of everyone at school. I laughed my ass off. I'd give anything to see her fabulous plop in the jail cafeteria hoping not to be shanked by the real queen bee of the prison."

She abruptly changes the subject, "So your dad said you are on the spectrum, you seem pretty normal to me, what's your gift?"

"Gift?"

"My dad says people on the spectrum are all gifted with something. He has a best friend whose son is autistic, level 2 low performing but has a mathematical ability and can solve problems his teachers cannot even fathom. Another friend of mine has a brother who can reproduce almost anything he hears

232

on a piano and hardly speaks. What can you do, other than time travel like a badass?"

"I think that's it. I don't have any other gift that anyone has noticed. It took me a long time to start talking, and my parents say I don't show affection to anyone. I think I am weird."

"Well I had a band-aid collection when I was thirteen, so I was weird, then got popular, then got weird again. Besides, you hugged me, so that's a start."

Yeah, but I felt like I knew you before you ever said a word. Mattis ignored his handler to jump on you, seems like he knew you too. Hold on Natalee, you collected band-aids?"

"Never mind the band-aids, it was a bad time in my life, like ew! I think Mattis can sense whatever we have, what did the old guy call it, an anomaly whatever that means?"

"An anomaly is something which is not normal or expected. The government thinks something is wrong with us so they want to test us. The old man says they want to use us to do bad things, Natalee. It scares me." Jeanne looks down at her knees where she is rubbing them quickly and it starts to get loud for her.

She's going into an anxiety episode; she is powerless to stop it. She starts flapping her hands by her ears to try and give her some sensory activity that might snap her back to the present. Mattis bounces up like he was shot out of a cannon and jumps on the bed, almost knocking Jeanne over, barks once, then puts his head on her shoulder and starts licking her ear.

Jeanne's panic attack starts to immediately ease up and

she puts her arms around Mattis, who licks her on the nose. Jeanne jumps a little bit, startled at the contact on her face.

"Jeanne, are you ok? Jeanne?" Nat says through the noise fog in Jeanne's head.

"Natalee?"

"Call me Nat you sweet girl." She places a hand on her knee, "You looked a little spaced out there for a second, but the doggo here must have sensed you were having an episode of some kind. How old are you anyway?"

"I am 16, and yeah, thinking about the government getting us was about to give me a panic attack. My brain is prone to allowing my senses to be overloaded, and panic disorder with anxiety all rolled into a wrecking ball that can take me over sometimes. I have a rescue drug for these, but my dad has them. Good thing Mattis jumped up here."

Nat says, "This dog is special. He needs to be your service dog, I think. I wonder if that cop out there would let him stay with you."

"I doubt it, they have to go to work."

"Now that the government is after them, I don't think life will be normal for them."

She pauses for a second, her eyes shifting back and forth. She looks up and says, "They have no idea who I am. Between the four of us, there is no way they'd be able to attack and us not be able to jump back to warn each other."

The sun is barely peeking on the horizon like a kid trying to sneak in the house after midnight using nothing but a covered cell phone light to navigate through the living room, but Savannah is already up and in the office. She is scribbling on the whiteboard and formulating the plan to present to ASAC Peabody this morning.

Her brain is working overtime on the issue, and her solution is brilliant yet simple. Use Vic's friends' hubris to bait him into giving up his position. Male bravado is a mighty and terrible thing, and her bet is Dan would not be able to control his urge to confront Vic after the debacle the day before.

She has agents from the San Antonio field office headed out to be stationed in Austin to ascertain if the K9 officer reports for duty Monday, but she bets they are holed up planning, just like she is.

Even though it is Sunday, she's requested a task force debrief this morning to get a situation report. She wants the identification of the vehicle that was used to escape. She needs anything about their unsub, the man who foiled the entire operation and made her look like a fool.

As the team begins to assemble at 8 am, Peabody and Newsome walk in together after sharing an elevator ride up, and Alicia starts talking as she walks into the room, "Listen up people, Agent Newsome has the plan to try and bait out our subjects using his friend's toxic masculinity against him, Vic can

235

you let us in on your plan?"

"Thank you, ASAC Peabody. In a nutshell, my friend Dan is a hot head. He can't see straight if he feels he's being challenged as a man. He can't handle it if he's not the guy with the answers. He also can't handle being second place and gets completely thrown off his game. His pride and his ego can't take the bruising that is required when you admit you don't know, or you finish in any position other than first, so this is where we hit him.

I'll call him and draw him to the phone. He should not talk to me, but like a moth to a flame, he'll be compelled to. When he does, we'll trace his location and move in with all agents armed with stun guns and tranq darts. Once we have them sleeping we've achieved our objective.

I talked to Savannah last night and we developed a plan around how to surveil them and potentially make a grab, but after consideration last night, I came to this, which, um, is already on the whiteboard." Vic seems startled to see his idea almost verbatim on the board but with more details and asset allocations.

Savannah chimes in, "Yes, Vic and I had an excellent conversation last night and into this morning after the op went sideways and I also arrived at the same conclusion, the wait-and-see approach was going to take too long and they could see us coming. As Vic states, his friend is the weak link given his propensity to go off half-cocked based on his short temper, so that's where we strike them, at their weakest point.

With the additional player, our third anomaly, the chances of surprising all of them will be remote, so decisive action is best before they can organize. As you can see here, my plan, er, our plan, is to draw Dan to contact Vic, or be open to getting a call from Vic. From there we can trace the call and location from the target's cell phone.

We can mobilize the task force and be in place for a quick surveillance action and breach at night when the element of surprise will be at its highest. I think the one we need to be most cognizant of is the dog, his senses will be attuned higher than the rest and if he somehow can warn them, we'll know we failed in the past."

Peabody interrupts, "What do you mean in the past?"

"Ma'am, what I mean is if the dog hears us coming, he may be able to jump back in his timeline, to us it will just look like he spotted us early and warned the group. If the unsub can control his anomaly, he may be able to jump further back and warn the group of the impending attack, and we're back at zero."

She turns to Alicia directly and says, "To answer your question, it will be the past to him, we just won't perceive it. Like the unsub who took down Richardson at the VIP seating area, for him it was undoubtedly his second or third time through the events of the day. For us, it appeared as though it was the first time through the timeline. Does that make a little more sense?"

"Yes, thank you, Savannah. Speaking of the past, how can we be sure these anomalies are not triggered subconsciously? I mean what if they can go back even though they are sleeping? Do we know that Savannah?"

"They cannot ma'am."

"How do you know that?"

Savannah looks down and around the room nervously as she searches for the right information, finally looks up and says, "Ma'am, we got that information from the Wannamaker family while researching the anomaly with Ira Wannamaker of flight 23 on September 11. One of the details they mentioned was that he always manifested this after going into a trance-like state while fully awake. Is this an assumption? Technically it is, but it's based on evidence. I'd call it a theory, well, it's more than a hunch but not yet a fact. We need to prove it out."

"You do realize, if I have this right, that you can't prove it?"

"Ma'am?"

"If you prove it, you won't know it, because if it manifests while she is sleeping, you'll only know it back on the main timeline. This will look like we missed and she jumped. We have no way to tell if she jumped while she was asleep."

Savannah looks perplexed for a moment, then looks right at Alicia and says, "Yes ma'am, I understand what you are saying, that's an excellent observation." She wants to say more, but her nervousness causes her to hold her tongue.

"OK then, we need to approach this next opportunity with stealth," Alicia begins. Meanwhile, Savannah turns in her chair, and lets out a sigh, almost one of relief, and contorts her face in a weird way that makes Vic chuckle.

Alicia spins around to him and annoyed, says, "Something funny there, Newsome?"

"No ma'am."

"As I was saying I'll be handling tactical control this time."

Savannah snaps back into reality for a moment and glares at Alicia with those piercing brown eyes that are about to bore a hole right through her skull. "Alicia, I can handle tactical ops."

"Not this time Custos, the buck stops with me. If they are going to evade us again for almost supernatural reasons, I am going to insulate you and the entire team from skepticism, and more importantly, from Sanumo. It will be hard enough to explain things to him if this goes south again without bringing in this nonsense of a band of unorganized time travelers and a dog giving the FBI the slip. Again."

"The brass thinks our task force is a bit out there," Savannah begins, "but you have to understand no one understands these people like I do. I've been studying this anomaly for years since coming over from the agency, talking to Ira's family again and again, and now that we finally have as close to a confirmed case as we've ever had, I am not willing to just let this go."

"Savannah, I agree with you, and you have been on this for your whole FBI career, but I lead this team and I won't have any of you affected negatively. I'll take the heat. It's my responsibility to you."

"Thanks, boss," Savannah says, quickly echoed by Vic

and the rest of the task force.

"Any more ideas or are we ready to work this thing? No? OK, let's go to work. Savannah, Vic, let's make the call this afternoon, Mahoney, let's coordinate with tactical and issue sleep dart guns and have some time to train with them before we deploy. Let's shoot for tonight people. Get to it!"

The room empties as they each start planning their portion of the raid.

Chapter 17

Best Laid Plans (Day +1)

Jeanne, Nat, and Mattis all fell asleep in the bedroom early in the morning, so they are still asleep when Dan starts making his morning coffee, he's already scowling at the package of instant coffee he is about to make and when he takes a sip his face shrinks as if he has just had sour milk and spits it out. He's contemplating dumping the rest of the cup out when Carlo walks in.

"Good morning, Dan."

"Morning," Dan grumbles back.

"I think your daughter, the new girl, and the dog all got along famously last night, they were talking well into the morning. My bet is they are all sleeping late, and don't drink that crap, I have real stuff in my bag, but it's decaf."

"What did you make of that Nat girl?"

"She's legit. Only someone who has started to learn control of the gift speaks of it like she does. I want to try and help her unlock more control. I think your daughter will be very special too if she learns to control her abilities."

"How do you control it, Carlo?"

"I told the girls this last night. I channel my concentration and think of the exact moment I want to travel back to and try to

241

calm my breathing, slow my heart rate, and let myself slip into an altered state of consciousness. When I see the halo or aura, I know it's starting to happen. My head always hurts too."

Dan's phone chirps. He feels for his pocket and pulls it out with his right hand after shifting his coffee to his left. Carlo turns to get his coffee from his bag when the cup Dan is holding smashes into a million pieces on the floor. Carlo startled, turns back to see Dan's face beet red as he furiously types on his phone.

"Dan, what's the matter?"

"My asshole friend who ratted us out is texting me trying to tell me he's sorry about what happened, he had no idea what was going to happen and says he mentioned Jeanne's ability to someone at the FBI and they are the ones who put this whole thing together. He's trying to apologize but I don't believe him at all. You said he was there."

"Dan, hold on a second. I never saw him; they just said the information came from him. You should not talk to him, that's a risk. Wait, have you had your phone on all night?"

"You're right. I'll hold my actions until I have him alone in an alley, and I'll put a hammer in his skull. No, I just turned my phone on a minute ago"

"Turn it off, now, and try and calm yourself. We need to come up with a plan to clear out of here and still be safe. I would expect the feds to be on your house, your family, and your friends. They have your phone, so make sure it stays off. Tony too, they'll have his precinct staked out."

242

Dan was already boiling, and this is a problem for all of them, but no one is aware of it. There is no stopping him from confronting Vic while he is in this frame of mind. Vic is counting on this, which is why he engineered this exchange to draw him into a phone call and their trap.

Dan is just small-minded and selfish enough that he is about to put them all in danger. He tries to calm down, even taking time to make another coffee and clean up the mess he left when his coffee cup shattered on the ground. Alas, the man is a hothead who is incapable of making adult decisions when he is angry.

He mumbles, "I'm going to get some air, I have to blow off some steam."

"Your coffee, Dan."

"That's not coffee," he says to Carlo and skulks out the front door. As he scratches at the stonework that makes up the path from the street to the porch, he takes a few steps and turns to his right, starts walking but his mind gets the best of him and he turns his phone back on and starts dialing.

Vic picks up, "Dan, I am glad you called me."

"Shut the hell up, you shithead. You endangered my kid and did the one thing, *THE ONE THING* I told you not to do. I am going to rip your goddamn heart out of your chest when I see you, hear me?"

"Dan, calm down, I had nothing to do with this crap. Some kid at the bureau wants to make a name for himself. I think

I've got them to back off of you, but listen you have to be smart here. I can't guarantee they won't try and find you again. I can arrange for some protection, but you'll have to work with me. All they want is a blood sample from Jeanne to see if she is sick and if they can help."

"We don't want help, we're going to use this to our advantage, not to hurt anyone."

Vic looks over at Savannah, who gives him a signal to keep him talking, and stretches out her hands, indicating they need a little more time. He continues, "Look, Dan, I am sorry, I'd never hurt Jeanne. They don't want to either, but they are scared about something like this being used in a nefarious way."

"Shut up, I am done talking. Never call or contact me again."

"OK man look, call me if you need anything, I can help you."

As he finishes the sentence, Savannah gives him the thumbs up, they've got a trace and a rough location on the cell signal. All they need is the carrier information and they'll have an exact location.

He nods at Savannah, then says, "Dan, I can help you."

"You've done enough. Piss off." Dan hangs up the phone, but the damage is done, and he forgets to turn his phone off. Savannah picks up the phone to inform Peabody they have the phone and will have an exact location within minutes. The team is already in full planning mode, gathering resources for the raid and they decide to call the task force back to a briefing at 11 am to plan out the exact responsibilities of everyone on the team.

In the meantime, they are gathering a schematic of the houses in the neighborhood. They've got drones on standby to do some high-level recon work, and are gathering the tactical units to arm up, document the breach plan, and obtain sign-off.

Dan almost slams his phone into the concrete, but he's oblivious to the fact he just gave the FBI a roadmap to their current location. He's so self-absorbed in his own emotion that he fails to see the fault with what he just did, and just murmurs to himself, "That douchebag."

He keeps walking to the end of the block, finding a hole-in-the-wall coffee bar that's already open, so he walks inside and takes a seat. He texts Jeanne to let her know he's going to get a real coffee and he'll be back in a while. She's still asleep, so no one is aware of what Dan just did, and no one is aware of where Dan is.

Vic leaps out of his chair. "He was outside, I could hear traffic. I guarantee you he's not going back inside, he'll go to some place and cool down, he has to. The guy is so predictable it's silly. We have to move now, this is our window."

Savannah shakes her head and says, "Half our guys have never fired a tranq gun before, this will be a disaster."

"No it won't. We can draw them outside. All we have to do is let a dog out and pull the 'hey we're looking for our lost dog' routine. We'll have breach teams in the front and back and we hit them decisively and quickly. Then we just keep them down for 48 hours to make sure we are in the clear and we're there."

"Interesting, let's go to Peabody."

Savannah and Vic lay out their plan to Alicia, who, shockingly gives the ok and mobilizes the FBI swat team for a briefing en route. In the meantime, the trace gives the location of the phone and they realize he's indeed at a bar, so they still have a bit of time. They'll have to deploy at least a couple of blocks over and take their positions, but Savannah has all those logistics covered. She is assuming the street the house will be on is within a quarter mile from the bar Dan is at.

"He's on the move," Mahoney calls out from his station in the tactical unit. "He looks like he is walking, traveling very slowly south on Abner St. off of Roosevelt."

"Let's deploy 2 blocks east and west for the front and rear breach teams. Mahoney, do you have the drones on station so we can plan our approach?" Peabody asks.

"We're almost there with the drones ma'am."

"Get on it."

Over the next 10 minutes, the drones reveal the path between houses they can use to approach the house where Dan's signal stops. Their target has about 6 meters of walkway in front, and the rear of the house is about 5 meters back from a detached garage and back chain link fence, so there will be no easy approach directly from the front or back.

The team decides to come in from the north and south, along the houses that flank either side of the target house. This

246

way, they can use the other houses as cover and only need to hop the fence in the backyard. The risk is the dog. He will be hypersensitive to noise, so they will send the distraction of Mahoney walking up to the front door trying to find his dog. They hope the target animal will move to the front of the house and allow them to take a position in the backyard unnoticed.

Peabody decides to use their tactical unit disguised as a plumbing truck to station three houses down from the targets to ensure they have a view and can be in position in case of egress by one or more of the targets. "All teams, this is ASAC Peabody, net control for this operation. Comms check, grab Team Alpha."

"This is Custos. Alpha two doors north of the location, moving into position."

"Team Bravo, comms check."

"Richardson here. Bravo is next door, with no dogs, in position. The Fence line is breached, we have access to the backyard."

"Team Charlie."

"This is Mahoney, Charlie is on station one house south of the target, I am ready to commence on your signal."

"All teams in position, Newsome and I are in the van, and Newsome is on the lookout for any external movement. Large windows on the front-facing side will make the approach difficult for you Alpha, be advised there appears to be a slit between the drapes where your approach will be visible unless you maintain a low profile."

"Roger that control. Alpha is proceeding around the

house and will take a position on the north side of the house from the backyard area, give us 2 minutes."

An excruciatingly slow two minutes begins to pass outside the house, as the final teams are getting into position. "Control, Charlie. We have movement on the front porch."

"I am telling you we don't have anything to worry about, I had it out with him and we're done," Dan is yelling. "Look I was two blocks away when I made the call, there is no way they traced the call to here. I am not stupid."

Mattis starts barking.

Carlo approaches the front door and looks outside with Dan. There does not appear to be any movement, but something catches Dan's eye in front of the house next door to the left as Mattis' barking now becomes more focused on the right side of the house. He senses the movement outside where Savannah's team is not yet in position and is alerting Tony that something is not right.

Mahoney decides now is the time to move, "Control I have to go, they've seen me, I am acting like I am looking in the bushes here Milo! Where did you go! Milo! Hey guys, sorry to bother you," as Mahoney approaches the walkway, about five feet to the left and in front of the house where Carlo and Dan are arguing on the porch, "I can't find my dog, he's a brown poodle, have you seen him?"

Dan looks at the guy for a fast second, sizes him up, and decides he's not someone to worry about since he's wearing a

Blackhawks tee shirt and torn jeans with sandals. "No man, but we don't live here, this is an R&R rental for us just for the day."

"Ah, well, I am sorry. My name is Daniel, Daniel Latrudo."

"Wait, you're the Karate Kid?"

"No, that was LaRusso, my name is Latrudo."

"Good one, position them in front of the porch facing south," Peabody asks from the van.

"Ah, well, my name is Dan too. This is Carlo."

"Pleasure guys, you just here for the day?" He extends his hand to shake but intentionally positions himself so the men have to turn their backs on Savannah's grab team. Dan and Carlo take two steps forward and as Dan is reaching his hand out, both men are hit with sleep darts in their backsides and go down, almost immediately and more importantly, silently.

"All teams, GO! GO!" Alicia commands, "Two subjects are down, your targets are the teen woman and the animal. The handler may be armed, use caution. Alpha has neutralized the unsub; two targets of importance remain."

"Roger that. Alpha breaching front."

"Bravo breaching rear entrance."

The house lights up as a flashbang goes off in the living room and a woman is screaming but is silenced.

"This is Bravo, we have two teenage females down."

A single shot rings out. "Control Alpha, we have a man down, we do not have--" Savannah's voice goes silent and the growl of an animal comes over the communication channel.

"Shit! Vic says in the van, the dog just went through the

window, we've lost contain! I am going after him!"

Alicia is almost dejected, "Don't bother Newsome. He's going to jump and the op is blown."

FBI Breach. Again.

"Comms check. Team Alpha." Alicia barks into their earpieces.

"This is Custos. Alpha two doors north of the location, moving into position."

"Team Bravo, comms check."

"Richardson here. Bravo is next door, with no dogs, in position. The Fence line is breached, we have access to the backyard."

"Team Charlie."

"This is Mahoney, Charlie is on station one house south of the target, I am ready to commence on your signal."

"All teams in position, Newsome and I are in the van, and Newsome is on the lookout for any external movement. Large windows on the front facing north side will make the approach difficult for you Alpha, be advised there appears to be a slit between the drapes where your approach will be visible unless you maintain a low profile."

"Roger that control, Alpha will take a low approach around the south side of the house. Mahoney, return to the south side of the house you are at, we have movement on the porch."

"Alpha, I don't see any movement at all," Vic says confused.

"Just wait for it, control," Savannah says confidently.

Inside the house, there is tension. Dan has let Carlo in on the fact he talked to his friend at the FBI to confront him and threatened if they ever made contact with him again, he'd be sorry. Carlo was not enthused at this at all and raised his voice, "You infantile moron. You just could not control that childish temper and now you've put us all at risk."

"What happened?" Tony enters the conversation.

"This asshat called the FBI, they are bound to have a fix on his location now," Carlo says, enraged.

Tony lowers his head. "Man, I have not known you very long, but that was a stupid move. He's right, they traced your location, when was this?"

"About 2 hours ago."

"We have to move, now. Natalee! Get Jeanne up, we have to go. Mattis! Hier!" But Mattis starts barking and darts to the front door, where he is expecting a breach to happen based on his last swim through this timeline.

"All teams hold!" Savannah barks.

"That's not your command to make, Alpha." Peabody calmly says on the channel.

"Trust me, ma'am. I hear the animal, he's going to move

251

to attack what he thinks is coming."

"How on earth would you know that, Custos?"

"Just trust me, I hear him. My guess is he's been through the timeline already and we messed up by moving too soon. We need to change tactics."

"All teams hold." Peabody commands.

Dan appears on the porch as Mattis charges outside but finds nothing. He puts his nose in the air and looks to the right. Carlo joins Dan on the porch. "Dan, what does Mattis have?" Mattis continues to bark like a crazy dog.

Tony comes out as well, his sidearm unholstered. "I know that bark, he's alerting me to something. Given what we've been through I think he anticipates a raid and expects them at the front door."

Savannah intentionally coughs and Mattis bolts to the right. "Alpha, engage all targets. Charlie, come in from the south, we've got one shot at this." Savannah shouts as she prepares to take aim at Mattis rounding the corner.

"All units GO! GO! GO!" Peabody commands.

Team Alpha emerges from the north face of the house and takes down all four targets, Tony gets off a shot as he is struck by a dart that puts him down, and that round hits Savannah as she hits Mattis with a dart.

She spins around and goes down.

Mahoney hits Dan from behind with a dart, and Carlo is hit twice by other members of Alpha. "Control, Alpha, four targets down, including our unsub and the target animal. We have an agent down, Custos took a round in the chest, we need a medic!"

Meanwhile, Bravo breaches the back of the house and takes Nat by surprise, putting her down with a dart immediately. "Control Bravo, we have neutralized a teen girl and the mother, but this is not our target, continuing through the house."

Jeanne hears some commotion after being startled awake by the gunshot, but she's still dazed when the door to the bedroom flies open. She can make out the silhouette of a man in a dark outfit and screams, but her eyes go dark as the fast-acting tranquilizer hits her in the neck and she is out cold.

"This is Bravo, we're clear. Two teen girls down and one older female including the third target."

"Nice work team, let's clean this up. Tactical, let's roll the transport up here and move these subjects to the phone store for testing. Let's roll medical for Savannah to the front of the house."

Peabody is beaming. She just engineered the takedown of some of the most difficult targets they would ever have to track but feels fortunate because they did not have time to organize. She is confident the older man is their leader, so to speak, as the one who could fairly obviously control his power, but she does not know the full ability of the girl or the dog.

She also did not know the father or the other female subject, so she made the call to keep them all sedated for 48 hours to ensure they had no issues. She turns her attention to Savannah, "Medical, give me a sitrep on Custos, what do we have?"

"Control this is Alpha. Custos is fine, she was hit in the

vest, it knocked her out for a second but no penetration, she had a double chest piece on."

"Great work everyone, let's send her to the hospital just in case."

"Roger that."

Chapter 18

The Phone Store (Day +2)

Savannah walks into the briefing as the task force is in mid-brief. Alicia is extolling the greatness of the team, the professionalism they exhibited, and the speed and efficiency at which they worked and sanitized the scene.

Aside from one injury which was not life-threatening, the team was able to subdue their targets and all are safely in custody and still sedated. "What's going on, it's all done?" Savannah asks.

"The woman of the hour," Alicia turns, beaming towards Savannah, and starts a clap that is echoed throughout the room, "without your call, I think the op would have been doomed to another opportunity for one or more of them to jump back and warn the others. Excellent work, Custos!"

"Thank you, ma'am."

"How did you decide to wear a double chest plate?"

"Police officers always go center mass. I figured if we gave him time to ready and fire, I'd take the brunt of it until the rest of the team was able to react. Honestly, after that first round hit me, I lost the rest of the event. I don't have any real memory of this until I got my wind back, but I was already being loaded in the Ambo."

Peabody replies, "We can have you review the body cams when you can, but we took all the subjects in the house, including one additional person we did not expect. We've identified her as Natalee Simon of McLean, Virginia. She's been reported missing just an hour or so, apparently her parents are unaware of her activities up here. According to the report she was to be with a friend, but their lie unraveled. We don't know how she arrived or why she is here, we'll wake her up shortly."

"No! No one wakes up until at least 24 hours have passed, if not the 48 we talked about. If she is one of them, she'll jump back. The parents and the handler are probably clean, but I want to be sure this time." She looks at Alicia, "Ma'am. That's my suggestion."

"After today, Custos, I'll be leaning on you a little more." She addresses the larger group, "OK people, let's keep them all down for another 24 hours and then wake up the cop and the dad. Mahoney, you reach out to Austin PD and give them the cover story?"

"Yes ma'am. I talked to Captain Stamis, their location commander."

"Very good. Let's move people, we have to make these people's families believe our story in the next few hours and we've got some catch-up work on the girl. Savannah, you're with me if you are able, let's head downstairs to the testing facility."

This facility, like many FBI black sites, was used to house criminals at one time that were used as informants and functioned as a safe house for a time. Fashioned from an abandoned telecommunications facility in Naperville, Illinois, it was a solid 45 minutes west and a little south of Chicago and the last place anyone would be looking for high-value FBI targets.

The facility itself was decommissioned four years previously and went unused until the task force had it reopened as a contingency for this op. Only the top brass are aware that it is operational again and they nicknamed it the phone store, given its past uses. The facility is 2 miles from the nearest highway, and tucked back, down a quarter-mile entry road with a gated entrance.

It is everything they need from a security standpoint and even has a helipad on site for emergency use. Over the last 48 hours, the medical units were set up in the basement and sub-basement and the hardened rooms that were emergency backup communication areas for the former building occupant were fashioned into patient suites. One drawback was that the rooms were interconnected, but the doors between rooms were secured and hidden.

They had not planned for the extra person, so some late prep is being done in a smaller room which used to be a server farm. This room is completely isolated, and they decided to place Natalee there since they knew nothing of her.

With Natalee at the end, the hallway has three rooms on each side plus her room at the end of the hall in the middle. Dan is in the room at the end near Natalee, Lynn is in the room next door, and Sgt. Scott is in the room at the other end of the hall, at its entrance from the descending stairs. Across the cold, gray concrete floor that seems to be lit by exceptionally green fluorescent lights are Carlo, Mattis, and Jeanne.

Savannah descends the stairs to the sub-basement with Alicia, who says "Savannah, these people would not be here if it was not for your fine work out there. I did not want to say this in front of the group, but I've recommended we move forward with your promotion to supervisory special agent. I want you to lead the testing and research portion of this task force while the others and I will remain vigilant in searching out other candidates that share the anomaly."

"SSA, wow. Alicia, thank you for your confidence. I thought I blew it when the op went sideways at the park."

"The important thing is we recovered. You got on Sanumo's radar too."

"Not sure that's a good thing, ma'am."

"You came back with poise and taking that round from Sergeant Scott while you concentrated on the target was first rate. Let me show you what we have here so far." She opens the door to room one, where Carlo is lying on the bed in the middle of the room, attached to monitors and an IV as if he was in the hospital.

Peabody points toward Carlo, "Here is our unsub, we've sent fingerprints off, but this man has not shown up on NCIC or the bureau. We've got Vic coordinating with SSA Mitch Linkletter, his former unit lead on running down identities from Interpol as well as the agency. I have no information on the progress.

We're starting a routine on all of them to build a DNA profile as well as to search for any known defects in their genes, and also comparing them to the known defects we found with Wannamaker. We'll get results tomorrow, we hope. The dog is in the next room and the girl in the last room."

"Which girl?"

"Ah, good point. The far room is Jeanne, the 16-year-old from Little Oak, just outside Chestertown. Across the hall here is the Austin PD sergeant, Lynn and Daniel McAlister are in these two rooms and the new girl is at the end of the hallway isolated. I want to wake her up and take a run at her."

"Don't. If she was drawn to them, she may also have the anomaly. You already started testing her as well?"

"We are testing them all. The DNA markers for mother, father, and daughter will be very powerful for us to establish a better baseline for defects. We also had flunitrazepam in the cocktail we gave them, and this should produce our desired amnesic effects, so they won't remember anything that happened to them. We'll need to validate that on the first two, we'll wake up and see if the cover story will stick."

"What's that story, Alicia?"

"Carbon monoxide leak in the house knocked them all out and they are lucky to be alive. All were in comas and have been brought back. We don't plan to tell any of them they are in FBI custody. When we get what we need, we'll knock them out again and transport them to Chicago Med where we have our secured private wing that will be legit. The families will be reunified there."

"You're just going to release them?"

"Sort of, we have a tracking chip implanted in each of them. Non-surgical, cutting edge. They should not notice or feel anything in their hips."

Alicia goes on to brief Savannah on her role in this. Her team will be taking the tissue, blood, and soon-to-be-captured brain samples and analyzing them for any abnormalities against the baseline DNA set forth by Dan and Lynn. Nat's samples are going to be analyzed with the assumption they will find abnormalities that indicate the same anomaly as Mattis, Jeanne, and their yet-to-be-identified unsub.

Mattis and Tony will be released first, and arrangements have been made to return them to Austin via FBI transportation. As for the other subjects, direct and threatening tactics will be used to try and trigger a jump.

"Hold on Peabody." Savannah interrupts. "The time paradox will not allow you to ever document a result on those. You realize when you trigger a jump, they'll likely jump back as far as they can, which will be before our interview and they'll be ready for the scare tactics the next time."

"We're counting on that. We have EEG leads on each of them, and we'll be monitoring for any abnormal brain patterns that we can reasonably detect and each time we measure one, we'll take a snapshot. We're hoping to do several over the next two days and hope we don't have them all jump back to the same point in time so we can measure multiple events."

"I'm not sure that is the soundest course of action,

260

ma'am."

"No?" Alicia fights back the urge to be annoyed.

"We're not basing the observations on any scientific method, just happenstance and coincidence."

"It's the best we have in the time we have Custos."

"Yes ma'am."

Operation Time Shield

Peabody has everyone gathered at the entrance to the lab area and starts to brief, "Team, listen up. We've got the mom, dad, and the cop in their rooms, and although the dad and the cop have been combative at times, they only want to see their loved ones. We're getting ready to wake the others up now. Make sure you keep the chatter to a minimum, although we've tried our best to make these rooms soundproof, they are not."

She looks down at her watch, then continues, "We'll have one hour for this exercise. Remember, we will get as much info as possible, approach to tell them we know about their anomaly, and proceed as quickly as possible to attempt to trigger a jump back to the beginning of that hour."

Peabody motions to Savannah, "Custos will be the supervisory agent on this round, please make all reports to her within 90 minutes of this first session. All right, everyone, Operation Time Shield is now a go. Remember, refer to all subjects as patients if this will work."

261

In the past 24 hours, both Tony and Dan have not revealed anything they knew about Carlo or Natalee to the "doctors" who were interviewing them. Tony began asking where the FBI was, sure that they were behind their capture. He was being especially belligerent, even when they hit him with the psychoactive drugs meant to induce the truth from him.

Dan was not as fortunate. He was combative from the start, demanding to see his wife and daughter. He did not believe a single shred of evidence they gave him about the carbon monoxide poisoning and demanded to see Jeanne.

Even after being dosed with scopolamine pentothal and midazolam, he only revealed he told an FBI agent about his daughter's gifted nature once, and also said that guy was a dead man next time he has the chance. They'd both been sedated again for the remainder of the night, but now they'd be observed interacting with the ones they wanted to see.

Each team administers the drugs intended to counteract the anesthetic and extubates each patient. Gradually, Dan and Tony are also brought back to their conscious states. They are all given an hour to acclimate to their surroundings and told they are in a recovery room at a hospital, where they have been taken after a carbon monoxide leak almost killed everyone in the house they were in.

In Carlo's room, cameras and recording devices are rolling the entire time as he stays in a transient state for over 90 minutes, refusing to speak or acknowledge anyone was in the room. The EEGs register repeated abnormalities. Finally, he ceases those brain patterns and speaks, "What am I doing here?"

"You're in the hospital sir, you've been in a carbon monoxide accident at the house you were staying at. You've been in a coma for a couple of days, and you're lucky to be alive."

"Where is the dog? I came to see the dog." He says groggily, but in reality, he is laser focused.

"The dog was rescued as well as two other men, a woman, and two girls. Were they all with you at the residence?"

"Most of them were, but one girl was tracking the dog, she was kind of stalking the dog if you ask me, and showed up at the door all of a sudden."

"What can you tell me about that girl?"

"Which girl?"

"The one that came to the house later that evening."

"Not much, the dog liked her. She spent most of the time talking to the other girl. The one with the hothead dad."

"Look, we were made aware that you can time travel sir. We also were informed you attempted to kill an FBI agent a few days ago in the park. They've been notified you are here and will be sending a team to talk to you later tonight. I suggest you let us in on what happened out there."

"Wait, you're FBI already, aren't you? This is not a hospital. You say I've been in a coma for how long?"

"Two days."

"No wonder."

"What, you can't jump back? We know you can only go back by a day at most. This accident did a number on you though, so nothing will help you get back, but I'll tell you what. If you just cooperate with us, we'll let you out of here when the feds come in to interview you."

Carlo looks at the eyes of the agent playing doctor in his room and suddenly leans out, catches him by surprise, and rips his mask from his face, "I know you, I saw you come out of the tent in Grant Park. You are FBI! I've got nothing to say to you. Take my blood and experiment on me, I don't care. You're not getting my gift."

"We'll get one of you to talk, even if we have to hurt the girls right in front of you. Let's see if we can hear one of them now." He reaches into his pocket and clicks a signal device that is almost immediately followed by a scream from outside the room. "That's little Jeanne. She'll suffer unless you play ball here sir."

"Screw yourself." He once again enters a trance-like state but fails to emerge. The doctors send a jolt of electricity through him to ensure he is still awake, and he yelps.

"There's more where that came from pal, we'll be back. Knock his ass out again."

Meanwhile, Tony is shown into Mattis' room. Mattis jumps up and greets his handler like he has not seen him in months. "Hey buddy, good to see you! These mean men have been testing you, haven't they?" Mattis barks as if he understands.

264

"Sergeant," the doctor says, "we've made arrangements with Austin PD and the FBI who held the event to fly you back to Austin tonight. We just need to ask how you came to be in the company of a known fugitive?"

"What? I know you guys are bureau. Wait. Who's a known fugitive? You guys just tried to kidnap my partner, how are you managing to wrangle out of this?"

"Don't worry about that officer, there is a chain of command and you'll be advised as to what the bureau needs from you going forward. You'll also be getting quite the opportunity to increase your presence and your reputation. The man who you were with, what is his name again, not Dan, the other one?"

"You expect me to give that up? If he's a fugitive, why don't you know his name? Let me guess, he's still unidentified? Yeah, that guy is called unsub. Leave this room right now before I give Mattis the command you don't want to hear. I'm assuming we're being watched, so I'll warn all of you watching to stay the hell out of this room."

He walks over to the agent masquerading as a doctor and with one hand throws him against the door. Mattis starts to charge but is restrained by a leash and harness. Tony reaches with the other hand to open the door, then removes the agent by his earlobe and shoves him into the hall. "You should probably restrain us. I am a law enforcement officer after all."

Meanwhile, in Jeanne's room, Savannah is playing doctor and building some rapport with the young girl. She's got some inside information from Newsome, so she talks about horses and animals, and why they were there to see the dogs. "In fact," she says, "that dog you wanted to meet is here now, if you can answer a couple of questions for me, you can see him, do you think that would be ok Jeanne?"

"Where's my dad?"

"He's still sick from the gasses that came into the house, you all were almost killed."

"How long have I been in here?" She can feel the anxiety building already, the fuse has been lit, and it's only a matter of time now. She starts flapping her hands and feeling it inching closer like a spider closing in on their prey trapped in the web. "I need my rescue drug, I am going to have an attack."

"Which one is yours?"

"Lorazepam, or Ativan if you don't have my pills."

"Ativan is usually used for seizures, but I have some, I can put it in your IV." Savannah has all the drugs she is on, they found them all at the house so they were prepared. She injects the medication and Jeanne seems to relax almost immediately. "There you go, I hope I can talk to you, and you are not scared. My name is Dr. Savannah."

"Hi, doctor. How did you know my name?"

"We retrieved all your personal items in the house, along with the medications. We did not know which one of you was which until we found Natalee's driver's license."

266

"What were you going to ask me?"

"Your ability to travel in time, your dad told us about it and we want to understand how it is possible, and if it poses a danger to you. We've found others that have this too, and they died because something in the body changed at the wrong time. Are you dealing with it ok?"

"People die from this?" She feels her anxiety rising again and starts to freak out.

Savannah speaks in a softer voice, "Only one so far, a long time ago. He saved a whole plane of people from crashing and it took a big toll on his body. We're just learning how to help you."

Jeanne knows that Natalee is right. These people are going to experiment on her, but her neurodiversity makes it very convenient for them in one key aspect. Her brain is wired differently, she is almost incapable of being subversive and telling bald-faced lies. "Well, my friend says that all you want to do is experiment on us."

"Who's your friend?" Savannah was getting internally excited as she felt like she was about to have intel on the other girl or their unsub. "The older man? James? We already talked to him."

"James?" She looks quizzically at Savannah and says, "You mean Carlo, and yes he says all you want is to exploit me and Mattis."

"Carlo, right, he goes by that. No, we are not here to take advantage of you. We ran some tests, but it is to help us understand how we can help you."

"I don't know if that is true or not, my brain does not work the way most people do, but I want to see my dad." She begins to twitch and moves her arms while shaking her head back and forth.

"One more thing, there was a girl in the house named Natalee. She says she has the same ability you and Carlo do. Do you know anything about her?"

"No, I just met her today. Wait, how long was I asleep?"

"About 2 days."

"Oh no." She looks down at the ground and her body starts to shake. She hears the noise and starts flapping almost uncontrollably. "That's too long. That's Too Long! THAT'S TOO LONG!!!" She starts screaming over and over and Savannah is forced to put her back to sleep. Still, she got much of what she needed, including a name for their unsub.

Savannah speaks into her lapel microphone, "Alicia, this is Savannah."

"Go Savannah."

"I have a name for the unsub. Carlo. No last."

"Great work! We'll get that to Vic immediately. Thanks, Savannah."

"Yes ma'am. Jeanne is out, she started to have a meltdown. We'll need to put the dad in play next time around. I'm going to take a look at the EEG, but I don't think she even tried to jump. I'll take a run at the other girl now." Savannah starts to ease down the hallway when she hears a crash across the hall.

"Come up here for a few minutes, I've scheduled a briefing to go over the comprehensive lab results," Peabody orders, so she heads upstairs without checking on the noise.

In Jeanne's room, as she is entering a forced sleep her mind is racing even though the drugs are designed to shut her brain down. *I have to go back. I have to go back. Think of the park. Find Nat. Oh no, it's too far.* Her favorite song starts playing in her head.

They've been outnumbered and cornered. Her mind starts playing back to the last days before her capture, the time she met Mattis. She thinks to herself *this fight isn't fair.* She sits up, startling the attendant, and says "Find what they never found!" Then she collapses back into bed and as the sleep takes her, the thought *They are stronger. We're faster…and I'm not scared anymore,* runs through the dying embers of her brain's conscious fire.

Chapter 19

The Anomaly is Exposed (Day +3)

Savannah makes the trek up to the lab to meet with Alicia and the other on-site members of the task force. She has only been at this facility for a few days but every time she walks in, she marvels at the equipment here, the DNA sequencers, genome mapping stations, mass spectrometers and flow cytometers, and the mountains of analytics that the computing power in the room can generate.

It also looks incredibly bright in the room, with everyone in their white coats, shiny equipment and bright lighting, even though the old factory they made this out of was a dump on the exterior. It makes for the perfect disguise to the real use of the facility. Black sites always work best when hidden in plain sight.

"What do we have?" She says to announce her presence.

Alicia responds, "Savannah, good work getting us a name to go on. We're chasing down DNA and facial on Carlo and other variations on the name." She turns to the group that has gathered in the lab and motions for everyone to take a seat at the conference table that lies just beyond the wall. They are set apart from the lab but have direct connections to all their data on a series of wall-mounted monitors.

"This is Dr. Ambie. She will be briefing us on the

preliminary results we have on the subjects. We have good sequencing on all four, and our suspicion Natalee has the anomaly has been all but confirmed even though Jeanne did not give that information up. Doctor, please brief us on the anomalous results you have."

"Thank you, Agent Peabody. I won't bore all of you with the details but we have several disparate genetic anomalies in all four of the subjects. The older gentleman Carlo exhibits the most changes by far, with changes to musculoskeletal DNA and a host of other systems, but only a couple of these are considered vital.

Interestingly, he shows some of the same blood markers we saw with Ira Wannamaker, in that his ASPM was very high with some PVNH, but not nearly as high a level. One other interesting bit is we found a blood protein we've never seen before that resembles netrin, a memory and neural connection booster. We've taken several tests and we've seen the levels dropping, but this is highly telling we see this new protein in all of our subjects. Subject 1 also has some pulmonary DNA changes that lead us to believe he will be passing away pretty soon."

Alicia interrupts, "By soon, are we talking days or weeks?"

"No ma'am, likely a couple of years." Then she continues, "Subject two, the animal named Mattis is an enigma. Although he has this protein and even though the canine DNA has been sequenced, there are so many breeds that we cannot baseline completely for alterations, so we are using other German shepherds within the FBI used as drug dogs as a comparison.

271

Like subject 1, Mattis shows several abnormalities, including a fairly significant change to his ability to manufacture bone cells. It is almost as if he has developed osteoporosis in his hip and leg. Talks with his handler indicate that he is favoring the leg at times, but the condition seems to rectify itself shortly after an event where he appears to time skip.

The animal exhibits some higher stem cell counts and elevated ASPM in comparison to the other control group animals. PVNH is exceedingly rare in canines and the cases we have found resulted in seizures in almost all the young dogs we found. There is no evidence of nodules with Mattis after several MRI scans. We don't want to rule this out as a cause because the other human subjects have nodules."

"Speaking of Periventricular nodules, subject 3, Jeanne has the most pronounced case. She is known to be neurodiverse, and we believe her to have ASD based on evaluation, we'd peg her as level 1 high-performing. Keep in mind the sample size is exceedingly small.

Her stem cells are extremely high, but she is the youngest of the group. Her ASPM was three times that of subject 1." She pauses as a researcher enters the room with a new test result. "Interesting, at the beginning of the interview, subject 1's EEG patterns were continuously in flux and after the interview, he exhibited EEG patterns that were much more abnormal, and his protein level spiked. We may have the trigger for the ability to change timelines. I would caution you this is only preliminary, and we need to run more tests as this was the only one that seems to have tried to jump."

She puts the test result down and refers back to the original folder, "Back to subject 3. Her protein level was not detectable for this new protein, which we are calling N-110142 or simply N42 for short. She had an episode at the end of her interview, after she was sedated where she seemed to exit the sedation for a moment and yell a phrase, then collapse back into sleep, but her brain function was too high for her to have been completely asleep. We don't yet know what this means, but her ratios are considerably higher than any of the other patients, although the protein was absent."

She pauses for a moment to pick up the file for Natalee, "Subject 4 is a bizarre case. We are not sure if she has the anomaly, but she shows far too many genetic markers to dismiss. ASPM is also high, but not as high as subject 1. She has a small nodule in her gray matter, but the clump is barely relevant. None of these patients exhibit the usual symptoms of this disease, being focal seizures that can progress to bilateral and generalized tonic-clonic ones. In the case of subject 4, her CSF has too many stem cells for a standard 18-year-old, but it is not considered to be at the same level that we see with subjects 1 or 3. We'll need more time to evaluate."

Savannah asks, "What conclusions can we draw from these results doctor?"

"Well, the data supports no conclusions as yet. We have a hypothesis we must test for, that the severity of the anomaly is magnified by the number of stem cells present, the magnitude of the nodules in the brain, and the abundance of ASPM in the blood. This loosely correlates to the ability of the brain to regenerate itself faster and stronger. We need to trigger a series of jumps in all our subjects to know with any degree of certainty."

"Thank you, doctor."

Dr. Ambie picks up her phone, "This is Ambie. Yes, right away." She looks up at Savannah and the group. "We have a situation with subject 4. She's broken the restraints on her bed and incapacitated the technician that was in there to draw her blood."

Savannah cocks her head, "I heard a crash about 10 minutes ago, why are we just now hearing about this?"

"She also shrouded the camera as she broke the restraints, she knew it was there."

"That has to be a jump. Does she think she can escape?"

The doctor thinks for a second and says, "I don't think there is any way she knows where she is unless she has been through this time loop multiple times and is anticipating what will happen next. We visually observed this through the peephole in the secondary door she still does not know exists."

"Gas the room."

"Savannah!" Peabody yells, "Why would you do that? We'll lose her for half a day!"

"We can run the tests and prove the hypothesis based on those protein levels which you think will now be elevated, and I assume the stem cell count will be down as she is in regeneration mode now, correct?"

"You're a fast study Agent Custos." Doctor Ambie responds.

As Nat's room fills with a cloudy substance, Nat holds her breath waiting for the gas to obscure the oxygen mask and when it does, she reaches for it and opens the flow, then positions herself so it is very difficult to see the mask is attached to her face, as if she simply fell against the back of the bed and became incapacitated there.

She hears the negative pressure pumps kick in to remove the excess substance from the room, *This is your one chance, Nat,* she thinks to herself. After what seems like half an hour, there is some noise in the hallway and muffled voices outside. She drops the oxygen mask, sure that the air was breathable since they were getting ready to come in.

She readies herself with her hands under her gown and out of sight as two people enter the room, Savannah and another tech who will be performing the blood tests. They approach Nat to roll her back on the bed that she is draped over, Savannah reaches over to pull the pillowcase off the camera location but as she turns back, she notices something. "Her hands are obscured, grab her arms and-"

"Not today girlfriend," Natalee calmly says as two needle safety guards hit the floor. "Sweet dreams bitches." Nat injects both of them with the same substance her technician has been inducing her to sleep with.

This is Nat's third time through this time loop, so she

275

knows the exact position each will be in, and now she has a chance to get out, or so she thinks. As she exits the room, she sees the only way out is up the stairs, so she runs to the stairwell as red flashing lights start to strobe and an audible alarm begins to wail.

She reaches the basement level and opens the door but her escape attempt is thwarted by three armed men who take her back into custody, waiting for her at the top of the stairs. As they are taking her back, she makes mental notes for her next try.

Escape Plans

Nat's room is filling with a gas-like substance, but she knows this can be defeated with oxygen so she holds her breath and waits for the gas to obscure the oxygen mask. Once it does, she carefully positions herself and thinks *They must have another camera in here.*

She's looking around when she spots a small dot in the lower third of the wall that looks like it has a seam. *Secret door, nice.* She waits for the gas to dissipate and decides that will be her course of escape this time.

The gas does not disperse this time like it did last time, *what the hell?* There is no way they changed their operating procedure midstream. She is thinking that maybe they did not notice as fast or they are being extra cautious this time around, no telling what the normals do on a moment-by-moment basis. Suddenly she hears footsteps, this time heavier. The door opens and two individuals wearing masks take aim and fire. She's asleep. Again.

As they clear the room of the gas, Savannah goes down the hall and the men are placing Nat on the bed when two syringes fall from her hands under her gown. "Good thing you sent us in masked and ready."

"She obviously jumped, well, we were pretty sure she did, so we were prepared for her knowing what procedure we were about to employ and changed the plan of attack. Good work agents." Savannah was complimentary, but she was taking no chances with the one who could control her ability.

"We need a full spectrum of tests on this one, let's get on this one stat. Wait. Something is different. Focus on the DNA for hair color." She felt proud of herself for using the word stat, something she secretly wished she could use based on her obsession with TV medical dramas and past desires to be a doctor. Of course, the technicians and phlebotomists knew it well, so they rushed the tests.

An hour later, Savannah and Alicia are sitting on a stool in the lab while the DNA sequencer is running and Dr. Ambie is peering through a microscope. Dr. Courtney Ambie is technically a geneticist but also has her MD. She stopped seeing patients several years ago to study the human genome and advance her desire to come up with a treatment for Alzheimer's disease, which claimed almost all her relatives on her father's side of the family and is starting to affect him as well.

His older brothers and sisters have all suffered from it and his mother died from complications from it. She has been dedicated to finding a genetic component that can be corrected before the hallmark markers are found in her or her siblings that indicate early onset.

She brushes her bright red locks to the side of her face back as she turns to meet the gaze of Savannah and Alicia, "Agents, there has been a physical mutation in the last hour with subject four. The MC1R, or hair-color gene for this subject shows several changes."

She pauses for a moment, then continues, "I am finding evidence that there have been partial alterations that have rendered this gene now able to produce multiple-color hair. I won't bore you with the details, but as we age, we all lose the ability to grow hair with the proper amount of melanin and we get grays that pop up here and there. Her genome looks like it can produce various levels and pigments, hence the subject should have blonde, brown, and black hair in addition to the gray in the sample you provided me. This one is most definitely broken and has been altered many times based on my opinion."

"What does that mean doctor?" Alicia asks.

"Well, again, I can't give you a definitive answer on that. I can say with relative certainty the temporal anomaly she experiences has changed her DNA in this gene. She has some other small changes, but not as many as the other subjects. Her temporal distortion seems pretty focused on this gene."

"What about the levels with other subjects, the nodules and stem cells?" Savannah asks.

"There we have a bit of a mystery. I expected to see high amounts of stem cells, as the hair underwent a metamorphosis, but we don't see any more than we saw earlier today. Now, the one piece of good news is that we did see a spike in the N42 protein after her time skip."

Savannah smiles, "So, you are ready to confirm that hypothesis."

"Hold your horses there, certainty for us is pretty big, so I'm not ready to prove a confirmation to the hypothesis based on a single result. We'll need a larger sample size, but yes, this is a good step in the right direction, and we will note this in our logs. The real question we should be asking is what happened to Natalee in the other timeline? What went on with all of us there? Or is this the only one now?"

Savannah is scratching her head, looking a little perplexed, "Hold on, you are talking about time travel and the idea of a paradox?"

"Exactly. There are three main schools of thought around this. One, the past is fixed and cannot be altered, say somebody goes back to prevent a terror attack, they may succeed in stopping someone, but the event will happen anyway. This was disproven with Ira Wannamaker, who thwarted what should have been another plane on September 11."

"Or was it?" Savannah asks.

"What do you mean?"

"We'll never know if that attack was meant to be stopped by some other event. Like what happened on United 93 where the passengers crashed the plane."

"True, we don't. It seems when you factor in what we just witnessed, and then add the events at the house where you made conscious decisions to alter your tactics, it follows that the past events were indeed changed and the subjects were also changing their actions. Subject 3 saved her father from dying. I think we can safely say that the first hypothesis has been disproven and the past can be altered."

"Fair, what is the second?" Savannah asks.

"The second is just that, the possibility events can change, but this introduces the paradox. If you go back and have an accident that causes a person to miscarry a baby, and it was to be your grandmother, then how can you be here?"

Savannah pops her head up and almost shouts with a smirk, "I saw this one, Marty McFly started to disappear when he could not get his parents to kiss on the dance floor!"

Dr. Ambie is unamused and says, "Something like that. This theory holds that the timeline will shift and past actions have repercussions on current events. I think we are close to this in our understanding. Ira Wannamaker had memories of both timelines. Not that this is relevant, but I remember a movie called Frequency that dealt with information relayed to a family member in the past."

She pauses and shakes her head. "I can't believe I am quoting a movie. Anyway, the boy's father did not die in the fire as he was supposed to and his son spontaneously found himself with new memories to go with the old ones. I am not advocating for this, the movie industry does what it does. It is obvious none of us have any memories of the past that are different, so we are narrowing in on the dynamic ability of time, or the third possibility."

"Which is?" Alicia Interrupts.

Dr. Ambie looks a little irritated at being interrupted, her red eyebrows a bit furrowed and her hazel eyes fixed on Agent Peabody, "Well, Agent Peabody, the third is a concept of multiple timelines or a multiverse as Hollywood calls it."

"No, don't invoke The Avengers on us." Savannah is shaking her head.

"This is not the movies; this is a theory that every change in time creates a new timeline. We are not aware of it because we are not on it. The people who experience one timeline and shift to another because of a change experience both. This theory holds that there are infinite numbers of timelines going, all with different results, hence my question about what Natalee is experiencing in the other timeline."

Savannah is fully engaged now, "So, what if person A changed something, then someone who suffered ill effects, person B, made a second change and went back through the same period, that creates three timelines or one dynamic line that changed twice?"

"Assuming both have the anomaly, then they could potentially work together, but I seriously doubt they would

281

remember each other's actions. Let's put it in terms of the events of today. Subject 4 has been through her attempted escape and capture and decides to try again, which it looks like she was doing based on the genetic markers we found. But hypothetically, let's say you also have the anomaly and did something to counter her change. Then, she would believe herself to be in her second or third time through, but in reality, this time through would be her fourth, because you made some alteration that materially affected her actions and resulted in her sedation. Now, if and when we wake her up, she may make another attempt and we'd be unaware of that as we'd just be experiencing the timeline for the first time through our eyes."

"OK, my head is hurting." Alicia quips.

Savannah smiles and nods her head.

"What do you know here Custos?" Alicia asks pointedly.

"Every time we try something, it is counteracted by them, but when we make a change to normal procedure, that's when it works out. So, when the dog charged out looking for someone, we altered our plan at the last moment and he was caught unaware. I think we need to be exceptionally cognizant of the body language and actions of the subjects to anticipate what they expect to happen. It's like chess. If they know the move we'll make, change our course. I don't think we can prove multiverse, multiple timelines or single dynamic timeline because if we...wait."

Savannah looks frozen.

"Savannah?" Peabody asks.

Savannah raises her hand, "One second please."

The room is silent for a few seconds and Savannah raises her head and speaks, "What if we get one of them to make a change for us, then we can see if anyone remembers the change, and if the change is material we can make a note of it. Like let's say we get subject 4 to adjust a coffee cup on a desk, and we give her a Go Pro to record it, then we can see her move the cup, but we'll never actually see a new position, we will remember it a certain way but the event will be recorded so we can see where she moved it. Hold on! I noticed her hair change color. I know that we had it on film when she got here, her hair was blonde with gray. Now it has three colors. I think we can demonstrate a single timeline. If it was a multiverse, we'd never see her change her hair, she'd just skip out of the timeline."

"That's kind of brilliant, Agent Custos," Dr. Ambie seems legitimately impressed, "it seems like you are a bit of a temporal enthusiast."

"I just find it fascinating. I think we can twist ourselves in knots over this, but we may be able to prove a theory that has heretofore been unprovable. I mean who has ever heard of time manipulation outside this team?"

"It's all been conjecture, but I am a geneticist. I do not have a great deal of knowledge in that field of study. No one seriously is, it's been considered the stuff of science fiction up to now."

Peabody stands and says, "OK people, I think we have a plan. Let's wake the girl up tomorrow and see what we can get if we offer her a chance to help us understand time travel and give her a sweet deal to work with us. She's a teenager, she may jump at the opportunity to explore her abilities."

"Time squad! Assemble!" Savannah says with volume higher than appropriate, drawing looks from everyone in the lab, especially Alicia, "So, I was just thinking we can build a team of time fixers that we can send in to correct events that are not in the interest of the United States."

"You mean Time cops?" Alicia can't hold it in and starts laughing.

"No, please don't bring that up." Savannah also couldn't keep a straight face, and soon the whole little group was chuckling.

Savannah stops and says, "Wait, was that a joke? From you?"

Peabody ignores her, "We have some work to do, Savannah, let's start brainstorming on how to make this offer to Natalee."

"Yes ma'am. If I am correct, the other kid could be stronger, so let's deal with her dad and see if they are willing to help us. The guy is a piece of work according to Vic, but I know the type. We can buy him off. The mom may be an issue, we know nothing of her. She's never been brought out of her coma."

Alicia nods her head in agreement and says, "You're right, she's an unknown, let's put the dad in play. OK. It's been a

284

day, and the subjects are all down. You look like you need a break too, that left eye of yours is all droopy. I did not notice that before, so let's reconvene in the morning, you've earned a rest."

Chapter 20

Recruiting (Day 3-5)

It is the middle of a fairly warm day in Chicagoland, or at least much warmer than the last few days, and Savannah is coming in from lunch, where she decides to treat herself to some pizza. She can usually eat just one slice since they are so thick, but today she brought one back to the office.

She is planning to stay late to try and get Natalee to cooperate and then turn her sights on Dan and Lynn with Jeanne. She was joking about forming a time team, but only partially so. She's always looking to the future, and she thinks this will allow her to put a stamp on what will eventually be a temporal enforcement division of the FBI.

She was up past midnight last night going over some terrorist attacks, mass shootings, and other heinous crimes that she thought they could stop with team members who were willing to bend time if they could. What she does not know is how long each member will be useful until genetic abnormalities cause them to either be unusable or pass away due to an unrecoverable flaw.

She has a design on taking a run at Tony Scott to see if they can employ Mattis as some manner of detection animal. The way she figures it, they've found some body chemistry differences in the subjects, and if Mattis can be trained to pick up on those distortions, he may be able to identify people who share those same anomalies, regardless of their ability to use it or if they are even aware of the gift they have. She also wants to breed Mattis to see if the anomaly can be reproduced.

Her first order of business is to talk to the police sergeant and his dog. As she walks in the room, they've been put together in the same room and Mattis is curled up on a blanket next to a couch they brought in for Tony, but he springs up and barks once as she enters.

"Hello, Mattis." She extends her hand to let him take a sniff, and he moves his head under her hand, seeking a pat on the head. He is still attached to the wall on a short leash and harness, but he has enough room to get up and take a couple of steps, which he did, and is now straining against the lash trying to move closer to this new person who he thinks is a friend and not a foe.

Tony sits up, "Hello doctor, wait, I know you. We met at the event. What is the meaning of this? Am I going to finally get some answers, or did you get all his blood and decide he's going to be a part of the FBI now?"

"Yes sir, I apologize for the subversion, but my name is Senior Special Agent Savannah Custos, and yes, we did meet at the event a few days ago. I am leading the research team trying to ascertain how Mattis here and some other people can effectively distort time to right the wrongs they see happen to loved ones. I have been authorized to brief you preliminarily in the hopes you will continue to work with us as an agent in the FBI, and we would like to make Mattis a special K9 agent as well. We'll handle any medical costs associated with him as your department did."

"Well, I don't think Austin PD will just let me go."

"Tony," she sits on the little stool in the room, "we have talked to your chief of police and the K9 Unit commander, and we intend to fly you home and let you tie up your affairs in Austin for the next few weeks, after which, we will begin relocation plans to Quantico, Virginia or here in Chicago if you agree."

"Respectfully, ma'am, my wife Mindy is probably going bananas right now."

Savannah interrupts him, "She is on her way here, we've told her about the happenings at the house and how you've been in recovery and unable to talk to her. She is meeting you tonight and is relieved you are going home."

"Ok, good then, but I don't appreciate how this has been handled. I don't remember the house events, but I seem to recall you tried to apprehend the girl there as well. What is the status?"

"Tony, we plan to form a team that can thwart people like these bank robbers Mattis stopped, and terror cells by reaching them before they can commit their crimes. We don't fully understand what the condition is or how it manifests, but it's safe to assume this circadian anomaly can be used for good things. Mattis here looks to be very well trained. Can he sense the anomaly in others?"

"Funny you should ask. I think so. He acts like he knows people when they have it. At least the couple that we've met." He's still not ready to give up Natalee when he gets a bit of a shock.

"Three, you mean. Natalee has it as well."

"Well, I don't know much about the girl, she had just shown up at the house before I lost my memory, but based on how Mattis is reacting right now, I'd venture to say four."

Savannah immediately retreats from Mattis and stammers for her words, "Look um, Tony…think about it, we'll get you, uh, set up in temporary housing before you, Mindy, and Preston find a home of your own."

She pauses, choosing her words, "We are still unsure where we are setting up the division. One of the girls is from Virginia, one of the girls is from here, and the older gentleman is still unknown to us beyond his first name Carlo."

"Yeah, you won't find him. I don't even know who he is. He's lived overseas in Asia since leaving the US. I also don't think he'd work for you."

"We're not planning on recruiting him, his genetic anomalies are far too advanced. We don't want to use Mattis like that either, he's already developing some nerve and bony defects in his hips based on the physical changes we are seeing with him. We want him to detect the anomaly in humans. That's it. Airports, museums, and anywhere a drug dog is tolerated, Mattis will be there. But we'll train a different alert for this anomaly. He'll alert to drugs and everything he does today, but when he finds a candidate for the anomaly, we want to talk to them. You'll be our point person on interviews."

"You mean kidnap them."

"No, we may have studied you and again, I apologize for the subversion, but we needed to gather information to further our study. We are at the point now where we are actively putting together a team. The job pays well Tony. Think about it, I'll be back after I speak with the others."

"You know Dan will never go for this, he's hellbent on revenge."

"Oh, I have a plan for him."

Savannah trots down the hall, knowing she has a yes from Sgt. Scott and Mattis. She calmly opens the door to find, once again, that Natalee has broken her restraints, but Savannah knew this, as new cameras were installed overnight and she was alerted. "Natalee, calm down, we want to help you, not hurt you. I am sorry this has been scary for you."

"Shut up, I want to go home. My parents are probably going crazy."

"We've talked to them; they are coming here to Chicago to pick you up. You'll be free to go once I talk to you, calmly."

"Wait. Really? You spoke with my parents?"

"Steve and Shay. Even your Uncle Pete, the cop. They were relieved when we told them we found you in a house where everyone almost died from carbon monoxide poisoning. It's all been smoothed over."

"You just want a lab rat."

"We already got the info we needed, Natalee. Would you like me to tell you that you have a genetic defect? We've named it the circadian anomaly, and it has to do with your daily biorhythms. We think we have a handle on what is causing it. We can't fix it, but we want to offer you the chance to fight crime before it happens. And we want you to do it for us, we're the FBI."

"I knew it, Jeanne's dad told us his friend was a rat and I heard you guys talking at the dog show. I went to warn them, and we don't have a defect, we have a gift. You government types won't understand. Where are my friends?"

"Carlo is older and not doing as well, but we're sending him home soon. I am about to talk to Jeanne's family and make them the same offer as you. We're making a task force that can go back in time and stop horrific acts of violence; mass shootings, terrorist events, things like that. We will never use you for anything other than the public well-being. We'll have a nice house for you and your family either here in Chicago or Virginia, not too far from where you live now."

"This is creepy."

"I know it must be, but trust me, I-"

"I will not trust you. All you had to do was come out and tell us you wanted our help due to our abilities, I bet we would have helped you, instead you tortured us and tried to take our blood. Did you get in my brain too? Is this what this bandage is?"

"I'm sorry we did that to you, we just needed to

291

understand if you had the power we thought you did. It's an incredible gift. We know you can't go back more than a day, but as I said this is caused by a distortion of your biorhythms. Our original case was simply diurnal and could only jump in the day or the night. We believe some will be ultradian, meaning less than a day but they can transcend the day/night barrier, and some of you are based on the circadian rhythm, basically a full 24-hour period. It has its entire foundation in those rhythms. We're learning more and more, but we need live tests to see you do what you do. This is on the verge of being the biggest science breakthrough of all time! And you and your friends will be a part of it."

"I don't want people to know I have it. People will want me to go back and just get the lottery numbers. Out of curiosity, what is the next longest biorhythm?"

"It's infradian, your monthly cycle that is based on the lunar cycle. We have yet to encounter anyone or have any evidence the body can tolerate jumping that far back. Can you control your gift well enough to get results like that?"

"Would I be here if I could? No, none of us can. It has to be a big stressor; you should know that. Carlo can jump pretty easily, he was about to start teaching us when you guys took us, but he warned us the one person in his group who tried to use it for personal gain died very quickly."

Savannah stirs in her chair, "I think I need to talk to Carlo about this group, he knew others that had the anomaly?"

"GIFT!" Nat says, raising her voice.

"Sorry, your gift. Look, we're going to give you a job, and we'll pay you over a hundred grand a year to do this. We're giving your family a house and setting you up in a swell situation."

"Swell? How old are you?"

"Doesn't matter. What do you say?"

"If Jeanne does it, I guess I'll do it. I don't want to be some oddball. I spent the last few weeks in high school as an outcast."

"Great! I am talking to Jeanne and her parents, and I'll be right back, and I'll see how close your folks are."

"OK." Natalee looks annoyed and she is scheming in her head what she can do to get out of this. If she is going to get a job like this and does not have to do any real work, then why shouldn't she? Her teenage mind is envisioning all the good things she can do with her time not having to go to college.

Her mind wanders to Shannon, how can she possibly explain this? Deep in the cluttered mind of Natalee Simon, there is a clear thought…she already knows. She may not be aware of exactly what this is, but Shannon senses she has some kind of ability. She told her once, but then she jumped to exact vengeance on Christina and erased the earlier discussion in Shannon's mind.

Savannah exits Natalee's room, turning her back to her, and makes the right turn to Jeanne's room, both doors are open for a moment as the hydraulics close the door to Nat's room, but

Savannah fails to notice Nat grabbed her door. Jeanne hears Nat scream, "Jeanne I am here, I'll do it with you!!" Savannah gives a half smirk and asks the attendant to get Dan as another agent grabs and pulls Nat's door shut but is distracted and does not realize the click of the lock did not engage.

"Do you want to see your dad?" Savannah asks.

"Yes. Please. Dr. Savannah, please!"

"Sure, they are bringing him over."

"GET OFF ME!" Dan is heard down the hall as they try to subdue him.

"Dad! Dad! I'm ok come here!" Jeanne calls out.

"Hey, baby girl! How's my sort of brown and green-eyed girl?"

"I am ok Dad. I was real scared yesterday or whenever, but Dr. Savannah is nice. I also think we're past the whole, brown-eyed girl thing, don't you?"

He looks down and says, "I suppose that's kind of done, now." He motions to Savannah, "Jeanne, she is not a doctor, she is an FBI agent. They were the ones who took us."

"I know Dad. I think I made a big discovery about my deals. I think I can control them. I had a breakthrough listening to Taylor in my mind last night."

Jeanne rolls her eyes, "OMG DAD THAT'S MILEY NOT TAYLOR!!"

"LOL. Sorry."

"Stop trying to talk in text speak, Dad."

He turns to Savannah, "What kind of bullshit did you feed

294

my kid, and get these shackles off me."

"I can't do that just yet Mr. McAlister. We have some items to discuss with you. I'll make it brief. We're offering your daughter a job with the FBI. She'll continue her education, and we'll also have specialists working with her to control her anomaly as well as her ASD. We think she is the strongest of the four of them based on the lab results we have."

"Of course, you experimented on her, you sacks of-"

"Mr. McAlister, it's ok. We have made several advances that can help us understand what is happening to your young lady. She can go back to fix things she experiences, we want her to do that for us, for the whole country. Stop violent crimes before they happen.

We'll pay off your house, pay her handsomely, and you'll be given a line of credit at Pimlico, up in Maryland, or your track Remington. Either track is a short drive from Quantico or Chicagoland where we will have a new house for you and the family. We are not sure where we will set up our division just yet."

"Why not here, you have all your equipment."

"Certainly a good choice just depends on the brass, they want us close to Washington." She looks at Jeanne, "You'll help defend the President young lady, working with the Secret Service."

"How can you say that? I mean last week this was all hooey. We had no idea what this was, just a few weird things that happened to her. I told a friend who passed that information along to you. WAIT! I want Vic removed from the FBI or we're not discussing anything with you."

"Dan, that's not reasonable."

"That son of a bitch put us in danger, I'll kill him if I see him."

"Can we talk to your wife about this?"

"Wait, she's here? How is she?"

"She took more carbon monoxide than you all did, but she just woke up, we're letting her rest and then you can see her."

He gets up, "Lynn!! Lynn!!" He is screaming and completely uncontrollable. The guards try to restrain him but lose their grip and Dan trips and falls over his leg shackles and hits the door frame."

"Dan!" Lynn was allowed out of her room to join the conversation as Dan ran himself into the door, "DAN!" she screamed as she found him motionless on the floor, blood already coming from his nose where he face-planted into the frame.

"Dad!" Jeanne starts to scream, but the guards have him up and her dad shakes his head a bit.

"I'm ok baby girl. Hey honey. We all almost died because of the furnace at that old house Carlo rented. Carbon monoxide. They got us out." He's panting now, breathing very heavily, but goes on. "The FBI wants to use Jeanne's deals to help them stop crimes before they are committed."

"And Natalee is coming too!"

Lynn is puzzled. "Who is Natalee? Who is Carlo?"

"Nat is my friend I met at the house. She has them too. Carlo is the old man. Mom, you were there, why don't you remember?"

"The last thing I remember is in the park and driving away with the old man, er Carlo. So," Lynn starts speaking slowly, "they want to use you to tell them when bad things are going to happen so you can stop them from happening. You've only been able to do that with Dad's heart attack and my hardware store robber guy."

"And the loan shark."

"WHAT!?"

"Yeah, mom, you know, the big win Dad had. It was because a loan shark was threatening us."

"You IDIOT! I told you that Jeanne was not a part of your betting crap. I don't want her to grow up to be like you." Lynn whacks him right on the chest and Dan starts seizing.

"MEDIC!" Savannah yells, "I think there is a closed head injury here!"

Jeanne is screaming for her dad. Nat, who is still free of her restraints, opens the door to her room finds a clear chance to escape amongst the chaos, and walks out of her room. Jeanne sees her and starts yelling at her. "Nat! NAT! Don't go. I am going to take care of all this. Remember what Carlo said, just visualize. I can do it!"

Nat takes a step to the doorway, "But Jeanne that was

297

like 4 or 5 days ago, no one can jump that far."

"I can."

"How do you know?"

"I just do."

Savannah hears what's going on behind her and turns around. "Wait, Jeanne, it's too dangerous, you can't do that, you'll hurt yourself if you even try and we know you cannot jump back that far. No one can."

"You've never met me. I can do anything; my brain is special. Nat, you asked me what my gift was. This is it. I will find you in the park before all this happens." She closes her eyes as they roll back in her head. Savannah freaks out and grabs a vial of pentothal and rams it in the IV still in Jeanne's arm.

Nat shrieks, "NO! You can't do that to her!"

Jeanne falls back in bed, clearly asleep.

"*NO!*" Nat says and falls to the ground where she stands.

Nat and the escape

The commotion in the hall gives Nat her chance, she can escape with all the chaos going on. She opens the door, having changed into the clothes of the attendant she overpowered and drugged. Instead, she calmly walks into Jeanne's room.

"MEDIC!" Savannah yells, "I think we have a closed head injury here!"

Nat gets Jeanne's attention and places her finger over

her mouth telling Jeanne to be quiet. She sneaks into the room even though there are 6 people in there already. The guards are distracted, and Savannah is already trying to lay Dan down. She walks up and puts her face right next to Jeanne's ear. "They won't let you go. I'll be with you, find me in the park, I know you had a breakthrough and you think you can jump that far, so go. Now. Hurry. You can save us all."

Savannah turns to see Jeanne's eyes rolling back, but as she is reaching for the pentothal, she realizes that Nat already has the vile in her hand. She closes her eyes but Nat says "I know what you are. Not this time." She jabs it in Savannah's neck.

"I'll see you again bitch. But this time, we'll be ready for you."

Jeanne sees Nat disable Savannah and her body starts to shake. Nat thinks there is a faint light around her head, like an angel's halo for just a second, but in an instant, it is gone, and Jeanne's body collapses against the back of the bed with a thud.

See you there girl. Nat is smiling from ear to ear as her world again crumbles up around her as if everything is made out of confetti.

Chapter 21

Third Time and Charms (Day 0)

Jeanne opens her eyes; she feels a little dizzy after making another jump within hours of making the largest jump she ever pulled off. Dan has his hand on her shoulder "Jeanne. Are you ok?"

"Yes, dad." She turns. "Mattis, you and I have to go find Nat. That escape did not work. You are not going to kill yourself for me again."

Tony stands there, mystified. Dan and Lynn look at each other in bewilderment as the sounds of the park dance around them. Jeanne stands up and looks around, thinking to herself, *You have to be here, you said you were lurking around, you know Mattis from TV, you have to be here.*

She decides on a different course of action. "Tony, you don't know me, but I have to tell you something. Mattis is going to be kidnapped by the FBI."

"What?" Tony responds surprised, yet with a sense of deja vu. "What do you mean?"

"Mattis and I have the same gift, we can go back in time and fix things that are about to go wrong, but the FBI wants to turn us all into a big lab experiment. Do you or can you trust me? I've been through this day already, in fact twice before. I've seen us run away and be caught. We also escaped and got into a car wreck that Mattis saved me from, and he died in. I have a different idea but I have to find another girl who I know is here, so excuse me for making a scene but I am about to fake a tantrum, one like I have not had since I was like 12."

"OK, but I'd suggest you go outside the cage here, so Mattis does not get spooked."

"Yes, but I need to give you some instructions. I am going to get Natalee to come to us. Maybe even Carlo, and when they do, we have to find their cars, and all go in different directions to escape. They are going to take you to the fountain, but when they do, fake a phone call and take Mattis for an emergency you have to attend to, go into the trees, and take his camera and harness off, they are tracking him. Dad, give him your number and we can text him and tell him where to go. Probably north, they have a soft spot up there."

"OK, young lady. I feel like I should trust you."

Jeanne starts to do something completely foreign to her, she is creating a fabrication, but it seems like that is what she has to do. She starts flailing and screaming, "NAT! NAT!" She gets on one knee, "Dad, NO!!" She screams at the top of her voice like she's being attacked by fire ants and screams "NATALEE!"

The commotion draws Savannah away from the control position for a moment as she sticks her head outside to see what the deal is. She sees Jeanne going through a breakdown of sorts and retreats back to her station. "Grab B, this is control. Move from your spot down toward the tent, we may have a chance to take the target under the guise of medical."

"Roger that control. Grab B en route."

Moving the grab team is a critical change that leaves the middle of their shield unattended, where Carlo has his car stationed. In the commotion, Natalee hears her name, but from a distance. She's lingering near the VIP area, but the screams get her attention and she starts to move in the direction of the big tent. She sees a girl seemingly in distress and wants to go help her but decides against it and walks casually towards the fences separating the dog runs for the handlers and animals in the competition.

One of the other agents exits the tent on instructions from Savannah and offers assistance. Jeanne stands up and says, "Thank you, I am sorry, sometimes my head and thoughts get away from me, did I cause a scene?"

Dan cocks his head to the side. Something is off. Jeanne does not act this way. If she is trying to fake a tantrum she is doing horribly at it. He goes with it and says, "Honey, do you want some water, we can walk over there and calm down."

"OK." She spots Carlo right where he said he was lingering, but she continues to look to the north and finally spots Nat. She looks at her dead in the eyes and yells "Nat! Come here!"

Natalee is shocked. This girl she does not know just called her by name, should she go? She thinks for a second and walks in that direction. "Um, hello?"

"Dad, can we walk over and get a funnel cake before the race?"

"It's starting in just a minute, honey," Lynn says, "do you want me to go and get one for you? I bet the VIP section will have them too."

"I need to go to the bathroom too, let's go real quick. Natalee, you come too."

As she is walking toward the edge of the tent she stops and says, "Hey, you are the man from the hotel. I want to ask you something, can you walk with me?"

"Sure," Carlo says, unsure of what is happening. This is not going the way the last couple of loops did. He looks around for a second or two and his face gets tense. He assumes this girl is the cause of this significant deviation that has him spooked.

They get on the other side of the tent and Jeanne looks to make sure the FBI agent is out of earshot. "Just walk slow. Nat we've met, but you don't remember because I jumped. We meet later but the FBI will take us all. They'll put us in a lab and test all of us, but they don't know that I can jump back almost a week now, and I'm getting stronger. We don't have time; they are watching us. Carlo, go get your car. Nat where are you parked?"

"I got lucky and got a spot in the public lot over on Roosevelt on the other side of the field with all the food vendors."

"Perfect. That's perfect. Carlo, just walk to the bushes and be casual, they don't know to look for you yet. Go north to Jackson, Mattis and Tony are going to be near the fountain, dad, text him and tell him to go to Columbus and meet Carlo. Carlo

303

you are going to get them and go north away from here. We're going to meet at the Home Run Inn in one hour. We'll be certain no one follows us. They are after me and Mattis, so I am sure they will notice us walking away and will track us. Actually, don't do that. Dad, tell them to go around the fence on the other side of the fountain and Carlo, you pick them up on Jackson. Tell them what they are looking for Dad."

"How can you possibly know this?" Lynn asks.

"Mom, so not important right now. I'll tell you all about it, but this is my third time through this day now. We have to get away clean."

Carlo and Dan exchange info about his car and that information is relayed to Tony who all of a sudden feigns an urgent phone call and changes his location while he and Mattis are about to get separated for their showcase. The agents try to give him some assistance to hold on to Mattis, but Tony insists it is safer, and he will be back for his run after he deals with this emergency.

"OK Mattis, it's time for us to get going." Tony takes all of Mattis' equipment off and leaves it in the tree they are next to, looking back for the trailing agent, who glances in his direction.

Tony takes a step back so he is completely in view, and waits for the agent to turn toward the competition, which he does moments later. "Mattis Geh Voraus" Mattis hears the go-ahead command and begins walking in the direction he is facing, and Tony follows him.

"Foos Mattis", Tony says and Mattis begins to keep pace with him as he starts running through the tree line, knowing he will be exposed in a matter of seconds as he reaches a clearing.

"Control. Briggs. The animal and handler appear to have moved north through the trees."

"What? Ops where is the GPS on the vest?"

"Control. Ops, we have a fix on the tracker. Stationary about 30 meters northeast of the command center."

"Briggs, check the tree line, are you certain?"

"One moment control." Briggs jogs over to where he saw Mattis and Tony last, "They ditched the vest, they've gone rogue."

"Vic, can you intercept, if they are moving north they have to cross Balbo."

"Roger that. Intercepting at Balbo." Vic barely has time to look up and he sees them going across the street, but he is still inside the fence line. "Stop! Freeze!" He draws his service weapon.

Tony looks at him, "You really want to shoot at a cop in broad daylight who is chasing his dog who got loose? Something is wrong with him; I'll be back as soon as I get him. MATTIS STOP!"

Vic has no idea that is not an official command, so Mattis appears to be off leash. "Control, the handler is pursuing the dog yelling for him to stop, he said the animal bolted off his harness and it broke."

"Control this is Briggs, the harness has been sheared

305

off."

"Vic, control. stay on them. Grab A, abandon the trap, and head to the other side of the fountain on the east side, move! Move! Use your tranquilizer darts on him when you make contact."

"Roger control, grab A on the way east." They are in a dead sprint away from the area so they have no way of hearing the car start in the brush only 20 meters from their previous position.

Carlo is in his car and leaves to the north on Columbus, getting to Jackson in less than a minute. He makes the turn right and sees Mattis and Tony going around the outside fence, with two agents closing from inside the fence line.

He pulls up to the curb and Tony and Mattis jump in the car.

"Control this is grab A, they just got into a blue Ford sedan and are going south on LSD, we could not see plates."

"What?" Savannah slams her fist on the table. "How did they know to ditch us, I could have sedated them in the damn tent! Grab B and C where is the girl?"

"Grab B, unknown."

"Grab C, we had her and lost her in the crowd, she has not returned north to the tent."

"No shit, they are headed south, go to LSD and Roosevelt now and try and get a plate for the blue Ford. Let's roll CPD."

Unknown to Savanna, Carlo pulled a U-turn at Balbo and was now headed back north along the shore of Lake Michigan. Jeanne and her parents are calmly walking towards Nat's car down on Roosevelt when Dan spots four agents running south through the field.

They were looking toward the lake, fixed on something, so he shielded Jeanne from their view and picked up the pace. Dan opened the passenger door and let Jeanne and Lynn in the back seat, then took shotgun and the four of them made a clean escape from the scene.

"Grab teams sitrep!" Savannah yells into her microphone.

"Grab A, they departed the area in the vehicle. We lost visual after they made the turn."

"Grab B, no blue fords fitting the description, we have stopped traffic at Roosevelt and are searching."

"Grab C, no joy. We do not have a visual on the target."

Savannah slams the headset down, "Damn!"

Alicia appears from the CCTV room, "Savannah, they exploited holes in the net that they could not have known were there."

"They jumped. I don't know how they did it, but the girl and the dog jumped. That's why the dog bolted, and that's why the girl fled from the VIP area, she knew that was the strike point. DAMMIT!"

"Savannah, I need you to calm down, what is our next step here?"

Savannah, seeing her career hang in the balance,

307

decides that she's going to take her punishment and come up with alternatives. "We know the dog and the officer have to return to Austin. We know we have the kid through Vic. What we don't know is if the family will know about everything at this time or just have a feeling from their daughter. It's clear to me that this young girl is in control of her anomaly."

"I'd agree. And the animal?"

"There's something else in play there. That handler had a car pick him up, he must have made a phone call, but how did he know the dog was a target? We could have picked him up in here. Let's get to the hotels."

She spins back over to the microphone, "Grab A and B, get to the girl's hotel. Grab C, go to the handler's room. Let's try and acquire them there. Otherwise, we'll have the San Antonio field office involved."

An hour later, in the parking lot of the Home Run Inn, the six of them plus Mattis gather around their two cars as the afternoon sun shines off the mirror, giving Jeanne a little headache from the glare, so she covers her eyes and moves away, but her dad notices something odd. "Jeanne, you are missing a finger!"

"Dad, we need to chat about a bunch of stuff, but first did everybody turn off your cell phones?"

Everyone nods that they did.

"OK, Dad, your friend Vic is going to try and bait you into talking to him, and you have to control yourself. I'll explain more later, but you cannot talk to him until we have an escape route. Right now the only phone that is safe is Nat's. Dad, Vic has your number, he can use that to get to Mom and Tony. Then, he can use Tony's to find Carlo."

Carlo interrupts. "Young lady, how do you know to call me Carlo?"

"This is a long story, but the short version is that you, me, Mattis, and Nat all have the same gift. The FBI calls it an anomaly, but they think it is only limited to a day because I guess no one has ever jumped back more than a day and they base it on biorhythms. Well, this is my third time through this day, and we've been both captured and killed, so we're doing better now. I can travel back longer than a day. I can jump maybe a week or even more. I know what they have planned for the next 4 or 5 days so I came back to change things."

"Jeanne, your hand." Her mom says.

"Jumping a long way can hurt us. Sometimes, we leave a piece of us behind if we want to jump and use our gifts but it's ok, a lot of the time when we lose things we gain things too. There is so much more that I learned from Nat and Carlo last week, I mean, this...um, whatever, but we don't have time. I'll tell you all about it after we're safe."

"It's so weird hearing you talk Jeanne," Nat says, "I've never met you in my time, but we're friends in your timeline."

"That's the thing, I think I figured out how time really works for us too. We can make a deal with the FBI, I want to scare them so they don't try and take us again. I am going to offer them solutions for mysteries the universe has never allowed us to solve, the types of questions I know they have been working on, but we have to bait the hook first."

She turns to her dad, "We're going to use your phone to call Vic. We're going to ask for their number and tell them we will call them tomorrow. We need a burner phone or five. After you make the call, we will turn all the phones back on, and leave them in the parking lot in the back of some pickup trucks so the FBI just chases their tail for a day or two. Then we'll be in a better position."

She thinks for a second and closes her eyes before sharply whipping her head around to Nat, "Also, Nat, you figured something out as I jumped. You discovered one of their agents has the gift, and I bet you they've been hiding it, so we're going to try and turn that agent to work for us and shield us."

"It's Savannah, isn't it?" Tony asks.

"Yes, how did you know?"

"Mattis has had a similar reaction to you, Nat, and Carlo. I noticed it with you in the cage and when he saw Carlo on the street this morning, he did the same thing. Look at him now, he's draped over Nat's shoulder. He does not do that. He did it to Savannah as well. Something inside you is detectable to him. He knows you have the gift. We can find others this way. I think our police life is done. We're about to be fugitives."

"So, I can't confront Vic?" Dan asks. It always has to be about him.

"Let it go, if I am reading between the lines here, you

blew this whole thing and either got us captured or killed because of your pigheaded pride Dan." Lynn is annoyed. "Listen to your daughter, she literally sacrificed a piece of herself for us and our safety."

She turns back to Jeanne, "I can't wait to hear what you have to tell us."

Jeanne calmly goes through several things for the group, "First, Officer Scott, the FBI will want Mattis to detect people for them. You can help us from the inside, so you will not be a fugitive at all. Second, that house you have is where Carlo? We'll go there after we make the call, let's get the phones on and in cars or trucks. Third, Dad, what do you want to say? I know what I want to say, but let's work on how you'll address Vic to get a good contact number out of him for tomorrow."

Chapter 22

Jeanne's Plan (Day 0)

Jeanne noticed something in addition to her missing pinky finger on her left hand; the noise in her head was diminished. She seemed focused in a way she never was before, even with the medication. She felt thankful right now; amid a situation that would normally be as stressful to her as she could imagine, she somehow kept her cool. "So, this place is a rental for you Carlo, how much longer do you have it?"

"Just tonight, I am scheduled to check out tomorrow. My goal was to meet you and Mattis and I've done that. Now, we need to see about rebuilding The Order."

"The what?" Dan interrupts.

"OK Dad, let me give you all the short version. Fair warning, Mom is going to hit you and call you names. Nat, you are about to learn a ton and Carlo, you'll be surprised too. Carlo found us because Mattis' bank robbery story went viral. He used to be in an organization that had many people like us in it, but all of them gradually died after they developed problems with their genetics after using their gifts too often or in an unlucky genetic mutation. He's the only one left from the group they called The Order."

Carlo nods his head. "Is this the part where your mom is

going to smack your dad?"

"Yes," Jeanne smiles, "Mom, Carlo also found out by lurking around the FBI tent that Vic was the one who told them about me winning a bunch of money at the track for Dad."

"Well that happened years ago sweetie, why would I be mad about that?" Lynn asked.

"Mom, the big jackpot was because he put me in a position to use the 3000 dollars he borrowed from a loan shark. Then, that guy and his fat bodyguard threatened to kill us if I did not win all of it back."

"You arrogant shit!" She hits him. Hard. "You have no right to exploit our daughter like that. Just for your stupid gambling habit!"

Tony cringed. Nat turned away and shook her head. Carlo smiled.

"I knew it would happen," Dan said.

"Did you also know that some genetic thing could end her? DID YOU!?"

"Well, no."

"Asshole."

Jeanne continues, "So, now that Vic learned we are aware of their plan, likely they will have to scrub the whole operation since they can't track us at the moment."

"Hold on baby girl." Dan interrupts again.

Jeanne is annoyed and does not hide it. "Dad, you have to get over yourself, you are not in charge anymore."

Those words cut right through his poor excuse for

manhood like an ax through a twig, "It's not about that. I noticed something earlier. You lied, well, you tried to even though you are terrible at it. And now you are like, super focused. Can these genetic changes be positive or negative?"

Carlo jumps in. "We've never recorded anyone having a physical imperfection caused by a jump fixed in a subsequent one, but one of our members did start to grow hair after cancer robbed him of the ability to do so. There is not enough evidence to say for sure, but I'd say if you have something wrong, it could be changed so that it is normal again, but that is a million-to-one shot."

"Dad, I know what you are talking about, and all day long, it has not been loud at all for me. I'm not ready to say it's fixed, or gone or whatever, but it is manageable without my headphones. Let's hope maybe one of the things that was different in my brain is not quite as bad as it was."

Lynn starts crying.

Dan puts his arm around his wife and whispers in her ear ever so slightly.

Lynn nods her head and softly says, "That was my prayer every day for her."

"Mom, it's ok. So, look. Last time we were here, we learned a lot about each other, and we can talk about all that again, but here's what they did to us. They captured us, ran all these blood tests, took pieces of our brains, and found out we have some kind of chemical or protein differences in our genes. They did not speak much about it, but Savannah was telling me a little bit when she was trying to convince me to be an agent with her. She wants us all to be a part of their group, er, *they* want us to work for them. I am certain she is one of us and is hiding it. When we escaped from the place, or when I discovered I could travel a long time back, Natalee told Savannah she knew what she was, and you'd see her again right as you knocked her unconscious with the medicine she must have used on me previously. This is where the time loops start to overlap. I think Savannah and Nat had a little battle where Savannah jumped to get the meds to knock me out so when I was trying to jump, Savannah stopped me with drugs, but Nat jumped back further and took the syringe off the table, and then put her to sleep so she could not go back, because she was closing her eyes and looking like she was about to jump when you zapped her."

"I did that?" Nat asks. She is pleased with herself even though she would never do what Jeanne said she did. "How do we reconcile the time slips? I did that, but I don't remember doing it."

"This is where Carlo and I can talk about what happens to the outside space-time continuum when we go back and forth, but we don't need to bore all of you with that. Again."

"OK, so, like we have something they want, and they have something we need, right?" Natalee asks.

"Yes! They have a big place somewhere around here, I never got out to see where it was but I am guessing it was close because when they offered me the job they said the lab would be here in Chicago or Washington DC."

"Wow, that's close to where I live. Damn, I should reach out to my folks, they'll be worried about me."

"I thought you snuck away and told them you were with a friend?" Jeanne said.

"Wait, how do you know that?"

Jeanne just stares at her.

"Oh. Right." Nat just looks down and excuses herself to call her folks.

Jeanne continues, "They have a lab that can test us, and tell us what genetic issues we have. They also want to figure out these proteins and genes. We need to understand what's wrong with us and we won't like it, but we should allow them to continue to test us as we go back in time to do good things. I want to talk to Savannah privately and enlist her support, then tell the FBI that we'll work with them if they leave us alone, and in return, we will supply all the blood tests they want, but no brain pieces."

Nat pokes her head around the wall dividing the living room and kitchen "Ooh, like the Time Avengers! Can I be Storm? My parents did not answer."

"Jeez Nat, Storm is an X-Men character. You're as bad as my dad confusing musicians."

"Well, my hair changes colors, so I like that badass white hair she has. And she was part of the Avengers for a while in the comics."

"But she went back to X-Men to fight against the Avengers, didn't she? OK, we're not superheroes, we are just people with a gift to use for good."

"Except for your father who uses it to make money," Tony says, obviously trolling Dan again.

Lynn thinks about slapping him again, but instead says, "I don't condone what my husband did, but it has led us to meet all of you. I've often wanted my daughter to have people she trusted and that she could call friends, and however it happened, here we are."

She turns to Dan and says, "But you are in the dog house."

Dan glares at Tony.

Tony continues, "Look, that's all good and I am happy if this is a net positive in your life, but I have a family as well and I have to say that I'm worried. What happens to them? The FBI is good, they will be all over them by tomorrow."

Jeanne looks him dead in the eye, which startles her father because he's never known her to do that. "That's part of the deal. We and our families are off limits if they want us to work with them. Period. End of story. We do need to wait until 24 hours from now to make the call, I don't want Savannah having delusions of grandeur that she can somehow trap us. If she does, we should threaten to expose her to the FBI."

Tony says, "No way she will expose herself. She's tough as nails that one. I just don't want them using my boy as a hostage because Mattis can help them."

"Mattis is not a big target for them, he can't talk. He's injured anyway, his usefulness as a police dog is limited."

"How do you know that?" Tony immediately starts looking at Mattis.

"I saw it. He has a limp and I think his hind leg has a problem now."

Tony begins to manipulate his legs back and forth, "I don't see anything."

"He needs a vet to make sure. I killed him last time I went back."

Tony, stunned, says," I'm sorry what?"

Jeanne explains, "I chose the wrong escape path and we got hit by a truck. Mattis tried to shield me and took the blow. For sure, he jumped back just to save me."

The group sits silent, digesting what Jeanne said.

Jeanne breaks the silence, "Ok, let's grab some shuteye, I am beat. We'll make contact with Savannah in the afternoon, Carlo can you rent this place another night?"

"I already did, we have it for two more days now, just in case."

"Mr. Scott, can you find where we should make the call from? I don't know if a burner phone is completely safe, especially when dealing with the FBI. Can they trace those?" Jeanne asks him.

"They can, but it's pretty tough without the right equipment. They are more likely going to try and triangulate our signal using the 911 technology, but that is not super accurate. Still, we need to make contact from a train station or on a bus, somewhere that is either in motion or a place that offers us a quick escape if they do capture our location in the few minutes we are on. And call me Tony young lady."

"Nat's car will work, correct?"

"Of course, they have not seen it!"

"OK, that's a plan." With that, Jeanne motions for Nat to go upstairs so they can catch up. Again.

The Feds Reflect

ASAC Peabody is steamed. The entire op was blown, no one got anything definitive, and the only piece of intel they got was that someone thought they saw out-of-state plates on a blue Ford. This is hardly an example of groundbreaking law enforcement work. She kept everyone on the task force in the tent after the event was over and laid down the law. "This was a disaster from the start. We know they can jump time, why were we not prepared?"

"Ma'am," Savannah starts, "We shifted and moved the net to try and anticipate their movement, but there is a possibility that they have gone back through this sequence of events multiple times until they got it right and learned our reactions and where our personnel, both fixed and mobile were. Officer Scott's using the fence was surely planned, it stopped us from intercepting him on his run. The girl wound up going south, mainly because we had absolutely nothing there."

"Grab teams, I'll expect your reports on your movements

319

and lack of intelligence on my desk in the morning. I don't care if it's Sunday, I want all the CCTV digital images, I want all the Chicago traffic cams, I want to know who was in the blue sedan and I want to know where they went."

Peabody's phone starts to chirp.

Vic's phone starts to vibrate on the table.

"Another thing," Peabody continues, ignoring her device for the time being, "where were our drones? I saw nothing at all from them, did we not need them?"

Another vibration from Vic.

"Ma'am, too much interference from foliage and human traffic."

Another buzz. Another ring.

"Vic, are we keeping you from something?"

"It's the dad. My friend, he's making contact with me now."

"Well, answer it, let's see about a trace, keep him on as long as you can." She looks at her phone and sees her worst fear on it, SAC Sanumo calling from Quantico.

"He's on my personal cell." Vic shrugs as he places the call on speaker, "Dan?"

"You piece of shit."

Multiple agents look at their feet and stifle their laughter.

"I trusted you with that information and you tried to take my kid. And the dog? Are you serious? I am assuming the rest of you in the tent are listening in and will have my location in about 3 minutes, so let me save you the time. Give me a good phone number to call your task force tomorrow, and I need to contact Savannah, a direct line for Dr. Savannah."

Savannah feels a rush of hotness course through her face, and she would not be surprised if someone says her hair is actually on fire. Her face and her scalp tingle at the mention, but a doctor? Where did that come from?

Dan continues, "At least she tried to convince my kid she was a medical professional. Funny thing, you guys have no idea that happened, but we do. I'm waiting for that number, er, those numbers. Dr. Savannah, you'll be hearing from Jeanne directly tomorrow. She has an offer for you since you realize the futility of direct action against a group of time-mobile people."

Vic pauses for a moment, thinking that he heard what sounded like a slap. "Dan, just call my number, I'll be here in the morning, what time?"

"Um, do you want me to give you an exact time to have your phone freaks all charged up to trace us? What's Savannah's contact number, or should I just call the Chicago field office and let them know a 16-year-old just ate your team for lunch today?"

"Fine, here it is, 312-555-1313."

"Thirteen, my daughter will remember that easily. It's her special number, her favorite artist on the planet says it's good luck, and she believes it. Be ready for an information dump that will leave you speechless tomorrow. Don't worry, you might triangulate us, but we'll be prepared for you…you know we will."

The click left everyone sitting there, stunned. Why focus

on Savannah? Why the doctor's reference? Most importantly, he mentioned a group of time-mobile people. The stunning wave rolled over them before Vic finally broke the silence, "A group of people, so either one of them spontaneously started jumping, or they found another person. Let's hit the CCTV and look at everyone she talked to at the event."

"The meltdown." Savannah says, "When she had the tantrum she was calling someone. Find that, we have a cam at the tent, she was right there."

The technicians bring up the footage, and they jack up the sound. Natalee. Vic starts smiling, once again his hot-headed friend sold out the group. It was only a matter of time before they got a match on Natalee, he knew it. "OK, we have the girl, who's this old timer she walks around the trailer with? Do we have a decent angle? He looks old."

Mahoney responds, "No sir, they drop out of view, we only get a partial profile, and the audio is too muddy with all the people there, we can't get it."

Vic shoots back, "Backtrack and follow the guy, all his movements. We're bound to get at least something we can make facial recognition on."

"Yes sir."

"Vic finally did something today people," Alicia sarcastically says, "anyone else going to have an original thought today or should we let operations tear this thing down and meet in the morning? I want all the CCTV analyzed and facial patterns running overnight with NCIC and the agency, I

322

don't care how it gets done, just do it. If we need to widen out to Interpol, make it so. This guy is 50 or 60, someone has him."

Alicia finally picks up her phone. "This is Peabody."

"You disappoint me, Alicia"

"How so, *Brett?*"

"Don't take that tone with me. You just allowed them to walk away. I see some serious incompetence here, wouldn't you agree?"

"I don't know how your Langley days went, sir, but if you had to track these people at the Agency, your career would be much different than today. You can't take brute force approaches with them."

"I'll be the judge of that. I authorized you to use up to and including lethality, you used none. Perhaps I need to take your command and award it to someone not quite as squeamish."

"No, we'll have a plan, we're tracking two new players on the field, possibly other anomalous individuals. Give us time."

"You have 48 hours to show results. I'd remind you that failure is not an option, Alicia."

"Yes sir."

Chapter 23

The Trap (Day 1)

It's Sunday morning, but Alicia does not have a religious bone in her body, so the entire task force is summoned to the conference room at 10 am. "OK. What kind of cluster did we have out there yesterday? Savannah, how did we lose control of the situation and do you think that girl is going to call today?"

"I do ma'am, I already have all calls to my number being traced, we'll be able to triangulate her position when she does."

"Are you recording them too?"

"No."

"Why not?" Alicia looks a little annoyed.

"That's not SOP, this is not a criminal probe or investigation. This is, at best, domestic surveillance. We don't have a mandate for a blanket wiretap."

"Let the technicians know and have them set up the taps on your line. Set one up for Vic's line too. Vic, does the dad have your office or just your cell?"

"My personal cell ma'am."

"Well damn, that'll take a day, jump on it, extend the tap to his personal device too, Custos."

"Yes, Ma'am." Dejected, Savannah gets up to leave the room.

"Where are you going?"

"You told me to get with the techs."

"I meant to call over there and engage them, right after this debrief. I hate that this entire team was outthought by a 12-year-old."

"She's 16." Vic interrupts.

"I don't give a shit. She made us all look like idiots. Is this what we have to look forward to out there if we continue trying to hunt down these people? At least we know where they live. They have to go home at some point."

"To the first question," Savannah begins, "we were reactive with the force we had in place, my opinion is the same today as it was yesterday. She has been through the timeline before, and this was a natural result of us not having all our bases covered. She eventually exploited the hole in our plan after testing the responses. Probably several times."

Alicia finally looks like she's ready to listen to rational thought, "Let's say for a second I believe this crap. Didn't she risk permanent change by going back more than once?"

"Yes, but if her other alternative timelines meant she was captured or someone was hurt, I mean if it were me I'd go back until I got out without issue."

Vic's phone rings.

"Vic, I swear if that's your guy again, we're going to destroy that thing and make you use your bureau device." Alicia is annoyed again.

"It's not a number I recognize, I'll get to it after a while ma'am."

"OK, what is our next move Savannah, what do you have? You don't sleep when you suffer a bad beat, so what have you come up with?"

Savannah gets up and takes the piece of charting paper off the whiteboard. "I think we are out of conventional options, it's time to start thinking about stealth and taking one of them by total surprise. I plan to back off them completely. Assuming they approach us by telephone later, we'll offer them the opportunity to work with us, nothing more. I'll try and get some information out of the girl if she does reach out. It's obvious she knows something, I'll have a good idea of our true next steps if we can talk to her."

"And if she does not make contact?"

"Well, Alicia, here is the deal." She goes over the positions and placements of assets and agents over the next 2 weeks to observe but not intervene in both Austin and Chestertown. Her plan is simple: let them re-enter their life somewhere and catch them in some normal activity where they will not be expecting the FBI to show up.

"Other teams, where are we on our facial recognition?" Alicia barks.

Mahoney pops his hand up.

Savannah looks at him and says, "What the hell are you doing?"

"It's not the worst idea in the world, Savannah." Alicia says. "Go on Mahoney."

"The girl does not have a record, but we got a hit on driver's license data out of Virginia. Natalee Simon from McLean, Virginia. We've got a good address and we also have a BOLO for her. We tried the parents, but they simply told us she was in Chicago. She gave them a cover story about being somewhere else. We got her vehicle information and issued an APB on the car with Chicago PD but a do-not-approach order on it. We just want to find her at this point. We have traffic cams online this morning and I'll have a team of three looking for license plate hits.

"You're assuming she's using her car?" Alicia asks.

"Why wouldn't she? The real question is why is she here? Why does Jeanne call out to her? My gut tells me she is the link between all this. This girl is another anomaly. Maybe the old guy is too, but he's not coming up on anything. We've run international records, US and Canadian driver's licenses, reached out to Langley, and the whole smash. Nada."

"The man is still a secondary objective, but for now, the two girls are known so they are the highest priority. Let's do some work, people. Savannah informs us the second you receive a call."

"Yes ma'am."

Half an hour later, the same number is buzzing on Vic's cell. He decides to answer.

"Hand the phone to Savannah." The voice on the other end tells him.

327

"Dan?"

"Don't waste time, asshole. Savannah. Now."

"She's not here."

"Go find her, you are working together after all."

Vic does not alert anyone that they are calling him. He wanders down to Savannah's station and motions for her to come over and mouths '*It's THEM!*'

She walks over and steps outside in the hallway. "This is Custos."

"Hello, Savannah. If you are nearly as competent as you sound, then you'll be tracing this so I will be brief. I am going to give you a number to text. It's a voice-over IP line, so don't bother tracing it. Text me a clean number we can call you on. We'll know if you trace it and believe me you don't want to experience the consequences of not following our instructions. Don't try and jump back, we're on to you."

She is writing on the palm of her hand and barely gets the last digit. She's breathing in to start talking when she hears the click. She considers for a moment whether she should expose herself to her bosses and the FBI and decides this is not the right time.

She knows the inevitability of her secret seeing the light of day but her mind races at the possibilities again. It's not the first time she's thought about what it means for her career to spill the beans, but she's also afraid of the repercussions. She goes back to her cube and pulls out a notebook with a black X drawn on the cover.

She begins rereading the plan for her to reveal her anomaly to the bureau. It is a blueprint of how she wants to parlay this into her own command, with her own task force and a healthy promotion, but it has a fundamental risk. She may become the lab rat.

Nat and Jeanne are getting ready to leave the house when Dan stops them, "Exactly where do you two think you are going?"

"We're going to call Savannah now and convince her to see things our way, she's one of us first, not them."

Dan gives her the look, that same look every father shoots at their daughter that means they are messing up big time and says, "Oh no you're not, not the two of you alone. We're damn fugitives."

"No we aren't, we've done nothing wrong."

"Maybe not, but you are wanted by the FBI, I'm going with you."

"So Am I." All three of them snap their heads around to find Tony and Mattis standing there. "You're not leaving without protection. You're about to reveal to them that you're the strongest person with this gift they've ever seen. Do you think they will just stop looking for you just because you threaten to expose one agent? Think again. You should have a backup."

"And if they do track us, I have a score to settle," Dan says.

"Come on Dad, we have to move forward through this, it

blew us up last time through this loop. People go on and on about, like, you have to forgive and forget to move past something."

"No you don't. You don't have to forgive and you don't have to forget to move on." His words and his face scream resolute, and Jeanne knows he's absolutely serious.

"I don't think you're ever moving on from this."

"Maybe not. That douchebag endangered all of us for what, a promotion? Screw him."

Tony begins again, "Look from a law enforcement perspective, you screamed Nat's name when you had your freak out by the kennels, and then she came into view of the tent. If it were me, I would have run your face to see if we could get a hit, and the FBI can always tap into nationwide stuff, so assume two things. First, they know who you are. Second, if your car is in your name, they have an APB on it as well. Heck let's just say that they do because they'll track you to your parents and then get any vehicles registered to your house. We had a pretty clean getaway using Carlo's car, maybe that's what we should use."

"That sounds like a plan. Where can we go, Tony?" Dan asks in a rare moment of deference.

"Using counter-surveillance techniques, I'd go at least 5 miles out. They'll expect 10 so staying in the radius may help us. Keep the kids in the back seat so traffic cams can't pick up facial recognition as easily. The guys can wear bandanas and caps. Let's all use PPE, it will look like we are all still paranoid from COVID and cover our faces."

330

"OK, it's been 24 hours. Let's move." Dan says.

"Girls, when you make the call, you'll have 3 minutes at the most before they'll be on us, so we will remain in motion and you'll toss the phone in a bush or something. Better yet, we can find the back of a pickup to throw it into."

The girls, Dan and Tony head out towards a suburb called Lemont to the south and east of where they were. Once they get off the highway Tony tells the girls it is safe to make the call to the number they received on the text. Dan's face is strained again, he wants to say something. As Jeanne dials, she starts to remember the entire conversation she planned out in her head as soon as Savannah answered.

Savannah is barricaded in her own office, expecting the call to come in soon. It's been 24 hours since the events of yesterday and they'd chosen that time frame for a reason: she can no longer stop them. The phone rings and even though she expects it, she still jumps in her chair. She answers it before the second ring, "This is Custos."

Jeanne begins, "Savannah, I am assuming you are tracing this, and for your sake, I hope this is not being recorded. I will be quick. You're one of us. I know you have the gift and you need to use it to try and catch us, but don't. I'll keep your secret if you help me keep ours."

"It's not that simple, Jeanne. You have a stronger ability than the rest of them. You called me doctor, why?"

"Because I jumped back almost a week when you had us

331

in the lab you set up to test us."

"I don't believe you. No one can jump that long."

"You're basing that on what, 3 people? How about this, envision what I am going to describe to you. A long hall at the bottom of the stairs, with a door at the end of the hallway you may have to use because you only have six rooms down there to hold us. I've been there. You can't go back as far as me, so I'll win any game you play."

Savannah pauses, the proof is in her words, she's seen the facility. "OK, I'm listening. What do you want?"

"Leave us alone, we will create a group that can assist you. We'll help you solve unsolvable events, but we don't want to be treated like animals."

"We have to understand what this is, Jeanne. We need to know if this is dangerous. What if other countries have other people like you who can anticipate our moves before anyone else?"

"Savannah, I don't have information about that, but if they find out about you, they will make your life as miserable as you are making mine. You tried at the park, you tried at the house, and you tried at the lab, and I got away. We've been playing games for a week, you just don't know it."

Savannah's desk phone blinks twice, and she continues, "Jeanne, I can't just stop looking for you."

"Tell them you gained my trust, and I will meet you and talk about working with you. That will buy you some time and I'll have a plan for you on how we can prove you are getting help from us."

"I'm sorry, we're going to find you, why don't you just come into our office and I assure you that you and your friends will be treated with respect and you won't be harmed, you have the opportunity to help your country."

"I've seen how you define respect and harm. You're not taking a piece of my brain."

Tony is waving at Jeanne that her time is up.

"Jeanne, please just come in. You don't want to be on the run for the rest of your life."

"I won't need to run if I give you to them. The best part is, I can prove it."

Click. The line is dead.

Savannah slowly puts her cell down and picks up her desk phone. "You have them?"

"It is a burner but we triangulated to an area near Lemont. It is still pinging the towers and it just shifted to a new tower to the south, they are on the move."

Savannah thinks to herself and mutters, "Clever girl, you are making us chase a phone again."

She stiffens and barks into the handset, "Set up surveillance on 55 and 355 running from Lamont to Downer's Grove or Naperville, they want us to believe they are headed in one direction when they are going in the opposite direction. We don't have the resources to cover everything, so we'll start with those two cities for now. Mahoney, you and your guys are going to be on the traffic cams southbound on Interstate 355 from

Woodbridge to 55 for the last 30 minutes before the call. The cop likely has them doing countersurveillance so we can assume they will throw us a decoy to the south when they are actually going north. Look for the blue Ford, they'll suspect we have Natalee's information by now, but keep an eye out for her car as well."

Meanwhile, in the car, Tony is finding a gas station to pull off the road as they head south. He finds someone gassing up and gets out to ask directions, casually dropping the phone in the bed of the pickup wrapped in a bag. He lingers for a minute to see the truck leave, heading back to the north, which is not the way he'd hoped for, but they were safe for now.

"We're going to need another vehicle," Tony says. "Call Carlo and let's see where he rented this from. Have him walk to an intersection close by and we'll pick him up."

"OK," Nat says as she picks up another burner and makes arrangements with Carlo to get him in 20 minutes.

Mahoney runs back to the team room, "Get Savannah in here, we've got them."

As Savannah gets back Mahoney briefs, "OK, we are 95% sure we have the vehicle," he points at the screen, "Here we have a vehicle that fits our description with two males wearing N95 masks, but it looks like there are a couple of passengers in the back, and we've traced the license plate back to a leasing agency and are following up with them now."

Savannah stirs in her chair, "How can we be certain of

this? Who do we have in the area that can try and intervene? If I were them, I'd be trying to get rid of the vehicle. How long until we have the rental company?"

"I have it," Mahoney chimes in, "the vehicle was rented for one day at O'Hare and extended for two more days just hours ago. I don't think they are going to ditch it, but we now have the same BOLO for this vehicle that we do on the girl's car."

"Mahoney you buried the lead, what name was the agreement under, we've been searching for this guy for a day. Let's dispatch a few teams so we can react quickly if we get a hit. One stays at the phone store, one goes toward Midway, and the other O'Hare, and with any luck they'll be back."

Savannah turns back to Mahoney, "Let's try and see about flagging the kid's parents as persons of interest so if they rent another car we will be alerted, but who's our unsub?"

"The vehicle was rented with a New York driver's license. Malcolm Goodwell. I didn't bring it up because that's a dead end, it's a fake ID."

Savannah scrunches her face, "Damn. That was worth a shot. How many locations can they switch cars at?"

"There are thirteen other locations, outside the airports."

"OK Mahoney, let's pick the closest three to Naperville and roll the dice. I want full teams with tranquilizer guns in vans ready to go."

Tony pulls into a gas station close to the house and Carlo jumps in, "Hey Tony," he turns, "was your call successful?"

"I don't think so, she kept saying she was coming for us."

"Well, it's dangerous having all of us together, you guys should go back with Dan to the house."

"I don't want to attract any more attention, we'll be ok," Tony says. Did you find a location that is neither near Naperville nor an airport for us to change the car at?"

"I did, we're headed south closer to Comiskey Park, I doubt they'd expect us to go all the way there, and there are too many facilities around Chicago for them to cover. We will have to stick to side streets so they don't get a hit on a license plate."

Dan is cocky again, "All right, I have a good feeling about this."

"I don't. They'll know immediately if we go and then within minutes what the tags are on this vehicle. I think we're safe going back to the house and switching plates with another vehicle, that'll be a better alternative."

As they arrive back at the house, Tony walks the neighborhood with Mattis and finds another blue car they can switch with of the same make and model. It's starting to get dark, so he leans over and takes the tool from his pocket, gives a quick pump or two, and switches the plates like it is nothing.

He pops the other one under his vest and starts his walk back to the house, mission accomplished, but something is bothering him. He hears a buzz that is a little too persistent to be a passing vehicle or a wind turbine being noisy, so he looks up in the darkening sky and his heart sinks as he realizes he's not as smart as he thinks he is. He feels the pinch in the back of his leg, but he and Mattis are both out before they even hit the ground.

Chapter 24

The Takedown (Day 1)

"The dog and the handler are down control."

"Copy," Savannah says with calm confidence before continuing, "This time we're taking them all down at the same time."

"Pardon, this time?"

"I mean, not like the park, we're getting them all at once instead of trying to wait until they separate themselves." Savannah dodged a bullet with that one. She'd been spending time in her office all day so she had exact moments she could jump back to and not draw suspicion.

She always told herself not to take a chance with a physical change in the middle of an op, but this one went sideways so bad she had to make an exception. Alicia almost busted her with her eye dropping last time through.

The risk of the girls exposing her after the fact was mitigated by her bringing three of them in at the same time. She was certain she'd get the command she was after and be able to evade the truly awful medical tests they would do on the others.

She had this one all figured out. "Grab A, wait for cover of darkness before moving in around the front. Grab B, you are safe to approach from the rear in 10. Final comms checks everyone."

Peabody comes in on the priority channel, "Team, you're not going to have backup this time from CPD, they are being called into an active shooter scenario at a mall about 8 miles from your location to assist Downers Grove. Preliminary reports indicate a diamond heist has gone bad and the subjects are trying to shoot their way out."

Great. Savannah thinks to herself. *We don't need any big events right now*, the distraction may allow them to slip in and out unnoticed by the neighborhood, but she dismisses the notion as immaterial.

What's for dinner, gang?" Dan says as he is looking at the fridge. "I think we should just get something delivered or maybe we can get something after Tony gets back with the new plates."

"I want pizza," Jeanne says.

"Again?" Lynn questions.

"Nat is not from Chicago; she has to experience all the best places. Lou Malnati's please!"

"I swear kid you are going to turn into a pizza." Carlo quips. "Do they deliver at least?"

"Oh yes, they all do." Dan answers.

Nat is surfing through the TV channels when there is a story about the big news in Chicago, an attempted robbery that has turned into a mass shooting in an open-air shopping area near Downers Grove.

"Hey Jeanne, this is our chance."

"What do you mean Nat?"

"Let's go back together. Let's jump back to the time right before we make the phone call and tell them about this. Maybe they'll believe us more if we can demonstrate we can do what we say we can do."

"Hold on, it's dangerous, you can lose a piece of yourself, remember?" Lynn is visibly disturbed at the idea.

Carlo offers some wisdom. "Lynn, I've jumped over a hundred times and I am still here. These small one- or two-hour time skips are pretty harmless, especially with no real psychological stress of a family member dying or anything. They can visualize exactly where they want to go, and as long as Jeanne has control now, they should be able to arrive together. The big question is whether they will both know they jumped or if they will jump into two alternate timelines. We still never figured that out in The Order, because no one ever was successful trying to do it. It always wound up with one person saying they made it and everyone else with no memory of it because the past changed. I'd love to see this work, but you have to go back to the same moment."

It's dark outside when Dan says, "Hey Tony's been gone for a while, I bet the pizza will be here soon. Did he take a burner with him when he went to scout the cars on the block?"

"No, he didn't." Carlo says, then turns to the girls, "I hate to add to the stress, but maybe you should jump back right now, and go up to your room."

"All right. Nat, you know exactly when we are going back to?"

"I do, the second Officer Tony tells us we are ok to make the call."

They run up to the bedroom. As enter the room and sit on the bed, the doorbell rings. Carlo opens the door and gets the early pizza delivery, but as he gives it to Dan, they are both knocked out as agents storm the front and back of the house. Lynn does not even have time to warn the girls, and the FBI intruders are silent as they use hand signals to start up the stairs after clearing the downstairs part of the house. "Unsub is down. Parents of the target are down, proceeding upstairs."

Savannah hears that and starts to smile, "Be fast, you won't have a second chance at this."

The grab team opens the second bedroom door and finds the girls sitting on the bed facing each other and darts are in their arms within 2 seconds, neither girl ever moves.

They Missed. Again.

Savannah's phone rings, "This is Custos."

"You missed."

"I'm sorry, who's this?"

"It's Jeanne and Natalee, we know you have our car, and we know you have our phones, did you like the trip around Home Run Inn last night?"

"Yes, it was lovely. All I want is for you to work for us."

"Cut the crap, we've had this conversation before, and you tracked us, and we're back telling you that you missed. Again. I am stronger than you, deal with it. You had to have jumped a couple of times to track us down that well. I don't care, because we're changing it all up now. I'm going to give you the chance to stop a major shooting in Downers Grove. If we do this for you, will you let us use our gifts in peace, without your constant stupid stalking?"

"Maybe. If this turns out to be a good lead, I'll think about it."

"You'd better think about it because if you don't, our next call is to your special agent in charge of your task force. Yes, we know who she is. She'll wonder how exactly you got the information about a robbery that was going to go bad, but we will tell her it was no accident at all if you know what I mean."

"Give me the details, we'll see how this goes."

The girls give the details and hang up before Tony waves time. Savannah's phone never blinks, so they never got the triangulation this time. Savannah feels an opportunity, so she walks into the team room.

"OK, new target. Jewelry place on Main Street in Downers Grove. I have good information that two subjects will be attempting a robbery there in the next 45 minutes, let's move swat and coordinate with DGPD on this thing, go!"

About an hour later, the FBI and law enforcement officers have staked out the jewelry store in question when a red van pulls up and two men jump out in full body armor. They enter the empty store and pause because not only is it empty, but there is no merchandise in the cases.

They look at each other confused for a fast second and are immediately engulfed in the deafening sound of a grenade and blinded by the illumination of the sun in their faces as a flash bang goes off, completely disorienting both of them. FBI agents leap from behind the counters and a team storms the van as well as breaches the now broken front door and the takedown is swift and severe.

In less than 15 seconds, all the subjects are in custody for a job they had scoped out for weeks. Each is armed with two assault-style weapons and multiple magazines on their vests. This was about to be a disaster, and Savannah just thwarted the whole thing.

Later, Savannah is filling out her report when ASAC Peabody walks in. "Let's cut the crap, how did you find out about the robbery?"

"OK, if we're cutting the crap, I am going to give you some information, and I want a promotion to SSA."

"Supervisory Special Agent Savannah Custos has a good ring to it, and after today I can probably make that happen for you, considering I had already put in the paperwork based on how well you faced the adversity of the park, and how you've been handling the task force."

"That's appreciated, Alicia."

"You've earned it, now cut the crap. Spill it."

"I've made contact with the girls. Jeanne and Natalee. They've agreed to give us intelligence in advance for major events if we agree not to pursue them."

"So, you want to run a black site team using the girls as your confidential informants? I mean, if we're cutting the crap."

"Yes ma'am."

"We still want the intel on what this thing is. How do you suppose we do that?"

"Long game Alicia, we play the long game. I'll earn their trust, then we'll have them come in for a little test because the genetic sequencing is getting messed up as they go back. I don't want to do invasive stuff unless we have to. We can start small and make them paid informants, I want this on the record."

"OK, let me make a couple of calls. In the meantime, try and make contact with the girls again. See if they'll agree to your terms."

"Yes ma'am."

Alicia closes Savannah's door and immediately picks up her phone. "Trace all outgoing calls from Custos' office. She is making contact with our targets right now."

"Hello?" Jeanne says.

"This is Savannah, Jeanne. The FBI would like to have you work for us, let me lay out the details." Savannah spends the next couple of minutes laying out the plan and says they will not hunt them or pursue them any longer, and they'll be free to re-enter their lives.

They'll have an agreement, in writing, that they can keep as evidence of the arrangement between them and the bureau. Natalee and Jeanne agree, but Dan interjects that he'll need it read over by their attorney before they sign anything.

Savannah agrees.

"Savannah, one more thing. We still know what you are, don't double-cross us here." Jeanne looks up to see Tony waving his hands to tell her to hang up.

"I won't lie to you, Jeanne. I promise. You'll be safe, but I do want to try and figure out what can happen to us so maybe you don't change when you go back, but we can do that down the road after we have a signed agreement."

Tony is about to grab the phone and has stopped the car now, "OK Savannah, thank you." She hangs up.

"We still can't trust them as a whole, ladies. This agent may be ok, but she has a supervisor and that guy has a boss. If there is anything I know about law enforcement, they won't stop until they get what they want.

If they want to test you and cut your brains open, they will still try and do that, unless Savannah is the one wanting to, but I guarantee she isn't. Let's ditch this phone and head back for new plates on this car just in case." Tony runs into a convenience store and slips the phone, on silent, into a woman's large shoulder bag without her noticing and goes back outside.

"Let's order some pizza and pick it up on the way back, what do you say? This is a celebration." Dan is cocky again.

"Let's not celebrate too early," Tony says.

"Pizza, yes. Nat has had Home Run Inn, we need Lou Malnati's or Giordano's this time."

"There's a good target." Tony finds a sedan in an alley, pulls up behind it, and makes the plate switch look easy. In 90 seconds, they are on the way again.

"We should have left the phone in that car," Tony says. "They'd be chasing their tails for a day."

"Is all this necessary?" Dan asks.

"You bet, you can't trust them until you have a deal in writing, and maybe not even then."

When they return to the house, the girls come in and immediately tell Carlo "It worked, we both went back to the same point in time, and we both remembered we had jumped. So, if we do it independently of one another, we may not remember, but if we go at the same time, it's the same timeline. This is huge, that means we can travel as a team unless it's too far back for everyone to jump to."

"That's great news ladies, do I smell a pizza?"

"You bet you do!" Dan says as Lynn enters the room.

"Hey, where is Tony?" Lynn says.

"I don't know, he said he was going to call his wife and take Mattis for a run, but he was with us a minute ago, they're probably fine."

Dan is getting drinks and ice when he sees a shadowy

figure outside the door. He immediately turns off the kitchen lights to see outside into the nearly dark expanse outside the window. "Babe, can you come in here for a second?" He calls out to Lynn.

"Sure." As Lynn comes in, she pauses, "Why is the light off?"

"Stop, look outside, do you see something moving?"

"Honey, you are blind at night, you know that."

"I know, but I swear I saw something."

Discount Doublecross

Savannah walks out to the team room to find Peabody, but the place is a ghost town. "Mahoney! Richardson! Where the hell are you guys?" She gets on the tactical channel, but they are either silent or out of range, and she realizes that she's given them the trace they needed with her long phone call. She reaches into her pocket and redials the number, no answer. "Dammit."

She calls Alicia's cell. No response.

She calls Vic. "Newsome here."

"Vic, it's Savannah."

"Hey there, good job today."

"What's your 20?"

"Alicia said she was sending everybody home, that you have a good lead with the girls, and that girls and we were going to transition the unit. I am about to get to the house."

"Ok, thank you."

"What's up?"

"I think Alicia is trying to double-cross them."

"That won't work out well. What can I do?"

"Nothing, I'll handle it."

Savannah goes into the technical area where Mahoney is running his team, looks around at the notes to find an address that is near Naperville, and wonders if this is the strike that Alicia wanted, *She wouldn't,* she thinks to herself as she grabs a jacket and a radio and heads down to the motor pool for her car.

Savannah is going 80 towards Naperville when she starts getting some intermittent traffic on her tactical channel, they're in an op somewhere within 5 miles of her. She draws on her instinct and goes south of town and begins to hear all the communications.

"Control this is Grab A, we are in position."

"Control, Grab B we have the officer and animal down."

"Control Grab C, in position on the back steps."

"Breach, Go! Go!"

Savannah slams her hand into the steering wheel but wonders if the girls are going to jump again.

"Control. Grab C, we have two subjects down in the kitchen."

Control! Grab A, we need an ambo, right now!!! The target took a dart to the carotid artery and ripped it out as she fell, she's bleeding out, get a medic in here now!"

Savannah's heart sank as she continued down the road, "Control this is Custos, what the hell have you done?"

"Custos, this op is moving forward."

"You just killed the target control. What are you going to do, wake them up so they can jump back again to avoid your foul-up?"

"You're out of line, Custos."

"Alicia, I had them lined up as CIs, we had everything we needed, you're the one who's out of line, what is your twenty? Grab A location! Screw it, I see your ambo, I'll be there in a minute."

Savannah pulls up to the scene as the paramedics are going up the sidewalk where the team brought Jeanne out. They are placing an IV and trying to get her heart back into rhythm, "Hang two bags of O neg now! I have the puncture glued, we have to save this girl."

"Custos I told you to step off this action, you're too close to it now."

"*I'm* too close!? Alicia Peabody, you're under arrest for conspiracy to commit murder."

"Alicia squirms out of her grasp, Custos if you value your career you'll think about your next words very carefully."

"Blow me!" She hits Alicia across the jaw with a haymaker that sends her down as Mahoney grabs her and tackles her to the ground. "Get off me Mahoney, this bitch just messed up the op for all of us. Now I have to fix this."

"What?" Mahoney is confused.

"You're an idiot Mahoney. Neither one of you is going to recall this, so kiss my ass."

Savannah takes a knee and closes her eyes. She starts to see the tunnel that she sees when she triggers this intentionally, and she has the same thoughts she always does when this happens. *Why do I always remember the boy who broke up with me over the phone in 25 seconds when I was 18?*

Savannah Makes Her Choice

Alicia walks out of Savannah's office and immediately calls Mahoney "Trace everything out of Custos' office, she's about to make contact with our targets."

"Roger that boss."

Her next call is to Sanumo, "We've got their trust, just as you predicted, they reached out and gave us the shooting as a show of good faith."

"I did not intend on burning two of Langley's assets in the process on this, Peabody."

"Wait, that was you? The shootout was the CIA. What the hell?"

"I take life when I must Alicia, grow up. You're about to enter the major leagues now. Secure our girls, and take the parents out if you have to, we can spin a cover story and I have a third asset we can burn as the perpetrator in a robbery gone

350

bad."

"Roger that sir, it's already in motion."

Savannah picks up a burner she keeps on her for emergencies and makes the call. "Hello?" Jeanne says.

"Jeanne, this is Savannah, I need to be brief. I want to partner with you, but there are people in the FBI who don't want that to happen. If I can get you an agreement that lays out everything you want, will you come on board with me and my team?"

Jeanne holds her hand over the phone, "Dad they want to work with us, but say others don't want to. She sounds like she's being secretive. Should I do it?"

"We need it in writing first, tell her," Dan says.

"We'll need this in writing before we agree."

"OK, and one more thing, I'll need a blood test. Just so we can try and help you not change your DNA every time you jump big amounts of time. Think about it and call this number. This is a burner the FBI does not track. You have no reason to trust me, but please consider it."

Savannah calls another number that she knows is the boyfriend of her best friend and talks for a few minutes, then hangs up the phone and marches out to the team room. "I got her. I will need a written CI agreement for her to become an informant. She gave us the robbery, she'll do more for us, including taking a blood test for us."

"How did you get that?" Peabody says.

"My charm and wit."

"What. Ever."

"Deal or no deal Alicia?"

"We'll run it up the flagpole, good work." She looks over to Mahoney who gives her a nod and Savannah retreats to her office with a smirk on her face knowing that they are about to go knock down the door of her best friend's boyfriend who happens to be cheating with an ex of his he swore was out of his life.

Savannah smiles as she thinks to herself, *Two birds with one stone.* She is pleased with herself at this moment and sets about the task of starting to go over her boss's head and Sanumo's to get a confidential informant deal on the record for Jeanne and Natalee.

Chapter 25

Bureau Politics (Day 3)

"It's been almost 12 hours since the FBI raided the home of Kevin Abernathy and Maureen Carlisle and little is known as to why they shot the owner of the property and an unidentified party with sleep darts, only to expose the fact that Kevin was engaged in an affair, destroying a young family in the making. Chicago bureau spokesperson Special Agent Josh Lemmon responded to CBS News' inquiry stating only that the investigation into the unsanctioned raid was in progress."

Savannah turned off her television and smiled to herself, wondering exactly what the fallout would be. Last night as she presented her findings to the Deputy Director due to Alicia's unexplained absence, she received the tentative blessing to draw up the agreement and deliver it if and when ASAC Peabody ok'd the deal.

This morning she'd find out who she had to get signoff from to make it a reality. As she drove into the office, she was conflicted about what she had done. She indirectly exposed a task force that was about as clandestine as the bureau had, but her defense was simple. She had not made contact with the informant and in fact, called a friend to ask for a favor because the CI demanded that no previous number was to be used.

As she walked into the team room for the task force, she was shocked to see SAC Sanumo and FBI Deputy Director Blakely were on hand to brief the troops. Blakely begins the briefing, "You've done great work over the last few days, stopping a robbery and securing the cooperation of the target of this entire task force. I'm here to articulate the next phase in our work. ASAC Peabody has been assigned to a new position in Quantico and the majority of this task force is going to be moving on to bigger and better things, but for those of you who remain, I would like to announce, and I am sorry to do this without briefing you first Agent Custos, that Special Agent Savannah Custos has received a promotion to SSA and will lead the newly formed select squad right here in Chicago."

The team gives a small applause, and Custos nods in thanks.

Blakely continues, "She will be tasked with leading the medical staff we already have and 6 agents, including tech and logistics, that will be continuing the mission of finding individuals with the anomaly and working with the three people who have shown interest in helping us thwart crime before it happens. They will be based out of the Phone Store black site in Naperville and will be known as the Temporal Enforcement Unit, or TEU for short. SSA Custos…"

"Thank you, Deputy Director Blakely. This is indeed a surprise to me, as I feel this team has been doing some seriously heavy lifting ever since our setback in the park on Saturday, but I want to commend you all! I'll be making selections for the team in the next day or two, but until then it's business as usual in tracking and finding anomalous individuals, and we still have to make contact with and hammer out a deal with Austin PD to make Tony and Mattis new agents for us. There is nothing to celebrate yet, let's get to it."

Savannah makes the phone call she's been waiting to make for what seems like a month. "Hello Mrs. McAlister, this is Agent Custos, I have some good news."

As Lynn hangs up, she smiles at Nat and hugs Jeanne. To her surprise, there is no recoil. "Nat, I just noticed your hair did not change during our ordeal. Was it because you made small jumps and no one was going to die that was close to you?"

"I don't know. The last time I did a bunch of jumps on the same day, it changed every time. That was my best friend and it dealt with her dying, so you could be right. We could never truly get what this thing is, but my folks are all excited I got out of the little mess I made for myself by coming up here."

Lynn nods and says, "Savannah told me the woman in charge of hunting you guys has been sent to FBI headquarters. Isn't that close to where you live?"

"It's less than an hour, but I think I am going to try and convince my parents to let me stay here in Chicago since I have a job and all now, or I will once we get the agreement."

Lynn shrugs, "Well, it won't exactly pay the bills and I think you have to risk your life every time you get paid, just like this one here," she pats Jeanne on the head and again, gets no

355

recoil.

Beaming, she continues, "ok, the last two jumps have made you different. You never allowed physical touch that was unexpected, what gives?"

"I don't know mom. There is this calm inside me now I've never experienced. The noise is even less, but it's still kind of there. I wish the FBI had a test of me before and after that big jump. That's when it happened. Don't worry, I am not feeling scared or proud or anything like that so my guess is maybe I'll figure it out."

Carlo steps up and says, "I want you guys to keep in touch with me. We need to have secret phones we never use except to talk to one another. I want to create a new version of The Order, but Jeanne, you need to be the leader of this going forward, I'm getting old and my time will come soon enough. You are the future of this, and you are the strongest I've ever seen. You'll need Mattis to help find more people." Carlo extends his hand to shake, and Jeanne hugs him instead.

Jeanne looks up at him, "Thank you, Carlo. One day you need to tell us your real name if you want to be in The New Order."

"I'll think about that after you have your signed agreement from the FBI. I am not a part of it yet, so they may still be after me. One day, we'll get together as a group and make our own little place we can work from. We really can make a difference in the world," he turns to Dan, "and that world does not include you manipulating your kid to win at the horse races."

Lynn's voice is stern, "You do that again and Jeanne will have to jump back and save your ass."

She smiles and looks to Tony, "Tony, are you heading back to Texas with Mattis?"

"We are. We are going to retire from the Police. I'm not sure if they'll let us but given his injury to his leg they won't keep him in service very long. The FBI has already reached out to offer us agent positions in the bureau. I think if I am inside this new unit I can protect you from unauthorized pursuit. I still don't trust that former task force commander. I don't care what they tell me. I'll be in touch with all of you. I have my burner number and yours."

The girls say their goodbyes to Mattis, and he nuzzles both of them, then jumps on Carlo one last time even though he's not supposed to jump on anybody.

Tony steps back, not bothering to correct Mattis, "Yeah, we're going to find new people with this gift. Maybe all over the world. I am not sure how this thing is going to work, but I promise you I won't let them harm anyone." He smiles at the thought.

"Goodbye, Tony, I'll miss you," Jeanne says. Nat hugs him too, and he heads out the door to meet his ride-share.

Dan asks, "Carlo, would you mind taking us to the hotel we left our stuff at? I don't know where it is now, but our car should still be there. Maybe."

"Sure, let's head out."

"Can I follow you guys?" Nat asks, "I want to stay with all of you until I leave the city."

Dan nods his head. "Of course, when we get to the hotel, why don't you park close by, and we can go inside and leave together? We'll drive with you to Indiana and you can head east from there."

"That's very nice of you."

"It's the least we can do," Lynn says.

Carlo says, "While we're getting ready girls, can I talk to you for a moment?" He motions them upstairs where they chat.

An hour later, they are driving back towards the loop and Lynn asks, "Carlo, what's next for you?"

"I am going back to Manila and am going to wrap up my affairs and try and sell my little house. Then I plan on coming back to the States. I'll be close, I hope. I may contact your FBI agent too, but I don't want to be recognized as one of their people. I made my life my own for the last 50 years and Manila is pretty westernized but there is still a culture shock here. Americans are not very nice compared to Pacific islanders."

"I think we are all in more of a hurry and based on our society, that makes us just seem rude."

"Fair enough."

As they pull up to the hotel, Carlo offers to drive them into the parking structure to find their vehicle, and it is indeed still there. He instructs Nat to park close, then he drops them all off at the front entrance and says, "I'll wait to make sure you are safe before I leave. I'll be in the lot right by your car."

"Thanks, Carlo," Dan says. "You've been a giant help to all of us, without you we would not be in this position right now."

The family, with Nat, goes into the hotel to check on their belongings, and as Dan approaches the desk, he is greeted by a slender woman with piercing brown eyes. "Mr. McAlister?"

"Yes. Wait, I know you from the park."

She extends her hand, he shakes it. "My name is Savannah Custos, I've been talking with your daughter and with you. I have something for you." She hands him a packet of information. "This is the agreement that has been authorized by the director of the FBI. Your family is safe from any further intervention, under the conditions we agreed to and as stipulated in the document you have before you. This offer is good for 72 hours from right now." She turns to Nat. "You must be Natalee Simon."

"Yes ma'am." She extends her hand to shake.

"So polite! I have the same paperwork for you too, have your parents or lawyer look over it. You are old enough to sign for yourself."

"Thank you. When do you have to do our bloodwork? I am not agreeing to anything invasive; does it say that here? No testing like that?"

"It calls out specifically what we can test you for. It says blood tests and any tests you request that can help us identify the anomaly."

"Can we call it something different, please? I've been

called special my whole life. That makes it sound like we are weird." Jeanne asks.

"Maybe, but the FBI is pretty set on it. I'll tell you what, when we talk we'll just refer to it as the thing."

Jeanne laughs a little bit, "OK. I have this thing."

"Exactly. Mr. and Mrs. McAlister, we've arranged all your articles from your room on this cart for you. Will you need anything else?"

"That was kind, did you bug all our stuff too?" Dan asks. "And what about Vic, I owe him a proper beatdown."

"Yeah, I don't think we're going to give you a shot at Vic for a while. He's chosen to accept a transfer to Quantico."

"No," Dan is shaking his head, "he's going with that crazy lady that used to run this outfit, isn't she? The one I met in the tent at the event?"

"I don't know, all I know is that he went back to headquarters."

"Thank you, agent Custos, I hope we will have a good working relationship," Dan says.

"Yes sir, thank you." Savannah shakes all their hands as she walks out with two other agents.

Dan and Lynn embrace the two girls and one of them whispers, "This thing is finally over, right?"

Nat and Jeanne look at each other knowingly and share a look of thanks and relief. Jeanne closes her eyes and sighs loudly.

Sanumo's Plan

Special agent in charge Sanumo comes into the room with his pressed suit and shoes that shine and sparkle like they are fresh from a rack at Paul Evans. His chiseled jaw is hidden behind the beard, but his lips are parsed and he looks very stern.

He beckons Alicia to sit next to him as he strides to the head of the large conference table looking out over the parking lot and the green space to the north of the black site they referred to as the phone store. He prepares two glasses and fills them with water from the pitcher in the center.

He motions for Alicia to take one as he takes the other and walks over to the projector to call up a graphic on the screen. As he's waiting for it to reach its desired brightness, he grabs a pill from his coat pocket and downs it.

"ASAC Peabody, we created this site for you to run this team, and it pains me that you're being removed from duty, but I have a proposal for you. I'll give you two CIA assets if you can assure me you can bring these two girls in, and I'll remind you that you have less than 72 hours before this monstrosity of a deal the director shackled us with is effective."

"Yes sir. I have resources in place at the home of the primary target and we've got units standing by at a highway closure to detain and sedate the other girl. We have a tracker on her vehicle, we won't lose them again." She feels her body tense up, bombarded by the glare of Sanumo's almost black eyes so she takes a drink of water and continues, "If we also have CIA assets, we can stop them en route and redirect them here."

He shakes his head, "Alicia, we can't bring them here. This site will be under Custos's command tomorrow. I have to figure out what to do with you. If she can jump longer than a day, assuming your scientist's biorhythm theory is accurate her anomaly could be infradian, so we'll have to induce a coma for a month to be sure we can keep her. Are you prepared to do this? I also want you to eliminate the family and stage an accident for the girl driving herself home, is that understood? You know I don't like sharing control of these operations with the CIA, but this is the place you put me in. Tell me about the cop and the unsub."

"Yes sir. The officer thinks he is in a rideshare to O'Hare, and we have assets waiting for the unsub to return the car at the airport and we'll take him right there. We just have to get the girls, and that should be easy enough as their guard is down. I knew full well this op was not over, it was just…"

She coughs and puts her head down, coughing more violently before grabbing another drink of water to continue "A setback sir, we had a setback." She feels sweat beading up on her forehead as she finds taking a breath to be more difficult. "Brett, I need some help here."

"No, you don't, Alicia. I told you not to mess this up." He looks over to the door and motions toward two men who are now stationed directly outside, "Meet the last two people you'll ever know. TART 3 and 6. Did I tell you the Temporal Agent Response Team has already been formed? The bad news for you is they will be handling this, but on the flip side your family will get your Memorial Star and you'll be on the Wall of Honor. Another detail you are not aware of…Wannamaker blew my op in 2001. That plane was meant for the White House, and the CIA brass were the target. I did not get my promotion that day, but instead, I began a pursuit that will find me in control of the most powerful resource in history…time."

Alicia gasps for her last breaths knowing she's been poisoned, the signature of one Brett Lucas Sanumo. She tries to reach for her weapon, but has no strength, and collapses on the table.

He looks down at her, then to the two agents and gives them a half head nod up and to the right; silent instructions they understand implicitly, then says, "Deal with the others. I want them at site foxtrot in 24 hours, you know how to clean this up."

He turns and looks out the window as a small smirk crosses the left side of his face.

Acknowledgements

This book and accompanying audiobook were funded via Kickstarter, and I'd like to acknowledge the people who helped fund this project to make it all happen. Thank you from the bottom of my heart.

Ruben Cavazos	Colin Osburn	Eric Krebs
Linda/Tony Villegas	Brent Bjornsen	Edward Hart
Corey Trumbley	Alyssa	Daryl Ewry
Tina/Matt Schreiner	Stephanie/Jason Hawver	
Carlos Villegas	Tami McKeon	Sarah Dimino
Paulie Pennington	Darren West	J.T. Dimino
Eric Thurston	Amy's Mom	Adie Mann
Teny Abraham	Ben Erickson	Chris/Krista Witt

Jeffrey Jones   Jody Kincaid   Brian Stiltz

Jeremy Bensley   Adam Brown   Vlad DeRosa

Jon Jordan   Kristine/Alex Gentry   Brev/Erin Tanner

Nicole Vrudney

21071749R00224